EMPLOYING PATIENCE

DIVORCED MEN'S CLUB
BOOK 4

SAXON JAMES

ABOUT THIS BOOK

Art:

When it comes to regrets, I have none. My life is perfect. I own a bar, work hard, party harder, and smother my niblings in all the love they deserve. I don't need to settle down, as much as my sister might want me to.
But then Joey Manning walks into my office and leaves me all but begging to give him a job … and wanting to give him so much more.
The self-professed straight man is in my head and while I know that I need to move on from him, my body isn't getting that message. It doesn't help that Joey is a grade A flirt who can banter with the best of them.
I've never had regrets. Not until Joey Manning.

Joey:

The bills keep piling up and the pressure to get my sisters through college before we're evicted is always on the back of my mind. Whoever said life was for living, clearly forgot that living's expensive.

My default mode is stressed AF and working myself to the bone, and there's only one person who gives me a break from all that.

Art de Almeida.

My boss.

The one man I shouldn't flirt with, but I can't seem to stop. I want to get under his skin. To leave him panting for me. Which wouldn't be such a bad thing except that he thinks I'm straight, and I've never bothered to correct him.

I need this job.

But some days I worry that I need Art more.

PROLOGUE

ART

I EYE THE MAN ACROSS FROM ME, NOT SURE HOW TO PLAY this. One part of me wants to hire him; the other part of me wants to say *fuck that shit*, strip him off, and take him to the stars.

Joey Manning is all grown up.

But.

But.

"Sorry," he says, wringing those sexy hands in front of him. What I could do with those hands. He's leaning forward, elbows on his knees. One chunk of hair has come loose from the short knot at the back of his head and hangs beside his face.

I could do a lot with that hair too.

"I know you're not technically hiring, but …" The self-deprecating laugh he lets out shows off a flash of white teeth. "I'm desperate."

"I like my men desperate."

This time, a real laugh. "I've heard the stories. But sorry. Straight. And desperately in need of a job."

Ah, well, there goes that fantasy. "Like you said, I'm not hiring."

"I waited ten minutes for service on Saturday night. It wasn't even that busy in here."

"Bullshit. It's always busy."

"Then you could always use the extra hands."

Sly little fucker. I like it. I think. Still, that doesn't mean I'm going to hire any guy who walks in off the street.

"Why are you desperate?" I ask.

"Money. Obviously."

"I can *give* you money. Why do you need a job? Here? In a bar?"

Joey's face twitches. "I've got bills like anyone else. And what's wrong with working in a bar?"

"Clearly nothing since I work in one."

"You *own* it though. Big difference."

I only own it because it's been in my family since my grandparents bought the brewery. It's not like I earned it or worked hard to buy it. It was nepotism. Pure and simple. "See, my problem is, if I hire you, I've gotta cut someone else's hours. I have all the staff I need." I deliberately don't give him a no. I could easily hire him, and it wouldn't impact anything. I want him to fight for it though.

The Killer Brew is Kilborough's go-to for coffee and alcohol. Sure, there are plenty of other places around town where people can get those things, but my business has never wavered. Add to that the rent I'm paid for the market in the spare warehouse attached, and when it comes to money, it's not something I'll ever need to worry about.

I wasn't exaggerating when I said I could give him

money. If he asked, I'd write a check right now, even though I barely know him.

I'd rather that than him working at a job he has no interest in. Turnover isn't something I'm interested in having, and neither is unreliable staff. If he wants to work here, I want to make sure he *wants* to work *here*, specifically. My people are tight-knit and rely on each other, and I do my best to keep them close because bar staff are an excellent source of gossip … and information.

Joey's eyes lock onto mine. "You're lying."

Well, hello. "Am I?"

"Yeah. You're Art de Almeida. Don't tell me the stories I've heard about you aren't true."

"What have you heard?"

"That you don't take no for an answer. That you're basically royalty in Kilborough. That you're the man who can make anything happen."

I run my gaze over him. "Including turning a straight boy?" I make it clear by my tone that I'm joking.

Joey's lips hitch up. "Even gods have their weaknesses."

"Gods, hey? Flattery will get you everywhere."

"In that case, I don't think I've mentioned how good-looking you are for an old man."

"Old? Men half my age have trouble keeping up with me."

His hum is gravelly and low. "I don't doubt it, *Mr.* de Almeida."

Something sparks in his eyes, and it's that exact moment I realize I'm fucked. Not only is he absolutely gorgeous, knowing he's off-limits *and* a cheeky flirt? The man is hitting all my weaknesses.

"How do I know you can tend a bar?" I ask.

"You don't."

"Got any experience?"

"Nope."

"This isn't looking good for you."

That cheeky smile again. "I disagree."

I need to get better at hiding my interest because he's got me pinned. In my defense, there aren't many times when I need to keep it under wraps. Whenever I meet someone new and hot, finding out their sexuality is always my first order of business. The straight or taken ones, I move on from. Easily.

But Joey's got me intrigued.

I've always liked a challenge.

"Tell me you at least have a high school diploma," I say.

"That, I can do."

I pretend to think about it. "Sorry, still not hiring."

Joey stands and then plants his hands on my desk. He leans over it, so close I catch a glimpse of yellow in his brown eyes. "We'll see about that."

Then he's gone as quickly as he came in, and I'm left stunned for a moment. That was … well, I'd expected more fight from him, if I'm honest. I'd hoped for it. Been dying for it.

That whole encounter has left me annoyed and sexually frustrated.

I lean back in my chair, scrolling through a mental Rolodex of my hookups and trying to picture which ones have longish hair. I'm in a specific mood tonight, and I want to get the frustration out as soon as possible.

I'm about to pick up my phone when I catch movement out of the corner of my eye. On the monitors, I watch as a familiar face charms one of my servers and ducks behind the bar. He grabs an apron from the hooks at the back, throws it on, and then finger guns the security camera.

I'm half-surprised, half-impressed as I watch Joey take an order and then move around the space like he's been working here his whole life. He's clearly trying to show off, spinning bottles and flipping cups, really putting on a show.

So much for no experience.

I've seen Joey around plenty but can't remember ever talking to him before. There's never been a need. I finished high school a few years before he started, and he's never been divorced, so he's not part of my group, which is who I spend the majority of my time with.

He said he's desperate for this job, but he's not acting the way I'd expect a desperate man to. He's not begging or bargaining; he's taking what he knows he deserves.

The confidence is a complete fucking turn-on.

For the first time since taking over the Killer Brew, I hope an employee doesn't last long.

Because as I stand from my desk chair and make my way through the mezzanine level and down the stairs, I already know that Joey is going to test me.

My patience, my sanity, my restraint.

I'm a dead man.

And yet, I reach the bar and set my card down in front of him anyway.

"Send through your details. You start Monday."

1

TEN MONTHS AGO

JOEY

"I'm telling you, it was Nevele Ounces."

I glance down the bar toward where a regular of ours, Tommy, is talking to the man beside him. Nevele Ounces is a name I've heard a few times now, but I have no fucking clue who it is.

"The dentist called and said it was all paid for. I just had to take Kristy in."

"That's unreal."

"I know. She really needed braces, but it wasn't covered by insurance, and I had no clue how we were going to pay for them ..."

Good for Tommy. And his daughter, I guess.

My attention is pulled away at a *thud*, and I sigh as I watch Marissa stumble into a bar table, bumping it so hard a customer's beer almost upends. She's in huge heels and has had way too much to drink, judging by the way she's swaying.

You'd think she'd be over this by now. Hanging out here every weekend and getting so drunk she can barely walk. I told Duncan to keep an eye on her to make sure she's not swiping drinks, but he's had a busy night as it is between the fight that broke out and those underaged guys who kept trying to sneak in.

"Court," I call to the other bartender.

As soon as I have her attention, I nod Marissa's way.

"Jesus," Court mutters. "If she doesn't pull her shit together soon, Art's going to ban her."

"I'm surprised he hasn't already."

"He acts tough, but he's a total softie underneath."

"I wouldn't know. I've hardly seen him since I started here."

She eyes me funny. "He's literally always here. *Always*. I usually see him when I open the bar because it's quieter, but I'll bet you tonight's tips that he's upstairs in his office."

I pull my eyes from Marissa long enough to send Courtney a skeptical look. "Right now?"

"Yep."

"There's no way. He'll be out hooking up, for sure." Because while I might not have seen much of Art de Almeida, I've seen way too much of his hookups. Men who pass through the bar and disappear upstairs for a few hours before returning disheveled and looking high as a kite. I swear guys hang around here just hoping to get on Art's radar.

Which is fucking weird. But the more people talk about him and the longer I go without actually *seeing* him has blown him up into mythical status in my mind. It's weird. The way I'm craving to catch a glimpse of my boss.

A loud shout jerks my attention back to Marissa. "I'm going to put her in a cab."

"Sure. I'll get Mitch to cover you."

Thankfully, Mitch, our barback, is a champ when it comes to this. It's not the first time he's covered me walking out a drunk patron, and it won't be the last. Ever since I started working here, it opened my eyes up to the number of creeps in the world. I have two younger sisters, one away at college and the other almost finished high school, so every time I see a drunk girl making a fool of herself, I think of them and how easily they could get hurt. I've taken it upon myself more than once to help them find a cab or to walk the sober ones to their cars once it's dark.

I weave my way through the Saturday night crowds and find Marissa staring vacantly into space, with a table of college-aged guys watching her.

"Hey," I say, and it takes a second for her eyes to focus on me.

"J-Joey."

"You didn't follow the rules again."

"I only had three."

I cock an eyebrow.

"Four. That's it. I swear."

"Well, if this is what four does to you, you might want to stick with one or two from now on. Come on, home time."

She pouts prettily up at me, but it has zero effect. She's gorgeous but a total mess. Not my style. I chuckle as I wrap an arm around her and steer her toward the doors.

"You can't even walk properly," I note.

"I don't need to walk to get on my knees for you. When are you going to take me up on my offer?"

"Tell you what; offer when you're sober, and I'll think about it." Thank goodness for me she forgets that every time.

She purrs, and I think it's supposed to be sexy. "Deal."

"Oookayyy." We get outside, and I pull open the door of the first cab waiting. "In you go."

"You could come with me, you know?"

"I know."

"So why don't you?"

"Because consent is what turns me on." I push the door closed, and her window lowers.

She folds her arms over the door and rests her cheek on them. "You're so pretty."

"You too."

"We'd make gorgeous babies."

I laugh because that's a new one. "Not something I'm thinking about, but thanks for the heads-up."

Because fuck. Another person to rely on me? No, thank you. It's bad enough that I'm covering for my sisters as much as I can, but the thought of a wife and kids on top of that? Hard no. I'm thirty-one, and every day that I get older, the less that image appeals to me.

I'm making good money here, but I don't want to be a bartender forever. I don't want to be the shithead who never finished high school and is resigned to hearing about everyone's amazing life stories rather than living my own. I love it here, but sometimes I want more.

The memory of the application stashed away in my room at home crops up again, and this time, I give it more than a second of thought.

Amelia is away at college, and Hannah is going into her senior year of high school—would it be totally mad to try and get my high school diploma or GED before my baby sister graduates?

Like every other time I've asked myself that question, a million and one excuses pop up.

It's not the right time.

I need to be working.

Amelia has textbooks to buy.

I promised myself my sisters would make it through college.

They're my focus.

Don't be selfish.

Some of the thoughts are beyond stupid, but they all hold weight. It's why I'm almost thirty-two and don't have a high school diploma. Even if I lied and said I did in order to get this job.

I turn to go back inside and almost run headfirst into my boss.

"Shit, sorry." I stumble back a step, thrown off by his sudden appearance. And like that day in his office, something stirs deep in my gut.

Art doesn't move, just folds those perfectly sculpted arms over his chest. "It's not clock-off time." His voice wraps around me. "What are you doing?"

I tilt my head. "You know what time I clock off?"

"I make the schedule."

"And memorize it, apparently."

He shrugs in a way that looks elegant and effortless all at once. "It's called duty of care."

"Funny. You don't seem to care much any other day."

"I care every day."

"I haven't seen you here once."

His lips pull up in the corners. "Almost sounds like you've been looking for me."

"Duh. How else will I know when to slack off?"

His dark-rimmed eyes narrow. "That's not your style."

"Says who?"

"Says my security cameras."

Interesting … I can't help the next words out of my mouth. "Is that what you do in your office all night?"

"Among other things."

"Things or men?"

His smile grows. "You really *have* been looking for me."

Shit. I can't even deny it because then I'll sound stupid. I try for a shrug like his instead, but I wind up feeling like a moody teenager. "I forget you exist most of the time, honestly. Like an old man locked away in the attic."

"Is that any way to talk to your boss?"

"Nah." I wink. "But I think you like it." Just like that day in his office, I'm a bit out of control of my own body. Art hasn't made a secret of the fact he finds me attractive, and … I kinda like it.

When his dark eyes slither over my body, I almost shiver.

"What are you doing out here, Joey?" he asks, voice darkly seductive.

A thought hits me. "How did you know I was here?"

"What?"

"You were watching me, weren't you? On your cameras? Did you follow me out here?"

To his credit, he doesn't deny it. "Like I said: duty of care."

"Do you watch my ass on those cameras too?"

Art's expression flickers.

"Jerk off over it?"

His laugh is raw and real. "You can't talk that way to your boss."

"Says who?"

"Says people."

I step closer, making sure I'm just inside that ring of personal space. It's surprising what Art does to me. Maybe I should overthink this urge to always flirt with him or question myself or something, but all I know is when he's around, it's as natural as breathing. And pumps me full of adrenaline. "You always do what people say?"

"Hardly ever. But in this case, I'll make an exception."

"Why?"

"Because you're straight." His eyes search mine for a second, and I don't look away. "Aren't you?"

"Completely." Mostly. Every time I've thought I've been attracted to men, the feeling passed before I could act on it.

He takes a step back. "Go inside, Joey."

"And if I don't?"

"I'll kick your ass to the curb."

I head for the door. "Bet that's not all you'd like to do to my ass."

His groan feels like a victory.

I've always identified as straight, with the occasional detour for a pretty face, but Art's not only pretty. He's *intimidating*. Stunning. The kind of man who doesn't seem real.

I've never gone there with a man, don't think I ever could, but the way my body is reacting to him so strongly is tempting.

Makes me curious.

I'm straight, but …

It doesn't hurt to wonder sometimes.

2

SIX MONTHS AGO

ART

I FEEL LIKE A STALKER.

Well, even more than when I'm *actually* trying to find out information on someone. I know Joey's shifts, I know when he'll be in the bar, and I plan my workdays around it. Not that it's a huge detour from my business as usual, but I'm present in the bar area a lot more than I used to be.

Because the monitors don't do him justice.

Joey's confidence and charisma have me like a moth to a motherfucking flame. I'd known as soon as I met him that I'd be a total sucker, but I'd never clued in on the kind of hole I was digging for myself.

And the smart-ass does not. Stop. Flirting.

I've been going out more and more lately to take the damn edge off.

"Hey," Orson says, sliding into the booth across from me. "Slow morning?"

I glance around the bar, but it looks like the usual lull before lunch.

He shakes his head. "I mean with you. I don't think I've seen you down here before."

"I work down here all the time." My tone is more defensive than I intended it to be. "I didn't realize you were keeping tabs on me. You don't need to be so coy. I told you I'm available."

"And I'm not." His smile is soft as he looks me over. "Everything okay with you?"

"Totally. Chill like the goddamn Dalai Lama."

"With way more cursing?"

"It's called creative expression."

He chuckles. "When your go-to word is 'fuck,' I don't think you can claim being creative."

"Hey, I throw some mothers and some shits in there too."

His brow wrinkles. "I'd hate for someone to be listening to this conversation out of context."

"I wouldn't." The thought lights me up. "Motherfucking shit cock. Cursing really helps let the tension out. Soothes the soul."

"Your soul needs soothing?"

"Every now and then, yeah."

Orson's gaze travels over me again, soft and curious. The bastard is way too perceptive for his own good, but lucky for me, he's not nosy. If it was Griff sitting across from me, he'd be straight on the attack. Instead, Orson lets out a brief "hmm" and then props his chin on his hand.

"Can I grab a breakfast sandwich?" he asks.

"Sure thing." I lift my hand, trying to get the attention of someone at the bar, and I'm equal parts relieved and disappointed when it's Travis and not Joey who signals me with an upnod.

The last thing I need is for Orson to witness how completely Joey disarms me because he'll pick up on it right away.

"Busy day?" I ask.

"Just work."

"My offer to go out at night still stands, you know. I'll even come to one of those straight bars with you."

He pretends to gasp. "And go a night without hooking up?"

My eyes flick back toward the bar before I catch myself. "Who says I won't hook up?"

"At a straight bar?"

I give him my cockiest grin. "You have a lot to learn, sweet cheeks. We're only as limited as our minds make us."

"At least you use all that motivational crap on yourself as well as the rest of us."

The thing I'll never tell them is that I believe most of it too. Boosting people up, being a cheerleader for my men, it's all the kind of thing people in high school used to sneer at me for. Call me names and make out like I wasn't as manly as the rest of them.

For a long time, I believed it.

Then I graduated college, came back home, and started learning how to run the brewery. Away from that toxic scramble of figuring myself out with other equally stupid young adults, I cottoned on to a few things.

No men I knew touched platonically.

Whenever Dad struggled, he did it alone.

Feelings were the worst kind of f-word.

And looking at that made me realize I didn't want to end up that way. I didn't want my friends to end up that way.

It took a long time to grow comfortable with who I am, and who I am is someone that will cheer hard for his friends. I love them. I love my whole group of divorced guys, and when I see them hit rock bottom and build themselves back up again, it fills me with the kind of elation I don't get from anything else.

When good things happen for me, sure, it makes me happy.

When good things happen for people I care about, I want to shout it from the damn rooftops.

"You summoned, oh powerful one?"

I almost huff at the sound of Joey's voice, and when he drops his ass against the table right beside me, that urge deepens.

"I summoned Travis," I say.

"Sorry, he's too busy right now."

I glance over to where he's wiping down the bar. "Doesn't look too busy."

"That's because you don't have my professional eye."

"Or annoying personality."

"You pronounced adorable wrong."

"I said what I said."

"Hi," Orson says, lifting his voice. "I'm Orson."

Joey glances over his shoulder at my friend. "Yeah, I've seen you around. How do you know boss man?"

"Friends." Orson's delighted as he looks between us. "And how do *you* know boss man?"

"He hired me."

"Right. And that's it?"

Joey nods. "Plus, he thinks I'm hot."

And there it is. "*You* think you're hot."

"No, *I* think *you're* hot."

"Back on this again?" I pretend to be exasperated, but I love it. All my staff flirt with me, and it's fun, harmless, the type of flirting that's more banter than anything else. With Joey? I have no fucking clue.

On my end, there's nothing innocent about the things I want to do with him, but it's impossible for me to pick what's going on in his head. I try not to draw attention to it because I crave his interest, but it's a dangerous game. He knows the thoughts I have. He flirts with me anyway.

He could be playing me like an idiot for all I know, and I'm giving him total power to do exactly that.

"You know," Orson says. "All I wanted was a bacon sandwich, but this is much more delicious."

"Glad you're enjoying yourself," I grumble.

"I don't think I'm the only one."

Joey smirks. "You're *definitely* not the only one." Then he holds my stare and slowly drags his teeth over his bottom lip. It should look sleazy as hell, but my brain isn't getting the message. Neither is my cock. It's like the second I get that hint of bergamot, I'm immediately at half-mast.

"Get the man a sandwich," I say.

"And for you?" Joey drops his voice. "Mr. de Almeida?"

The way he pronounces it perfectly, light accent and all, is too much. Every time my name comes from those sinful lips is another nail in my coffin.

Because Joey's going to kill me.

"An employee who does his damn job?"

"Travis already has that covered." The gorgeous bastard leaves with the final word.

"Well, that was interesting." Orson turns to watch Joey walk away.

"No, it wasn't."

"Should we ask the group chat what they think?"

My hand flies out to cover his phone before he can pick it up. "Don't you dare."

He grins angelically at me, so I tell him the one thing that will get him to back off. "Joey's straight."

"*I* was straight. Can't say I've ever flirted with a man like that before Ford."

"No, you just did a lot more."

Orson shrugs. 'That was work."

"So is this. He's only flirting to get more shifts. They all do it. Think if I like them that I'll start playing favorites."

"And do you?"

At least that I can answer honestly. "I have favorites, but that doesn't affect how I run my business. I make sure they're all scheduled equally."

"You know, some days I think you're a complete dick, and other days you say things like that, and I know you mean it."

Fair point. "I'm multifaceted."

"You're definitely something. Including into your bartender."

"So what if I am? I can't do anything about it."

"Maybe not. But you owe it to yourself to know the truth. If he is only doing that for more shifts, you need to cut it off before it messes with your head."

"Stop being logical."

"Why? You do it to us all the time."

When Joey comes back with Orson's sandwich, Orson takes it and throws me a look as he stands up from the other side of the booth. I know what that look is. I *give* that look. It's the "listen to me, for I am wise" look, and I don't appreciate it being directed my way.

Still, when Orson leaves, I know he's right.

There isn't a single part of me that wants to get up and follow Joey, but I do it anyway.

He's in a stockroom down the hall by the time I catch up with him, and I almost want to ask him to step back out into the hall to give us some more space. But at least in here, we have limited privacy—for when I'm about to make a fool of myself.

"Hey."

He mustn't know I've followed him because he jumps about a foot in the air, then immediately starts to laugh. "Holy fuck, you creep!"

"I wasn't exactly quiet."

Joey turns his back to the shelving and leans against it, crossing his arms over his chest. "Trying to get me alone, huh?"

"Not in that way."

"Then …"

I huff because this is going to be a pain to say, and I already hate myself. "I think it's clear I'm attracted to you, and while it's all fun and games, the flirting needs to stop."

Whatever he'd been expecting, it wasn't that. "Wha-why?"

"You're not an idiot, Joey. Because I want to sleep with you, and stringing me along isn't fair."

"Who says I'm stringing you along?"

I turn it back on him. "Have you ever been with a man?" Because I know better than anyone that even straight men can get curious.

"No."

"And would you?"

Doubt crosses his face, and for maybe the first time since we met, his answer feels genuine. "I don't know."

My voice is deeper when I speak again. "If I got down on my knees, right now, and pulled out your cock … would you let me suck it?"

Joey's hesitation makes me think it's going to be a yes, when that sly smile reappears. The one he wears when he's flirting and carefree. The one I don't trust.

All my hopes and expectations crash.

"Why don't you try it and see?" he asks.

Well, fuck.

While he might not have been direct, I got my answer.

Joey's playing games with me.

"Excuse me." I leave, inhaling the clear, bergamot-less air of the hall, and put as much distance between us as possible.

So I've wasted a stupid amount of time lusting after this guy, no big deal. He's just one less guy I have on my booty call list, and since he's an employee, it's probably for the best.

I move my work back up into my office where it belongs and force myself to get my head on straight.

But I keep slipping. My gaze keeps flicking to the monitors, and when I turn those off, my mind wanders back downstairs to his scent, that wayward chunk of hair, the muscles bunching in his forearms, and the way he tosses his head back slightly when he laughs.

Fuck this.

I get up to go in search of coffee, not-so-secretly hoping to catch a glimpse of him, but as I reach the bottom of the stairs and go to turn the corner, his voice comes from up ahead.

"Don't be stupid."

"You flirt with him all the time though," Courtney says.

"So do you," Joey throws back.

"Ah, yeah, but he's gay. Flirting with him is fun because it's never going to lead anywhere. Not for any of us. But …"

"Don't look at me like that. I'm straight."

"Straight but want his dick."

Joey huffs, and it's the most frustrated I've ever heard him. "Jesus, Courtney. He's the boss. I'm a shitkicker. None of us have a chance with the great *Art de Almeida*." He doesn't pronounce it right this time. The bitterness chokes up the syllables. "He's another rich dude who gets what he wants. Well, maybe I want to get what I want for once."

"And what do you want?"

I hold my breath as I wait for Joey to answer.

"A raise. More time off. Better shifts. And hey, maybe if he thinks I'll put out, he'll give me those things."

Courtney's giggle is loud. "And if you got those things, would you put out?"

"God, no. Straight, remember?"

Straight.

My molars are grinding.

If that little shit thinks he can play me and I'm some big, dumb idiot who will fall for it, he's in for a shock.

Let the little straight boy flirt.

Next time, I won't back down. I'll call every one of his bluffs.

MY IDIOTS CHAT

Griff: *Anyone else noticed how hot Art's new bartender is?*

Art: *He's straight.*

Payne: *When's that ever stopped you before?*

Art: *It doesn't when they're interested.*

Griff: *So you would do him?*

Art: *Did I say that?*

Payne: *It's Art and Joey has a pulse. Of course he wants to do him.*

Griff: *Still offended I seem to be the only person on earth that Art doesn't want to sleep with.*

Orson: *I think if you ask Heath, he'll agree Art has a valid reason for that.*

Griff: *I'm not saying I want to sleep with him, I'm just saying I want him to want to sleep with me.*

Art: *Eeeeverybody wants A's D.*

Payne: *And A wants J's.*

Art removed Payne from chat.

Orson added Payne to chat.

Payne: *Rude.*

Art: *Traitor.*

Payne: *Can you blame me? I'm just glad we're not talking about Beau for a change.*

Griff: *Speaking of Beau, tell him I say hey ;)*

3

PRESENT DAY

JOEY

No job I've held in my life is as wholly frustrating as this one.

I'm good at it, I like the people I work with, and I even like the customers nine times out of ten. It's not a long commute, it pays well, and I picked it up like second nature.

The frustrating part … is my boss.

What started as harmless flirting that I'd expected to die off has morphed into something less fake. Less forced. *Way* more interested. I've never been like this before. Any man I'd felt a stirring of attraction for in the past was gone from my mind by the next week. It worked for me. It was supposed to work again.

But I can't deny Artur de Almeida is under my skin. A burning, fizzing fixture that makes my whole body hum with awareness the second I walk in the front door. I'm always on alert for him, eyes constantly scanning, waiting, because if there's one thing I know, it's that he's always here. The anticipation of when I'll see him means I'm on edge every shift.

A whole year of this. A whole year of quick glimpses and brushed shoulders and his deep, sexy voice throwing back some incredible banter.

I'm beginning to suspect I *actually* want to fuck my boss.

A man.

Art has me more curious than I've ever been before.

"Ah, *shit*," Courtney mutters.

I glance over from serving the guy in front of me and find her holding a small knife she was using to cut a lime. She's slipped and sliced her palm, leaving behind a thin trail of blood.

"You okay?" I grab a wad of paper towel and shove it against the cut.

"Eh, not the first time it's happened. I'm going to go pop a Band-Aid on it. You know what Art will say if I bleed all over his bar."

"What *will* he say?"

The sudden deep voice makes me jump, and there he is.

Full lips, dark skin, and hair that's never out of place. And those *eyes*. Every time ours connect, it's like my gut hollows out and I'm in free fall.

Art … God, I've *never* felt lust like this before. And the more I flirt, the more he turns me down, which is driving that need higher. I can respect a "no," I can pick up on the signs and know when to back off, but Art gives me all of the signs to keep going.

Like right now, when those stunning eyes sweep over me, his full lips pulling up just a little on one side, before … *wham*. His eyes hit mine, and the air is punched from my lungs.

I've never been a dramatic man, but Art brings it out in me.

Art's pink tongue swipes over his light brown bottom lip, and I have to hold in my moan. My dick is thickening from being in his presence, and it's ridiculous the way his proximity ripples through the air and brushes my skin like he's really touching me.

My jeans are normally snug, but they're getting almost *too* tight down one leg as they stretch around my hard cock.

Courtney giggles, stealing Art's attention. "It's no secret you like things clean around here." She leans forward, tits almost spilling out of her top. "I can't imagine you'd be too happy about me bleeding all over the place."

"It's a fireable offense, you know. No bleeding in my bar. It's the number one rule."

"I thought the number one rule was no fucking your employees?" I ask.

That gets his attention back on me.

There's something lurking there, something promising in his expression that I catch glimpses of every now and then. "Don't remember ever making that a rule, actually."

"Ah, so it's a me-specific thing, is it?

He winks. "Now you're getting it."

"Joey, stop flirting with the boss," Courtney says like she wasn't doing the exact same thing. Only, in my case, I have a chance.

Art's gayer than gay, and with the number of men he has in and out of here, no one is likely to forget it anytime soon. Every time I have to serve one of those bastards or watch them sneak down the stairs at the end of the night, I try my hardest not to get resentful.

I'm not trying to lock the guy down or anything; I just

need to do something to relieve all this consuming want. I'd like, just once, to get through a shift focused on my job and not constantly waiting for him to appear.

The consuming need to reach out and touch him simmers through me, so I sling my rag over my shoulder and tuck my hands into the back pockets of my jeans. My tank top is loose, and in this position, my arms are on full display. I barely feel the cold, which helps when I want to show off for my boss.

Something he doesn't hesitate to admire.

Art's white teeth flash at me. "Yeah, Joey, stop flirting with the boss." He shifts away slightly, and his full attention returns to Courtney, leaving me empty and frustrated. "How's the hand?"

She lifts the paper towel, and they both lean in to inspect the cut.

I desperately wish I could take her place.

That's it, I'm the only one cutting limes from now on.

"Stopped bleeding," he murmurs. "Go put some anti-septic on it and a couple of Band-Aids."

Courtney twirls her hair with her good hand. "Thanks, boss man, I will."

Normally I like Courtney, but as she walks away, I want to roll my eyes. I know there's nothing behind her flirting; almost everyone here does it. Art is hot as fuck, our boss, and ... he's the kind of guy you *want* to have favorites, and you want that favorite to be you.

"You gonna jump back here and help me out, then?" I suggest, but I'm being a smart-ass. There are another two people serving down the other end of the bar, so it's not like I'm struggling without her.

But Art just gives me that confusing, cocky look of his, rounds the bar, and pulls on an apron.

"If you're done standing around checking me out, we have customers waiting."

And a few of them since we've been talking. Great. Nothing like a full bar with a raging hard-on pressed against my thigh.

We work in tandem for a few minutes before Art reaches around me for the bottle of rum on my other side. He's taller than me, wider, and smells like goddamn candy apples, and when he tilts his mouth close to my ear, I get a hint of mint.

"Might want to work on your phrasing too. Asking a red-blooded gay man to *help you out* could end in ways you're not prepared for."

"Or ways I've been picturing for a while now."

Because yeah, I've jerked off over him. Many, many times. And on the odd occasion I take someone home, there've been moments I've slipped. Times I've regretted. Where I've been with a beautiful woman and couldn't stop from wondering what it'd be like to plow him instead.

Art's eyes darken. Send my pulse rate skyrocketing. If I don't pass out from having all the blood in my cock, he's going to kill me from a damn heart attack.

His lips and his throat and his chest, all right there within licking distance.

"Careful, you cocky little shit," he says in warning.

"What are you going to do?" He's had more than enough reasons to fire me and hasn't.

Art swallows. "I haven't figured that out yet."

"Okay, okay, sorry, I'm back." Courtney pushes her way between us and sets her hand on Art's arm. "I can't believe you covered for me. Absolute angel."

He chuckles, turning kind eyes on her. A look he's never once given me. "I'm no stranger to hard work."

She hums and gives his bicep a playful squeeze. "I'll say."

Art takes off the apron he borrowed and hangs it back on a hook. With every step he moves away, my disappointment grows heavier. I've got it bad.

"I'll leave it to you both. We all know my customers would rather see your pretty faces than my old one."

Courtney flicks her hair, and I can't stop my mouth from opening.

"You think I'm pretty?"

"You're fucking gorgeous." Art sneers. "That's part of the problem."

He leaves, and like that, the sizzling band of need loosens.

Courtney laughs as soon as he walks away. "Still straight?"

I send a teasing smile her way. "You know I'm playing."

While I might tell my colleagues I'm straight, it's only so they don't look too closely. Don't see my rejection every time Art barely looks my way. They don't need to know the inappropriate thoughts I'm having about my boss, especially when I have no clue if I'd actually follow through.

There are so many labels I've played with for my sexuality over the years, but every time I try one on, I feel like a fraud. As far as I look from the outside, I'm straight. So that's what I tell people. I have no clue what's the truth, so I've stopped thinking about it at all.

"I don't blame you. He's a fun man to shoot the shit with because he knows how to give it back."

I agree, trying to resist having my eyes follow him. Seek him out. Beg him to come back.

Because the only thing worse than being caught in his orbit is when I'm not.

The whole thing is a mindfuck. I'm too old for crushes, but that's exactly what this is. The same rampant hormones and uncontained lust as a goddamn teenager. I'm thirty-*two*. I need to get this thing under control.

But you don't really want to do that.

I tell the voice of honesty to fuck right off.

The night moves at a snail's pace with no more glimpses of Art. It's painful. The knowing that he's here somewhere but having no clue where. Or with whom.

When the night wraps up and I've finished packing up the bar, a drunk straggler staggers against it. "J-Joey?" she slurs.

"That's me."

"My friend … Marissa. Marissa said you'd—" She hiccups. "—help … cab."

Hoo, boy. My reputation precedes me. "Gimme a sec." I hold a finger up so she catches my drift, but she's so out of it I doubt she has any clue what's going on. None of us here would have served her in this state, so either she slipped past the doorman already wasted, or she's been swiping drinks.

I make my way over to where Mitch is kneeling beside a crate. "You okay if I head off?"

"Yeah, man. Almost done. You in tomorrow?"

"Nope, two days off."

"See you, then."

I remove my apron and join the girl waiting for me, who immediately throws herself into my arms. Most of her weight is on me, and I try not to curse as she slurs something about *hero* and *tampons*. I have no idea what's going on.

When she's back on her feet, I wrap my arm around her and steer her toward the door. It's not until we've almost made it out that a prickling creeps along my neck.

I pause, reaching for the door handle, and glance back to find Art upstairs on the mezzanine level, arms crossed over the handrail, eyes fixed on the two of us.

Before I can overthink it, I send a wink his way.

Then help Drunky McDrunktits out the door.

4

ART

I walk into my sister's house, hating these days where I'm too antsy for my skin and need to get out of Kilborough for a bit. She lives on a property on the outskirts of town, with nothing but grass and trees and hills for miles. I used to love the view of those hills. Now, it makes me frustrated.

Because the only times I come out here are on the days Joey is rostered off, and I know he's becoming a huge problem.

I've never thought of myself as a weak man. I'm confident, determined, show all the emotion I like, and wring every last drop of fun out of life, but the last six months have been torturous. I'm a gay stereotype, crushing on the straight man.

No matter how much I put steps in place to move on from this … *need*, it's only getting worse.

"You're early," Mariana says, twisting her dark hair up into a knot in the hallway mirror.

"What can I say? I missed my niblings."

She chuckles. "You had them a few days ago."

"A few days too many."

My sister finishes with her hair and approaches to kiss my cheek. "The pastéis de nata stuff is in the fridge."

I fist pump, and she chuckles.

"I think they know it's your favorite."

"Hey, I'll cook anything with those little ankle-biters."

She fixes her eyes on me, and the way her mouth sets reminds me of when Mom tried to get information out of us when we were kids. Usually incriminating information. And she'd always succeed.

"You're an amazing uncle, so this isn't about that, but … you've been coming around a lot lately. You hang out with the munchkins all the time …" And while her leading sentence is something Mom used to do, unfortunately for Mariana, I'm not a dumb kid anymore.

"Is that your way of saying you don't want me here as much?"

"*Definitely* not. We all love having you here, and the time you spend with them is invaluable. I just …"

Another leading sentence. I keep my trap shut.

"I'm worried you're leaving it too late."

"What too late?"

"Kids, Artur! You want them. I see how you are with those two, and it would break my heart if you never got that for yourself."

I stare at my sister and slowly let the relief sink into me. "You think I want *kids*?"

"Isn't that why you've been coming around so much? You're getting the male equivalent of baby fever. Don't you think it's time you settled down? The stories about you out there …" She shakes her head, and I can't help it. The thought of me settled down with kids makes my head fall back with a laugh.

"I don't want kids."

"Then …"

"No kids. None. Ever. And it's going to take a one-of-a-kind type of man to make me settle down; you'll have to get better at blocking out the stories."

She sighs. "I just wish there weren't *so many* to block out."

"What can I say? Your brother is in high demand."

Mariana cringes and grabs her bag. "The keys are by the door if you end up going out somewhere. I'll be back later."

"*Até logo.*"

She leaves, and my grin immediately takes over my face. As much as coming here has been my escape, hanging out with these two is never a hardship, and my heart aches over the day they're too old to want to spend time with me.

"Where are the little monsters?" I shout, stomping down the hall. There's a flurry of movement from the TV room, and when I walk inside, Gus's giggles immediately give him away—along with the foot sticking out from under the couch.

Alice is more tricky. I pace from one side of the living room to the other, Gus's giggles getting louder every time I approach, and when he sounds like he's on the verge of wetting himself, I drop suddenly, chest to the rug and face-to-face with the silly kid.

He screams and scrambles to crawl out the other side, and I latch onto his misplaced foot and drag him out toward me. He writhes and squirms as I tickle him before throwing him over my shoulders like a lamb.

"*Ti-ti-tio Artur!*" he gasps through his laughter.

"Now, where's Alice?"

"Th-there!"

Ah, five-year-olds. No concept of loyalty. I kick open the trunk by the window, and Alice glares out at me.

"No fair! He gave me away!"

I cock an eyebrow at her. "Would you rather hide or be baking?"

To her credit, she makes a valiant effort to hold on to her annoyance. "Why can't Gus ever play right?"

"He does play right because there's no wrong way to play."

"There is in Monopoly."

"We're not playing Monopoly." I can already tell she's in an argumentative mood today, and while I know she drives Mariana up the wall when she gets like this, I recognize it for what it is. Her negotiation and reasoning skills are in overdrive as her mind starts opening up to the world outside of, well, her. Parenting books and child psychology videos for the win.

The promise of sugary pastry has her backing down faster than she normally would, and when she climbs out of the trunk, I set Gus back on his feet.

"So, what first?"

"We have costumes!" Alice says. "Mom picked them up."

"Oh, yeah? Who are we being today?"

Alice and Gus share matching evil looks before tearing off down the hall, immediately united through mischief. Mariana and I were exactly the same.

They come back with an Olaf onesie.

Merda.

Alice and Gus dress up as Anna and Elsa while I pull on the white polyester suit, praying nothing today catches on fire. Then we get to baking. Pastéis de nata are easy enough to make, but everything takes twice as long with a five- and eight-year-old who are determined to do everything themselves.

"So ..." Alice starts, getting that same mouth pinch as Mariana and Mom. "Why don't you have any kids, Tio?"

Unlike when my sister or other adults ask, I don't mind the question.

"Because kids are hard work. And unless you're ready to rebuild your entire life around someone else, I don't think you should have them."

"What do you mean?"

Okay, in a way for them to understand ... "If I have kids, I have to stop coming around. I can't cook pastéis de nata with you anymore; I'll have to do it with them."

Gus wrinkles up his nose. "Tha-that doesn't sound fun."

"It doesn't. So no kids for me."

"But I want cousins," Alice whines.

"And I want—" I cut that thought off before I say something not appropriate for little ears. "To spoil you."

"Do you have a boyfriend?" Gus asks with his usual bulldozer tone.

"Nope."

"But *why*?" Alice pushes. And yep, I can see why these moods drive Mariana up the wall.

"Because I have a lot of boyfriends." *Aaand I probably shouldn't have said that.*

"Do you *kiss* them?" Gus teases.

"All the time. But I'm a grown-up, and I can do what I want."

"I don't see what's so great about being a grown-up," Alice says. "I don't want to kiss anyone or have bills or responsibilities. I only want to cook and have babies."

I snort. "You're kidding yourself if you think babies aren't a responsibility."

"I want to-want to be a dog!" Gus shouts. Then he jumps off his stool and starts wandering around the house on all fours.

Alice watches him go before turning to me. "Mommy thinks you're lonely."

I go to deny it like I do with everyone. It's automatic at this point and mostly true. I'm *not* lonely. I just … there's this pit deepening in my chest every time I see one of my divorced guys finding love again. I've never been in love. My marriage was a whim. An exciting spur-of-the-moment decision that ended not long after. It wasn't love. It was fun. Like most of my life has been.

Instead of telling her to mind her own business, I set my arms on the flour-covered counter and lean toward her. "You know what, *minha linda*? Sometimes I am."

"So why don't you marry one of your boyfriends?"

The married part isn't something I think I'll ever do again, but the boyfriend part? I've never wanted it before. Never thought I'd be the settling-down type. But there are times, especially lately, when I look up from my desk at ten at night and stare at my empty office and wonder what the point of it all is. My empty office, my empty house, my empty bed.

"When you're an adult, things that appear easy aren't always like that. People play games. And not games like Monopoly where there are rules, but games where you think you know the rules, and then those rules are changed on you.

Sometimes, it's easier to forget you're lonely and focus on the good stuff you have."

"Like …"

"Like you two. Our family. My friends. Killer Brew. The ability to help people." When I list it out like that, I can't deny I have a full life. A happy one.

I've never been the guy who wants more.

I wish I could hold on to that.

THE SORRY SUCKAS GROUP CHAT

Orson: *What costume was it this time?*

Art: *Olaf onesie. It was bulky, but not one of the worst.*

Griff: *Still waiting on that photo of you as My Little Pony.*

Art: *You should hold your breath while you wait.*

Payne: *That sounds healthy.*

Orson: *I'm still waiting to be invited to one of these dress-up cooking parties. They sound fun.*

Griff: *Art doesn't share his niblings.*

Orson: *Pity, I'm great with kids.*

Griff: *Yeah, maybe you can teach them how to dance ...*

Payne: *Oooh, low blow.*

Orson: *Ford happens to love my dancing.*

Griff: *Maybe we need a demonstration.*

Payne: *Jfc does your dick ever switch off?*

Griff: *Well, Art's not sharing his cooking, Orson's not sharing his dancing, you're not sharing your Beau. It's like we're drifting apart!*

Payne: *Wish it would happen a bit faster.*

Orson: *You love us.*

Payne: *Apparently I'm getting poor taste in my old age.*

Art: *Old is just a mindset, a limitation, an excuse we use to hold ourselves back.*

Payne: *He's checked out, hasn't he?*

Orson: *A good five minutes ago.*

Art: *Listen to me, for I am wise. Also: get your own fucking niblings.*

5

JOEY

I HATE DAYS OFF. OTHER THAN COURSEWORK, THERE'S nothing to do. Hannah's at school, and I'm glad she convinced me to get my diploma because at least the classes I'm taking now keep me occupied, but it's a struggle to stay focused. Art pays us well, but the bills keep coming in, and Amelia's list of college textbooks keeps growing—even e-copies of those things cost more than my grocery bill—and while my classes are at night, I still have a lot of coursework to get through each day. Exams to study for and assignments to get through. It means missing work. It means being unreli-able. It means a cut to my paycheck.

Hannah has offered to pick up a part-time job, which I flat-out refused, so now I'm focused on keeping my prob-lems from her as well. Other than the few kinda-friends in class, I have no one to talk to about any of it. My friends from high school either moved away, or we grew apart when

… well, when my sisters and I moved away from our parents. When I dropped out of school.

It seems like no matter how hard I work, I can't get a grasp on anything.

I close my laptop screen, which I've been staring at vacantly for the last hour, then pull the paper and pen I've been scribbling with toward me. There's a blank space in the corner where I list my stresses.

Money.

Time.

Classes.

Sisters graduating.

I hesitate and add another one.

Art.

Because I should *not* be crushing on my boss. I reread the list, hopelessness creeping over me, knowing there isn't much I can do about any of it.

Art's flirty but completely closed down, and other than that one time in the stockroom, I haven't been able to catch him alone. My sisters are doing well; so long as I continue to hide my worries from them, I can't see that changing. Classes … I could quit. And feel like more of a failure than I already do. I can't make time. Money … well, that's one I can fix. Maybe.

I hate days off, and another job *would* help each week. It won't make much of a dent in my sister's or my student loans, but a little more to go toward rent and utilities always helps.

Another job will eat into my time though. And my classes. But if I can find something flexible, something where I could duck in and out for a couple of hours when I'm sitting here uselessly … that would be ideal.

I can't imagine a job like that exists though.

Resigned to at least try, I open my laptop and start searching. Cafe, nope. Retail, nope. Scrolling and scrolling and—

Convenience store assistant—early hours.

Hmm … taking stock deliveries and organizing inventory. Between five and eight each morning.

That could work. If I close the bar the night before, it'll be tough, but those hours don't clash with anything. My shifts at Killer Brew don't start until after nine.

I fill out the application details and send it off, but then grab my stuff and head down to Kilborough Convenience. Can't help to give my application the personalized touch, right? Freddy has owned the convenience store since before I was born, and I thank the universe that I've always been friendly with him whenever I've been in there. Most people rush in and out, knowing how Freddy likes to talk, but I give myself the extra time.

Hopefully, that's about to pay off.

It's a small shop: five rows of goods, a newsstand, and homewares jammed in by the front counter, and the heavy smell of lemon cleaner on the air.

"Ah, Joey," Freddy says, perking up the second I walk in. "Good day, huh?"

"Yeah, it's great out there. How is everyone?"

Freddy smiles, and I lean against the counter as he makes his way through updating me on everyone in his family. Wife, kids, grandkids, *great*-grandkids. Pictures and all. He's proud of them.

And as he talks, I glance around the store, breathing in the scent of lemons, and decide I could work here. It won't be glamorous, but it'll be mindless enough work for a few dollars.

It also comes with the benefit of not wanting to climb the boss like a tree, which will be a big improvement.

I wait for a natural lull in the conversation before making my move.

"I saw you're looking for an assistant?"

His craggy face brightens. "Yes! My last one moved away, and I'm getting too old to do it all myself."

"What's involved? Taking deliveries?"

"Deliveries, stocking the shelves, and making a few home runs that I have on my books."

I pretend to think it over, even though it's basically a no-brainer by this point. "I'll take it."

"You will?"

"Sure will. I can even start tomorrow if you need me."

"Ah, Joey …" He climbs off his chair and rounds the counter to swamp me in a hug. "You've always been such a good fellow. Listen, Tony is handling all this stuff for me, so …" Freddy grabs a scrap of paper and shakily jots a number down. "You give him a call and tell him I've hired you. He'll sort out all the other stuff."

Relief—and also panic—settles over me. "Thanks so much, Freddy. I really need this."

"You and me both." He chuckles and picks up a choco-late bar, which he presses into my palm. "On the house. I'll see you in the morning."

I leave him to it, resigned to spending the next … *fuck*.

Years. Years and years.

Just trying to get ahead.

Normally, I love opens at the bar. It's the one time the place is quiet enough that Art works downstairs and I'm treated to unobstructed eye candy. Everything he does, from staring at his computer to scrolling through his phone to flipping through his notebook, is so damn erotic I revel in watching him.

While I try to concentrate on working.

But today … I've come here straight from Freddy's for the third day in a row. It's only been a month of juggling both jobs and classes, but I'm feeling the effects of burning the candle at both ends.

My muscles are tired. I'm sluggish. I don't even know if the assignment I turned in last night makes sense. There's this cloud over my brain constantly, and I can't shake it. I'm just … *bleh*.

My phone dings with an email, and I pull it out to find one from Art to the team, requesting a server upstairs tonight. Overtime rates.

Before anyone else can offer, I reply all and volunteer before stuffing my phone back in my pocket. With my assignment turned in, I can take an hour or two for a quick nap this afternoon before coming back. No problem.

I instinctively glance at Art and know that he's read my reply when he looks over at me. I go for a cocky grin and a salute, but I don't know if I pull it off because his frown deepens.

Damn that man looks good when he frowns.

I stifle another yawn and get on with the day. I'm on my feet all through lunch, almost smashing two glasses in the process and colliding with Courtney so hard she's knocked clean off her feet.

"Fuck." I grab her and help her back upright. "Are you okay?"

"Fine." She shakes me off, face flaming. "What's up with you today?"

"Just having an off day."

"Well, get your shit together, Manning."

She has every right to be pissed, and when Art comes down half an hour before my shift ends and tells me to head off early, I don't hang around to argue. Or flirt. Which is wild for me when I take every opportunity I can get.

But back home, it's too bright in my bedroom, and my brain refuses to switch off. I drift in and out of a haze, the bang of the front door letting me know Hannah's home, the beep of the microwave as she heats up a snack, the constant hum of cars making their way home from work.

A light knock on my door snaps me out of the half-awake, half-asleep phase, and I push myself up onto my elbows.

"Yep?"

Hannah nudges the door open. "You home for dinner?"

My yawn cuts off my reply, so I shake my head instead.

"Joey …"

"I'm good."

Hannah's eyebrows knot. "You're not. You've hardly been home in weeks."

"I'm working."

"You're working *too much*."

I force a laugh and flop back against my mattress, body rebelling at the thought of having to get up soon. "You know how much I enjoy the eye candy."

"Yeah, Freddy's a real dreamboat," she throws back

dryly. "You know you'd get a lot more eye candy if you dated."

"No time for that." Surprisingly, I haven't had the urge to go out with someone in … a while.

"Yeah, because you have no time for anything right now."

I have zero energy to spare for this. "Done nagging yet?"

"Nagging?" She makes a choking noise. "If you weren't my brother, I'd kick your ass."

"And if you weren't my sister, I'd kick you out."

She rolls her eyes at the empty threat. "You're running yourself into the ground. The only thing you should be worried about is your classes. Doing your best. Getting out of this shithole town."

It's not the first time Hannah's said something like that, and just like every other time, her words give me pause. It's no secret Kilborough isn't exactly ideal for a seventeen-year-old, but this is our home. What's she going to do? Go away for college and never come back? My chest gets uncomfortably tight at that. So I ignore it. Hope she gets over … whatever this is.

"Sure, I'll just let our landlord know, will I? Sorry, buddy, can't pay you this week. My little sister said I have to study."

She scowls and *plonks* the plate she's holding onto my dressing table. "Eat."

Hannah turns on her heel and leaves me with the smell of melted parmesan and tomato sauce.

My groaning stomach outweighs my need to go back to sleep, so I reluctantly get up, grab the plate, and carry it out into the kitchen.

I eat in complete silence, trying to ignore Hannah's

closed bedroom door. The dishes in the sink. The sheets I nailed over the windows for curtains and never got around to replacing.

The list of everything I didn't do keeps growing.

I ignore that too.

6

ART

MACK COLLAPSES ON ONE OF THE COUCHES BESIDE THE large mullioned window. He's half an hour earlier than I told everyone to get here, and my *you've got a friend in me* radar is tingling. I bypass the bar to grab two beers, and when Joey hands them over without glancing in my direction, let alone sparing a smart-ass come-on, a whole bunch of other radars starts going off.

But I can only deal with one thing at a time.

And as much as I'd like to keep pushing Joey and calling his bluff, Mack needs me. DMC are more important letters than HJ, BJ, or D-I-C-K. So I take the beers without comment and head for my boy.

"What's wrong with you?"

Mack's head jerks up like it's somehow surprising to see me here. In my own bar. "Ah, nothing."

I hand his drink over before dropping down to sit opposite. "If you didn't want to talk about it, you wouldn't have flopped in here like a wet rag and done everything you could to make sure I knew you were upset. Out with it. The kids again?"

Mack's pale blue eyes fly wide. "Gee, at least let a man *think* he's being subtle."

"Bullshitting's not my style."

His laugh is feeble at best. "I … I dunno. Things are still so hard."

"With Davey?"

Mack hesitates for a second, then nods. He and Davey separated amicably because Davey's job constantly has him away for work, and they even joined the DMC together. They're closer than any other divorced couple I know.

"I thought everything was okay there?" I ask.

"Ninety percent of the time, it is. But because we're still friends, the kids don't understand. They want Daddy at home with us when he's back, so he comes over and then—"

"Then you end up being the one all confused." Makes sense why he got here so early now. Mack's the kind of guy who doesn't want anyone to see him as anything less than happy. He's a man made of sunshine, easily confused, doesn't always know what's going on, but is pure in the way most people aren't.

"What do I do?" he whispers.

"Tell him to stop coming around. Cut the cord. You've been separated for a year now. It might be time to move on."

"And what if I don't want to?"

"Probably shouldn't have gotten divorced."

Mack huffs. "You wanna know something dumb?"

"Always. It makes me feel better about myself."

"The whole reason I suggested the divorce was … was …"

My intuition kicks in before his words do. "Tell me you didn't suggest it hoping that he'd quit his whole career to stay here with you?"

Mack rapidly turns red. "*No*. Well, no, not *exactly* ..."

Yep. He definitely brews slower than the average beer. I'm a good enough friend to hold in my sigh.

"So that plan didn't work. What's next?"

"I don't have anything else," he wails, hanging his head back. "I had to get out of the house. Everything was so ... so normal."

It's obvious Mack is clinging to any hope he has of everyone forgetting the divorce happened in the first place, but that behavior isn't healthy. Unlike this flirting game I've been playing with Joey, which is the healthiest relationship I've had ... ever, actually. Because it doesn't exist.

"Fucked anyone else yet?" I ask.

Mack's gaze meets mine. "You offering?"

"You know my cock's always willing to serve—" Especially since, with Mack in love with Davey, there's no risk he'd fall in love with me. "—but it was a serious question."

"And I think you know the answer."

"Then it's no wonder you're conflicted. Your dick is desperately seeking out the person he knows he can get a good time from." Unfortunately, my comment does the opposite of what I'm hoping.

Mack's eyes get a faraway look about them. "It was a really, *really* good time."

"And it's in the past. Leave it there, and trust me when I say there are plenty of other guys who can take you to the moon and back. You just need to be open to new experiences. Take that heart of yours off hold."

"I'm not ready."

"What about Davey?" I lift my eyebrows Mack's way. "How many men has *he* fucked?"

I feel bad as soon as Mack's face pales, but I only want to get through to him. He can't keep sitting on the fence like this, waiting for Davey to completely crush his fragile heart for good.

"I ... we don't talk about that."

"You thought he was cheating already though, right?"

"*No.*" Mack sits forward, finally showing a flicker of passion. "I never believed that. That was ... I was an ass. I used to say that to make him angry, because when he was angry, I'd get attention, and then we'd—"

"Have explosive makeup sex?"

Mack groans and covers his face with his hands. "No wonder he was so quick to divorce me."

I wouldn't say years of trying to make it work was quick, but what would I know? Thing is, Mack and Davey are both my friends. They both get along, and there's never any drama with those two. In fact, if I didn't know they were divorced, there's no way I would have picked it. And sure, Griff and his ex-wife are still on good terms, but not like those two ... Mack being confused isn't a surprise when they still act like they're together.

"Let's go out," I announce, and my next words are probably louder than they need to be. "We'll get your dick sucked, and if you strike out, I'll do the job my goddamn self." Then, because I'm the shit-stirrer I am, I glance toward the bar, expecting to find Joey giving me "a look," but he's not there. No one is.

I made sure the small bar was stocked myself before anyone arrived, so there's no reason for him to duck off.

"I dunno, Art ..."

"It's simple. Either you want to move on and find someone who deserves you, or you hate yourself so much that you pine after your ex-husband until the day he shows up with someone new, and it makes you so bitter and angry you inevitably end up in jail." I squeeze Mack's arm. "You both have a great relationship. Don't ruin it by holding on to something that doesn't exist. Hakuna Matata."

His smile is fast like I'd hoped it would be. "You had me right up until the end there."

"Should I have said something about the circle of sex-life instead?"

"I don't even know what that means."

"I don't know what half the shit I say means."

Mack's gaze drops to his lap. "So ... this weekend?"

"Works for me."

"And you'd really ..." He gestures toward his crotch. "*You know.*"

"Sure." I shrug. "It's just sex."

"Right. Yeah."

"You good now?" I ask. "I've gotta go check on something."

"Yeah. Totally. I'm fine."

He's not, but he will be. Mack and Davey are both great guys. I find it hard to believe neither of them has found someone of their own yet, but it'll happen. Probably sooner than Mack is prepared for, so the quicker we can get him to move on, the better.

Joey still isn't back, so I jump up and go in search of him. A quick glance over the banister shows he's not downstairs, so I follow the short hall behind the bar down to the storeroom, where we keep a couple of the more popular items on hand up here.

And there, sitting back against the shelf, legs sprawled over the floor and chin tucked to his chest, is Joey.

Sound asleep.

About a thousand "what-in-the-fuckeries" cross my mind at an *employee* actually *sleeping* at work. I mean, sure, I do it. In the bed that I have here specifically for that purpose. But it's only ever after I've been working so late there's no point driving home and then driving back in the morning.

I clear my throat, and when that doesn't work, I kick the idiot's shoe. Joey snuffles and shifts, eyes slowly blinking open until they focus on my legs—then shoot upward.

"Art. Shit. I—"

"Fell asleep?"

He clears his throat, and his usual confident smile flickers to life. "Just a power nap."

"On my time."

"Ohhh, that sounded super Dommy of you. How will you punish me? Spanking? Flogging?"

"Suspension without pay …"

And even though I threaten him all the time with being fired, a hint of worry graces his expression before disappearing again. "Suspension games? Haven't tried those before."

Of course he'd go there. Joey is shameless, and I hate how much I like that about him. "I obviously don't have enough Dominant energy if you think flirting with me is at all appropriate."

"Tell me to stop, then."

He's got me there. The word *stop* is right on the tip of my tongue, but it won't come out. "I think you should *start* by telling me why you're sleeping when I'm paying you double time to be here."

By avoiding Joey's challenge though, I've obviously given him confidence. He pushes smoothly to his feet, way too close, and lifts his arms over his head to stretch them out. His T-shirt pulls up, but I refuse to glance down at the sight I know he's revealed. Smooth stomach, barely there abs, and the lightest dusting of hair that disappears under his pants. I've seen that sight way too many times for my comfort. Instead, my eyes stay locked on his.

"You know how it is." Joey winks. "The girlfriend's been keeping me up all night. Sleep hasn't been on the agenda for weeks. Thought I'd catch up a little before I head home to do it all again."

A ... *girlfriend?*

That one word is the slap across the face I need to snap me out of this shit. Every time the reminder comes up, every time I overhear that he's straight, that he's playing me, every time I see him leave the bar at all hours with his arm wrapped around yet another woman, I think that'll be it. That'll be the reminder I need to get over him.

It never lasts long.

So instead of huffing and leaving as fast as possible like I normally would, I lean right into Joey's space. Right into the scent of his cheap spray deodorant and bergamot bodywash. "Looks like you need to work on your stamina."

His lips twitch, and those loose strands of hair that always fall around his face taunt me to reach out and touch them. "Am I receiving one of the great Art de Almeida's come-ons?"

"If you were, straight boy, you'd be on your knees by now."

Joey unconsciously licks his lips, and *damn* does that mess with my head. There are moments like these that make me wonder. That drive me goddamn crazy with want. They're the moments that force me out at night for a quick fix, but then I find myself back in the exact same place.

There is no cure for Joey Manning.

And I fucking hate him for it.

7

JOEY

ANOTHER DAY, ANOTHER RESTLESS NIGHT'S SLEEP, SEXUALLY frustrated over my boss, followed by an early morning argument with Hannah. What the hell she was doing up at four thirty, I'll never know, but hopefully, she followed my big-brotherly advice to "get your entitled ass back to bed."

I'm killing it at this pseudo-parenting thing.

Despite the lack of sleep, I'm enjoying these early mornings at Freddy's. It's still dark for half of my shift, and people don't usually start to come in until eight anyway, when people are heading to work and school drop-offs. I help out where I can, even if that means being drawn into long conversations with Freddy so the customers don't get stuck talking to him.

Sometimes that means my shifts run over, but I don't mind.

Until today.

The flash of a familiar face on the other side of the front

door has me dropping to my knees behind the counter. Freddy blinks down at me, thick glasses magnifying his eyes and wrinkles magnifying his frown.

"Hip give out?" he asks. "Happens to me on occasion."

"No, just—" I hold my finger to my lips, and Freddy taps the side of his nose. He clearly assumes he's onto something, but I can guaran-fucking-tee it's not what he thinks it is.

Freddy wishes Art good morning as he steps into the store.

"Oh! And if you smell something, it was only me. No one else. Side effect of getting old, don't you know?"

I face-palm.

Art chuckles. "Good to know."

There's a high-pitched squeal, and Art mutters something I miss.

"I promised a treat for school," he says in a long-suffering voice. "Where can I find something that will win me points with the kids but won't make my sister want to kill me?"

Freddy starts on a rant about chocolate and candy and *his day* …

I pinch his leg and whisper, "Aisle two."

"Ouch! Oh! Umm, aisle two. That one."

Art thanks him, and I let out a breath as I hear footsteps walk further into the shop. The problem now is getting out of here before Art pays because he's tall enough he'll be able to see over the counter to where I'm crouching like an idiot.

I'm not even sure what prompted me to hit the deck like I was on storm-ravaged seas, but seeing Art misplaces my brain cells, and while they're rattling around out of place, I do the dumbest shit.

Which is why, after a glance around the counter to make

sure the coast is clear, I crawl as fast as I can into the closest aisle.

Freddy's wheezing laughter follows me the whole way.

Being on hands and knees in aisle four does not fill me with confidence for the rest of my day, so, with as much dignity as I have left—by my calculations, 0.1 percent—I climb to my feet. Only I get halfway and glimpse what has to be the single cutest sight I've ever seen through a small gap in the shelves.

A teeny, tiny mini Art.

He's got chubby cheeks and messy black hair, but there's no denying the family resemblance in those golden-brown eyes, brown skin, and shrewd little expression.

"But-but-but Gabby said I'm not allowed to like Elsa. Gabby said I have to like Kristoff. I don't like Kristoff. He-he-he has a moose, and mooses smell. I don't like smelly things."

"Gabby's wrong," comes Art's smooth voice. "And I'm sure Kristoff takes excellent care of his animals."

I lean closer, way more interested in a conversation I know nothing about than I should be.

"S-s-she said Elsa is for girls."

"Let's check the next aisle."

Oh, fuck.

I shoot upward and time it so I sidestep into the aisle they've just left before they step into mine. Even with my heart hammering and other people in the shop, I stoop again to try and catch more of their conversation.

"—harmful stereotypes."

"She's an idiot," the boy says.

"She's not an idiot; she's simply misinformed."

"What does that mean?"

"It means she's been told the wrong thing. If you want your favorite character to be an immensely powerful witch, don't let anyone tell you differently."

"Who's your favorite character?"

"I like …" Art sighs. "The sleeping one."

"Snow White or Sleeping Beauty? Because they-they-they both sleep."

"Either. What about these?"

I can't see what Art is holding up, but the kid scrunches up his nose. "I want tarts."

"I told you, we don't have time to cook them before school. We'll make some this week."

"But I want *taaarts*."

"Keep going, Gustavo, and you'll have nothing."

The kid roars and starts kicking the bottom shelf at the same time as a high-pitched scream comes from the end of the aisle.

A girl who looks like *Gustavo* but older starts to yell, "*Tio*! *Tio*, there's a strange man watching Gus between the shelves! What if he wants to steal him? Help! *Help*!"

Oh, no, no, no.

I shoot upward and accidentally stumble into the woman behind me, who I grab before she can fall into the shelf. "Shit, sorry, I—"

"Were you watching that little boy?" she gasps, horrified.

"Stranger danger! *Heeelp*!"

"No," I assure the woman before holding both hands up and taking a step toward the girl. "You've got it wrong. If you could—"

Something slugs the back of my head, and I freeze for a second, wondering what the hell just happened.

"Creep!" the woman shouts, lifting her bag for another go.

"Stop!" I hold up a hand. "This is all *wildly* getting out of hand. If everyone could just keep their voices …"

My words trail off as Art steps into the entrance of the aisle. The girl, who's obviously his niece, ducks behind him as he folds his arms over his chest.

"Out of hand?" The woman raises her bag. "You were *creeping* on a little boy."

"I *wasn't*."

"Then who—"

"Him!" I throw my arm toward Art, face feeling volcanic-level hot. "I was looking at *him*, okay?"

Art has the fucking audacity to smirk. "Who could blame him, really?"

The woman doesn't look ready to back down, but at least she lowers her bag.

"This was *totally* taken out of context. If everyone could *calm* down." Holy hell, my voice is coming out all panicked.

"Sounds like the only one not calm yet is you, Joey." Art turns a sincere smile on the woman. "I appreciate you looking out for my nephew."

"Again, *nothing* to look out for." My voice still hasn't gotten its shit together.

"Just a suggestion," the woman spits, pulling her bag onto her shoulder, face almost as red as mine feels. "If you weren't spying on *anyone*, this wouldn't have happened." She leaves in a huff, and all I can do is cover my face with my hands. I count to five, hoping by some miracle Art's left me to my shame, but when I risk looking out again, he's standing right in front of me.

I glare up at him. "Couldn't leave me to drown in embarrassment, could you?"

"It's more fun this way." His eyes trail over my face. "I don't think I've ever seen you so bright red."

I throw my hands out to the side. "Well, there's one for your bucket list."

"Two, actually."

"Two?"

Art's smile is dangerously handsome. "You admitted to checking me out. I'm flattered."

"I'm pretty sure I said *looking*."

"Looking, checking out. All the same in my books."

"Your ego enjoys fiction, huh?"

"Whatever keeps it alive."

It's tempting to roll my eyes and play it off. I'm still so flustered that the encounter, combined with the brain-cell-less-conundrum he leaves me with, gives him the upper hand. "Trust me when I say there's no way your ego is endangered."

"Lucky for me, then. It'll come in handy this weekend."

This weekend. When he goes out and hooks up, and all I can hope for is that he doesn't bring the men back to the bar with him. A small part of me dies inside at the knowledge that no matter how much my libido goes into overdrive for him, this will never happen.

"Planning on propositioning me at work, are you?"

"You'd love that." His infuriating smirk is back as he reaches up and tucks my loose hair behind my ear. He leans in. "Don't worry, I won't tell your girlfriend the whole store caught you checking me out."

I'm too wrapped up in his proximity, too distracted by the rapid *thunk thunk* of my heart, to register his words. By the time my brain has made sense of them, Art is already approaching the counter.

Girlfriend.

Shit. That person I told him I have and couldn't be less interested in having. That stupid word that slipped out in an attempt to get one over on him. My big goddamn mouth.

I leave the aisle of misery and walk into the main part of the store, where Freddy is chatting to the kids about school.

I wave his way, trying to subtly catch his attention and gesture I'm leaving, but when my erratic movements catch his eye, Freddy apparently decides I haven't been humiliated enough for one day.

"Joseph, good, you're not crawling around on the floor anymore. Be a good lad and grab this delivery before you clock out, would you? It's on your route home."

And like that, the cat's out of the bag.

I give one of my bosses as friendly a goodbye as I can manage while the other looks on in curiosity.

Then I grab the delivery and get the fuck outta hell.

8

ART

My mind is running at a million miles an hour by the time I drop off my niblings and get to work. I've always thought of myself as a smart man, someone who's well-informed about nearly everyone in town since drunk people tend to spill the deepest secrets.

But Joey … I don't know nearly enough about Joey.

I have only the vaguest recollections of him around town when we were younger. Christmas parties our parents dragged us to, where teen me was way too cool to pay attention to the kid in the corner. I have no idea where his parents are now because it's suddenly occurring to me that I don't think I've seen them in a long time. Did they move? *Die?* I have all these questions, and it's killing me.

I know *everything.*

But all I currently know about Joey is that he's working two jobs, and while I want to cling to my anger over him having a girlfriend, the math in my head is coming up with a different answer to why he fell asleep on the job.

First job, plus second job, equals tired employee.

I stomp up the stairs to the mezzanine at work, trying to figure out the *whys*. The possibilities could be endless though, and the only thing I know for sure is that he must be doing it because he needs the money.

Even before I'm consciously aware of it, my brain is tallying up how much of a pay raise I'd need to give everyone in order to cover Joey's wage at the convenience store. It's a fatal flaw of mine. Wanting to give everything to everyone. The thing is, I have the money to do it; what I don't have is the justification. I already pay well above standard wages, have excellent insurance and paid days off, but I had to fight with my grandparents to get those things.

They're good people, and they believe in helping others, but they're extremely risk-averse. Adding another increase on top of the standard annual one isn't something that will happen.

A Christmas bonus could.

Or ... Nevele Ounces could pay him a visit ...

Stupid name. I shoot that idea down as soon as I have it because without knowing *why* Joey needs the money, there's no way to know if he meets Nevele's code.

There has to be *something* I can do.

It's not until I glimpse Joey on the security monitors later that afternoon that an idea hits me. I pull up the bar schedule on my computer and find his roster for the next two weeks. All closing shifts.

With 5:00 a.m. starts at the store.

And the late-night overtime shift last night.

Well, that won't do.

If that stupid, stubborn man had come to me and told me he was picking up hours somewhere else, I would have worked with him. Or organized more events upstairs that I needed the extra help with.

I rub my jaw, agitated, then—

"Fuck it."

Starting from next week, I change his remaining shifts for the month to 9:00 a.m. starts. That gives him time to duck home and change, and he has the afternoon and nights off—to hopefully sleep, and *not* with his supposed girlfriend.

It doesn't fix the two-jobs thing, but *hopefully*, now he won't be dead on his feet.

My phone lights up with a text from one of the group chats, and without fail, it brings a smile to my face. I have an amazing network of men at my beck and call, and I know how lucky I am to have them, which is why I make sure I'm available when they need me.

Even if it's only to give them shit.

Which I do.

A lot.

And with one group of men all successfully loved up, I move my attention to another of my chats. Keller, Mack, and Carlton. While I love the shit out of Orson, Payne, and Griff, they've happily caught "couple's disease." The infectious mindset that all anyone needs is the right cock to be happy. I love that they've found that and that it makes *them* happy, but I've jumped on a lot of dicks in my day, and that's not the way to my inner goddess of contentment.

So instead, I'll turn to the single men.

Me: *Who's coming out this weekend? We've got slutting it up to do!*

Mack: *Me! I'll be there!*

Me: *Now that's the level of enthusiasm I expect at the prospect of a blow job by yours truly.*

Keller: *Not sure I want to know.*

Carlton: *What's to know? Art's obviously been offering out blow jobs again.*

Keller: *Well, in that case, I'll take one!*

Carlton: *Ooh, me too!*

Me: *Hey, hey, just how easy do you think I am?*

Mack: *It feels mean to be honest here.*

Keller: *Why? Art's proud that he's the cheapest rich guy in Massachusetts.*

Me: *It'll be the world next, baby!*

Carlton: *One cock at a time.*

And like that, my mood is one hundred times better. Mysteries about Joey Manning are temporary, like every other pretty face in my life. These guys are the real deal. Now, if only I could find a way to make the DMC my entire life and not worry about anything else.

Well, anything other than the Killer Brew. I like being rich. I like that everyone knows me. I like that in this tiny slice of town, I'm able to make a difference and feel like I'm somewhere I belong.

There's commotion on one of the cameras, and I watch as Joey scrambles around, picking up shards of the glass he's dropped. This new schedule can't come into effect soon enough.

My body sags as I force myself to my feet, preparing to do something I really, *really* don't want to do.

If he's desperate enough to be working two jobs, he can't afford to go home early, but as much as I feel for him, I have other employees to think about—not to mention his *fucking health.*

Safety is number one for me though, and if he's at the point of breaking glasses, unfortunately, he's gotta go. I can't risk someone being hurt because of my negligence.

As much as I'm sure Joey will flirt and blow it off like it's nothing, there's a seed of regret burrowed deep inside me that won't shift. I'm at the top of the stairs before I pause, an idea sinking in. I cast my eyes back to the small serving area up here, then change direction.

It takes ten minutes, but I mess up the area enough that it should be an easy hour of work for him, and then I jog down the stairs and into the bar.

"Joey?"

He curses under his breath, dumps what he's holding into the trash, and approaches. "Look, I'm sorry, it just—"

"Why didn't you clean up last night?"

That question throws him. "What?"

"The bar upstairs is a pigsty. You're exhausted if you're falling asleep and breaking glasses, so I need to cut your shift short tonight. But you can fix upstairs first."

"But I—"

"Unless you want to go home right now?"

"I want to finish my shift. I can't leave them to—"

I cut him off again, but I soften my voice this time. "We both know you're causing more issues than helping. You're tired. You need sleep."

"Pfft. I'll sleep when I'm dead."

"Keep making mistakes like breaking my glasses and you'll sleep when you're fired."

He scowls.

I grin. "Now, are you going home, or do you want the extra hour upstairs, away from everyone, cleaning up the mess?"

He eyes me. "I'll go upstairs."

"Good choice."

He takes the glass out to the dumpsters, and I'm already upstairs waiting for him by the time he joins me. Instead of going back into my office, I take a seat on the couch that has the best view of the bar. Which I know because I've made use of it at many, *many* of my parties.

"We going to talk about this morning?" I ask.

"Nope."

"You don't crawl around on the floors here, do you? I can't imagine they're sanitary."

"Like the convenience store would be any better." He's keeping his back to me, tidying up the chocolate powder I sprinkled all over the countertops.

"Why'd you do it? Got some kind of animal kink I should know about it?"

"And why should *you* know about it?" he throws back.

"Call it professional curiosity."

That gets enough of his attention that he throws me a look over his shoulder. "Do *you* have any secret animal kink I should know about?"

"That's on a need-to-know basis. And until the day I ask you to put on animal ears and a tail, you don't need to know."

"Ah, but you're saying the day will come."

"You should hold your breath while you wait."

He chuckles.

I'm not deterred. "If you don't answer my question, I'm going to assume I hit the nail on the head."

Joey throws me a wink. "It's a need-to-know basis. Sorry, boss man."

"You call Freddy boss man?"

"No." For some reason, that makes me happy. "I actually have respect for him."

"Ouch. Direct hit."

"Feed your ego some more fiction, and I'm sure it'll recover."

"Eh, all I need to do is remember you were checking me out between the shelves at the convenience store for my ego to be properly inflated."

"*Only* your ego?"

That opening is so tempting. A wily call to flirt while we're alone and no one else can hear us. Where I can really play chicken with his attempts to bait me. And *because* it's so tempting, I ignore it.

"So, what is it?" I ask instead. "Cat? Or a cute little pup?"

He gives me adorable puppy dog eyes and a tiny yap.

"Maybe a horse?"

He brays.

"Or something kinkier." My smile grows. "A dragon? Do you lay eggs?"

This time, he flips me off and goes back to cleaning.

"What? No fire to breathe? Don't worry, I'm sure you'll get there one day."

He drops his head back on a groan. "I don't get it."

"What?"

"How I can be *so* attracted to someone *so* annoying."

Suddenly, I don't have a reply.

It's not what he's said, because he's come at me with shit like that loads of times, but it's *how* he said it. Like a casual, offhand comment.

Like he *means* it.

Which goes against literally everything else I've been feeding my narrative of denial. That I *can't* have him.

Joey's straight.

Joey's my employee.

Joey's queerbaiting me with my favorite brand of lure.

Flirty, witty banter.

I'm eating it up, knowing it means nothing.

Fortified against my want for him by the simple fact it'll go nowhere.

My defenses worked.

But with one sentence, he's put a crack in them.

I was supposed to be the one calling his bluff, but now the tables have turned, and I'm struggling to keep up.

"I'm going to go," I say suddenly.

"What? Why?"

He sounds genuinely surprised, and I take a moment to run my gaze over him. "Because I'm about to do something I'll regret."

Then I leave him, finally silent, and lock myself away in my office, begging the universe for a scrap of strength.

BITCHIN' BACHELORS GROUP CHAT

Carlton: *I'm out for tonight. I didn't realise when I took the job with Payne that a large part of my day would be spent making sure Beau doesn't kill himself, but here we are ...*

Keller: *The camp hasn't even opened yet.*

Carlton: *I'm just telling myself that it's a warm-up for when we have school kids in here being idiots every week.*

Mack: *Bummer! I needed all my boys there tonight.*

Art: *You've got me for a backup, who else do you need?*

Mack: *Everyone. I feel sick.*

Keller: *You're getting in your head about it.*

Mack: *But I don't want to sleep with anyone else. It feels like cheating.*

Carlton: *As much as I reeeeally hate to remind you of this—you can't cheat on someone when you're not together.*

Mack: *So I'm just supposed to leave him home with the kids while I go out and get my dick sucked?*

Art: *To start off with, you'll be sucking mine.*

Mack: *Gahhh is everyone I meet going to be like Art?*

Keller: *No one's like Art.*

Art: *One of a kind, baby.*

Carlton: *That didn't feel like a compliment to me.*

Mack: *This doesn't feel right.*

Art: *The best steps forward are usually the hardest—literally. Your dick will tell you what to do.*

Mack: *My dick's been wrong before.*

Art: *Not surprising when you talk about him like that.*

Mack: *What am I meant to say? Good boy, peenie?*

Keller: *Literally never that.*

Art: *I dunno, I thought it had character.*

9

JOEY

MY SHIFTS HAVE CHANGED, WHICH IS … ODD. BUT according to Art, he made a mistake with the schedule for what would have to be the first time ever, and now I'm miraculously scheduled through the day. My bullshit detectors are running hot, but him changing them *for* me doesn't make sense. Art loves his employees, but he's a businessman. He's fair.

Moving my shifts just to suit me isn't fair.

A blond guy plonks down at the bar right in front of me.

"You okay?" I ask, eying his downturned mouth.

"Just get me as drunk as possible."

"Legally can't, sorry. But I can get you *a* drink." I give him a once-over, and even though I'd guess that he's roughly my age, I hit him up for ID anyway.

He pulls it out with zero enthusiasm, showing me he's twenty-seven. "Makes sense. Everything else is going wrong, so why not struggle to get fucked-up too?"

There's something Southern about his voice.

"Beer?"

He gives a halfhearted gesture, so I start pouring.

"You not from around here?" I ask.

"Yeah. Well, *now* I am. Or at least, currently. Maybe not for much longer." He sighs and takes the glass from me. "I don't even know what's gonna happen."

"I'm listening, if you need it?"

He looks down and takes a sip. I'm about to walk away when he says, "I'm Will."

"Joey."

"Yeah, I know."

"You do?"

Will shrugs. "I've seen you around."

I tuck my dishcloth into the band of my apron and lean my elbows on the counter. "You've got a story, and I've got some free time. Shoot, Will."

He stares at the beer before taking another sip. "My best friend is moving away."

"Ah."

"I can't afford the apartment on my own, so ..."

Okay, so there's the problem. "Why don't you put out an ad? See if you can't find someone to take his room?"

"I'd feel awkward living with a stranger."

"Could you find somewhere cheaper?"

He shrugs again, but it's more hesitant this time.

"It's a tough situation. Why's he moving away?"

"To get a fresh start."

"And you don't want a fresh start with him?"

"I was never offered one." His thumb absentmindedly draws lines in the condensation on the glass. "A friend from college offered Mols the room, and he said yes. He's moving to Seattle and *leaving* me here."

I can't help my chuckle at how pathetic he sounds. "You in love with this guy?"

He shakes his head roughly. "No, he's not my type. I … Never mind. But if I can't afford to stay here, I'll have to …"

I wait him out.

"I'll have to move home. And I'm not exactly welcome there."

"Why?"

"Because I'm gay."

My heart sinks for the guy. "I'm sorry."

"You and me both."

"Kinda makes me wish I had a room to offer you."

"I've already been offered a room, but—" He cuts off and doesn't continue, even when I give him a few seconds.

"Then what's the problem?"

"It's … it's with Mol's dad."

"Cool."

Will's whole face goes bright, bright red.

"Oh." I can read that reaction. "*Very* cool?"

His gaze shoots to mine. "Very, very *not* cool."

I laugh. "I can see why your best friend isn't your type."

He shushes me and hurries to glance around. "No one can know."

"I'm not telling anyone."

"Good." He drops his voice. "Molly would kill me. It's why I can't take the room. Molly offered, not Keller. It … it wouldn't be right. On both of them." Will drains his drink, and I pour him another one.

"Did you say Keller?"

Will's head snaps up. "You know him?"

"If it's the guy I'm thinking of, he's friends with my boss."

"That's the one." Will slumps even further on the stool. "They're going out together tonight."

"Interesting …"

"Is it?"

Given the bitterness in his tone, I'm going to go ahead and assume he finds it far from interesting. I chew on my tongue, trying to hold my question in, but it doesn't help. "Do you know where they're going?"

"Yeah, a gay bar in Springfield."

Doubly interesting. I busy myself by serving a group who come over instead of latching onto the idea trying to take over. But it keeps burrowing in, overriding my thoughts, distracting me from the task at hand.

Once the group moves on, I gravitate back to Will. "Hey."

He glances up. "Umm, hi?"

"I've had a thought."

"That doesn't sound too good."

"Hey, I'm a smart guy."

Will readjusts his backward cap, and a slight smile twitches his lips. "Tell me, then."

"Feel like making a nuisance of yourself?"

"I'm not following."

I throw a quick glance around to make sure no one is eavesdropping before leaning in. "You're interested in a certain someone, and it's possible I might be interested in a certain someone he's out with."

Will suddenly perks up.

"You're also down a best friend, and truthfully, I don't have a lot of friends myself. And when I say not a lot, it's basically none. It could be fun to go out, have a dance ... maybe accidentally-on-purpose bump into some people we know."

"I ... I don't know ..."

"The way I see it, they've gone out for one reason. Now, we can either do nothing and let it happen. Or we can do our best to get in the way of that."

"I don't think that's the way to get their attention."

I imagine Art's irritation at having every prospect cock-blocked. "Actually, I think it's exactly the way."

"It doesn't matter, anyway. He doesn't see me like that."

"Have you asked him?"

"Well, *no*, of course not, but—"

"Then you don't actually know." I wave a hand toward him. "You're a good-looking guy." Objectively. "And chances are if you're only ever hanging around with his son, Keller only sees you as his kid's friend. He has to see you outside of that. If he sees you dancing all hot and sexy with other guys, it'll show him *you're* someone hot and sexy."

I can tell he's thinking about it. His whole face has lit up with hope, and fuck, I'm crossing my fingers I'm right because otherwise I'm going to feel terrible. If it's my fault he has to watch Keller go home with someone else, that'll be the fastest-ended friendship in history.

"Molly will kill me," he says, but it's clear by his tone that he wants me to reassure him. Which is easy to do because while I get it would be weird to see your friend with your parent, they're both adults, and they get to make their own decisions.

"Kill you for what? I'm not telling you to try and get in his pants. Just come out, we'll dance, get their attention, and then I plan to annoy the shit out of Art until he goes home solo."

"Dance. Get his attention." Will gnaws on his lip. "I think ... I think that's okay."

"Of course it is. So you're in?"

"Looks like it." He slides his empty glass toward me. "What time do you finish?"

"Five thirty. Then I'll need to run home and get ready. Wanna book an Uber from here at eight?"

Will sucks down a long breath, and it's kinda funny seeing a six-foot, muscular, frat-esque dude look so sweet and uncertain. "I guess we're doing this."

I'M NERVOUS THE WHOLE WAY OUT TO SPRINGFIELD. THERE'S no real reason to be, but I'm convinced we'll get there and be too late, or Art will have changed his mind and gone somewhere else, or he'll see me and laugh in my face about how pathetic and desperate I am.

But I've reached the point where it's time to acknowledge this crush or whatever isn't going away. It hasn't passed on like all the others. It hasn't lessened.

At this point, all I want is to have sex with a man. *That* man. And hope to hell it gets my head screwed back on properly. Even when I'm not at work, my mind is full of piercing eyes and a teasing smile. His height, elegance, control, and that goddamn filthy mouth.

I want my life back, so it's time for him to learn all my flirting bullshit ... isn't bullshit.

We pull up out the front of the gay bar, and Will is slow to get out of the car.

"You doing okay?"

"Still walking off those beers from earlier."

"You only had two."

"Yeah, but I don't … I'm not much of a drinker."

"Lightweight?" He's larger than me, so should technically be able to put more away, but I've also been drinking since before I should have been drinking. "You'll have to go easy tonight."

"Yeah, one drink will be my limit, I think."

"Good plan. You ready to do this?"

"Not really. I've never been to a gay bar without Molly."

Oh, wow. "Well, I've *never* been to a gay bar, so you're one up on me."

"Really?"

"Would you believe me if I told you I was straight?"

He blinks at me. "Umm … aren't you here for a guy?"

"I am."

"That doesn't sound so straight to me."

I know he's right. "Here's the thing. I know bi fits me, but my attraction to men very, very rarely happens. Sometimes I find myself drawn to one, maybe attracted, and when I am, I get over it quickly, but that's not happening with Art. So, I figure I need to sleep with him to move on. Other than these slight, uh, *sexuality hiccups*, I've always been with and wanted to be with women. It feels assumptive to call myself bi when I have exactly zero experience with the label."

We approach the bouncer, and I pay Will's cover before we go in. I figure it's the least I can do for dragging him here.

But once we're inside, Will doesn't follow me. He's watching me closely, backward-hat-covered head tilted to one side. "You do know there isn't a quota, right?"

"What do you mean?"

"You could go your whole life only ever being with women, but if you're attracted to men … good chance you're bi. Or pan. Or … whatever. Look, it's not my business to label you, but I just want you to know it's okay. There isn't a bi-test to complete before you get your validation card."

I can't argue with any of that. Logically, I know he's right. But when I haven't faced the biphobia, when I haven't embraced that side of me, when I haven't even considered the idea of settling down with a man, I feel like a fraud.

I know how ridiculous it sounds when I say I'm straight —especially since I barely believe it. But I don't know how to claim this bi side of me without having to explain that no, I haven't been with a man. No, I'm not sure if I ever will. No, my crushes don't last long.

So instead, all I say is "Sexuality is a headfuck, huh?"

"You have *no* idea." He claps my shoulder and passes me, walking down the hall into the club. The whole time I follow him, I mouth one thing, over and over.

Bi. I'm bi. Bisexual.

Even silent, the words feel fake.

10

ART

I LOVE THIS CLUB. HANGING OUT WITH MY BOYS IS ALWAYS A worthwhile time, but when I come here, I know I'm getting laid. There's a mix of people, body types, personalities, and sexualities. Whatever I'm in the mood for, I can usually find, and I'm blessed that it's rare I walk away from a night like this alone.

And tonight, I'm looking for a guy just like—

"Motherfucker."

At first, I think my eyes must be playing tricks on me, but no matter how many times I blink, he's still there. Hair loose and sexily messed up, straight-boy shorts that make him look like a dad, but a tank that's hanging loose enough I can make out a nipple, even from this far away. Lucky it's hot in here and he won't freeze those nipples right off.

I have to bite my fist to hold back a moan.

"What is it?" Keller asks. His long black hair is out

tonight too, and he's already had to fend off two twinks and a leather daddy since we got here.

"My goddamn employee."

"Where?" Mack immediately—and obviously—spins in his seat to look. And of course, Joey takes that exact moment to spot us. His eyes flick over the group before landing on mine. Then he lifts his thumb to his mouth, licks it, and casually drags it over his exposed nipple.

I pull my gaze away.

"It's suddenly hot in here," Keller teases, still watching Joey. Then his whole face falls. "What the hell is he doing here?"

I brave a quick look back Joey's way and see Will join him. He passes over a drink, and the two of them laugh over something.

Something funny.

Something *together*.

"He shouldn't be in a place like this," Keller says, about to stand up.

I yank him back down beside me. "A place like what?"

"Like …" He gestures to me and Mack. "A place with horny old dudes who'll want to get in his pants."

I lift my glass to my mouth, pretending to take a drink as I mutter, "Like you, you mean?"

"Fuck off." Keller scowls. "I'm just looking out for him."

"Looking out for his dick!" Mack shouts without an ounce of subtlety.

To take the attention off Keller, I reach for my fly. "What's that? You want to see a dick?"

"I know *I* do." Joey drops into the seat beside Mack.

"Well, that's one of us," Mack says. "My answer might change later, depending on how desperate I get."

"What does that mean?" Joey asks.

I make a slashing motion at my throat, but Mack doesn't notice.

"If I don't find someone to hook up with, Art's going to help me move on himself."

Well, fuck. I can't read the look Joey sends my way.

Will hovers by Joey's side, trying not to look at Keller.

Keller doesn't let him succeed. "Will."

His gaze snaps to Keller. "Ah, hey. How are you? I'm, uh, out with a friend."

"Where's Molly?"

The change in Will is immediate. "How should I know? Packing?"

"He doesn't leave for months."

"I'm allowed to have other friends." Will sulks.

Keller doesn't answer, just watches him before dropping his gaze and finishing his drink. "I'm going to dance."

"Are we going to do that?" Mack asks me.

"Sure are. Now." I stand and send a wink Joey's way. "Have a good night, boys."

"Oh, we will."

Joey's tone isn't concerning at all. He's up to something, and him being here cannot be a coincidence, but at the end of the night, I'm going home with someone, and he'll be leaving here solo. If he wants to waste his night on … whatever he's doing, that's his problem.

Mack follows me onto the dance floor, looking bewildered and staring at everyone we pass. "It's been so long since I've been out like this," he says. "Did *we* used to wear next to nothing at these places?"

"Nope." I pull him close enough to dance. "We could hardly find a safe place like this, especially not around Kilborough. And we were scared in our twenties. Cautious. We have a lot to be grateful for."

"I'll say."

It takes Mack some time to loosen up and not look like he's one of those bobblehead dogs people put in cars. Though I'm not convinced the arm-flailing inflatable tube man impression is any better. Hey, if you can't caution them, join them. Who cares if I look like an idiot if it means saving Mack the embarrassment. It's his first night out, and I want it to go well. He's got singledom ahead of him, and he's not going to meet men sitting in his living room.

To my complete fucking surprise, a man around our age cuts between me and Mack. He's cute, hair receding a bit, and his sights are set on my friend. My friend who blushes right to his hairline the second this guy sets his hands on Mack's hips.

That was a thousand times easier than I thought it would be.

I turn and start dancing with a twinkish-looking guy, who leaves to get us drinks and never comes back. I'm approached by a shy man in his twenties, but he's too inno-cent-seeming for me. The next guy I walk up to abruptly turns his back on me and leaves, and then a hottie silver fox —after grinding against my leg for a good twenty minutes— mimes he needs the bathroom, then returns with a glass of water that he promptly throws in my face.

"*Pig.*"

He leaves me standing there, a little damp and a *lot* confused.

Something strange is going on.

I swipe the water from my face and glance around at some of the amused looks I'm getting. Then I shrug.

"What can I say?" I shout over the music. "My cock wrecked him for other men. Consider this a public service announcement."

"I like those kinds of announcements," a gorgeous guy says, stepping close and brushing off the damp spot on my chest.

My interest immediately clicks in. He's about my height, slightly younger, with the same jaw-length brown hair as Joey, only his is brushed neat rather than looking like an electrified mess. This man is clean-shaven and wearing gold contacts, but ... I can work with this.

"Art," I say.

"I know." He winds his free hand around my waist. "I've seen you around."

"Not hard when I've been around. A lot."

"So I've heard." He leans in. "Your so-called public service announcement."

"Just want people to know what they're getting themselves into."

"You trying to convince me you're packing?"

"Nope. My length and girth is a dream, but the thing that will wreck you is that I know how to use them."

"Oh, really?"

"I'm a master of my tools."

"I can't wait to—"

We're knocked from the side, and I stumble into the people dancing beside me. The guy I was with releases his grip as he spins around, looking pissed as hell and gearing up for a fight. And the split second his attention is off me, arms close around me from behind.

Cheap spray deodorant and bergamot fill my senses as lips press close to my ear.

"Feisty guy you've got there."

"Can't say I much appreciate being pushed either."

"It was only a little nudge," he says. He's laughing.

The guy I was with spins around, and his gaze lands on the two of us.

"Fuck off, dude, he's with me." Faux-Joey stares down real Joey, and I'm the unlucky—or lucky, actually, depending on what angle I look at it from—guy in the middle.

Joey hums, hands sliding down my front to rest above the band of my shorts. "You sure about that?"

Faux-Joey turns wide eyes on me. "Tell him, Art."

Yikes. Well, that puts me in a shitty spot. On the one hand, I'm right where I wanna be. On the other … admitting that out loud is definitely a trap.

"Remember when you two were fighting over me?" I ask. "Let's go back to that."

Joey chuckles while the other guy levels me with a glare. And seeing him take this so seriously makes it very obvious which way I'm going to go if I have to choose. If you can't take humor over shitty situations, life is going to make an orgy out of you.

The way Joey licks my ear tells me he gets that.

The way douchebag cat-eyes crosses his arms tells me he doesn't.

I pat Joey's hand and step out of his grip. "It's been fun, gents."

Then I turn my back on them both and walk away.

Doesn't help though. I can still smell him. And if you'd ever told me I'd be a fan of Axe or whatever the hell that is,

I would have cut off my nose to stop it from happening. It reminds me of being back in high school, crushing on the straight boys in the locker room.

Joey's clearly here to play games with me, and I wish I hated it. Really wish I could tell him to fuck off with his head tricks and take his queerbaiting somewhere else, but I'm a whore for the attention. For thinking there's an actual possibility he could want me as badly as I want him.

And there *is* a possibility, isn't there?

He's here. Would he really have given up his entire night to follow some old man around, cockblocking him at every turn? The more I think about the guys tonight, the more sure I am that's what's happening. I've never been through so many potentials before getting my dick sucked.

I tap my fingers against my thigh and figure out how I'm going to play this.

Grabbing Joey and dragging him into a back room is tempting; it'd get me answers once and for all. I'm not interested in harassment charges though, and Joey's clearly wanting to play a game.

I *love* games.

My gaze zeroes in on Will. He's sitting at the bar, staring glumly at the drink in front of him, which he tips back before calling for another.

Target acquired.

The guy's completely off-limits, considering he's Keller's kid's friend, but when it comes to pissing Joey off, he's fair prey.

I just have to hope Keller doesn't spot me first.

Even *I* can't pull off a black eye.

"Hey there, cutie," I say, slipping between him and the guy on the stool next to him.

"Oh, umm. Hi. Hi, uh, there. Art?"

I try for a winning smile, even though I'm worried he's stroking out. "The one and only. Will?"

"I am." He laughs. "Will I am. Like the singer. Or swiss."

"Swiss?"

"You know … doctor. Doctor swiss."

It's a real challenge to keep a flirty look on my face. "Dr. *Seuss*?"

Instead of an answer, all Will gives me is a large burp before face-planting on the bar.

Aaand there goes that plan.

"Hey." I pat him on the shoulder, drawing out a pathetic noise and nothing else.

At least I know he's still alive.

I'm about to go find Joey and tell him to take his friend home when I spot Keller, shirtless, on the edge of the dance floor.

I wave to get his attention and watch as his focus slips from me and lands on Will.

He's over in a flash. "What's going on?"

"He's drunk."

"Will?"

An indistinguishable noise answers him.

"Want me to get Joey or—"

"No, I've got this." Keller runs his hand over Will's back. "Let's get you home."

Will's head shoots up, and he blinks bleary-eyed at Keller. "Am I dreaming?"

"Just drunk." Keller loops an arm around him. "Come on."

But instead of standing, Will falls backward off the stool and into Keller's arms. "My hero."

Keller hoists him into a bridal carry. Which is a feat since Will isn't exactly a small guy. "And my pain in the ass."

I grin at how Will is rubbing his face on Keller's chest. "Don't pull a muscle, old man."

"Fuck you too, Art." Then he leaves, carrying Will like he weighs nothing. They'll probably be hit up on the way out to make sure Will's not being taken advantage of, but at least I know he's in good hands.

A loud groan comes from beside me. "I think I just found another man crush."

"Yeah, me too." I turn to Joey and find him already looking at me. "You're not going to leave me alone so I can hook up, are you?"

"Nope. But you can hook up with me."

I shake my head and stalk away from him, but Joey keeps up.

"I'm relentless, aren't I?" he asks.

"You say that like it's a good thing."

"Because we both know it is."

"No, we both know you're a tease with no follow-through. What did I do to deserve this?"

Joey grabs my arm and tugs me into the corridor that leads to the bathrooms. Then he presses me up against the wall. "Who says I won't?"

"You. Countless times."

"You sure about that?"

"What do you think being straight means, genius?"

The teasing slides from his face. "I—"

"What do you want, Joey?"

"You." And when his eyes meet mine, I think I believe him. But that answer could mean many, many things.

"And what do you plan on doing with me once you have me?"

He swallows. "My brain doesn't know, but my body is screaming for *everything*."

The hope inside me ebbs. His lips are right there, his face, his body already so close to mine his heat is like a furnace. But if his head isn't sure, this can't happen.

I press against him, backing him into the opposite wall until our positions are reversed. He's so close I can count every eyelash, can make out the faded freckles underneath his eyes. The want running hot through me is struggling to take over, knowing he'll let me, but I refuse to give in.

"It's no secret that I want you," I rasp, freeing the words. It feels both good and terrifying to say out loud. "But that doesn't change anything. Until your head and your body are on the same page, I don't want a part in your game."

"And when they are?"

My breath hitches as his fingers sneak under my shirt, running over the sensitive skin on my stomach. "Then you better be fucking ready. Because I *will* give you everything. And it'll leave you begging for more."

11

JOEY

Do I GO HOME AND JERK OFF OVER THAT PROMISE? YOU CAN bet your ass I do. *I'll give you everything.* Damn, those are some sexy words to come out of that sexy mouth. Having someone so handsome and powerful pressed up against me like that, knowing that he had complete control over the situation, was something else. I've never had a thrill like that. Not when we've been flirting, not with any of my previous relationships, and not with any of my other crushes.

If Art had kissed me, if he'd wanted more, I would have gone through with anything and everything.

The only problem is, I don't know if I would have regretted it after.

I'd like to think I wouldn't. I'd like to think that sleeping with my boss, let alone a man, is something that wouldn't affect me, but until I've been there, done that, how the hell do I actually know?

This obsession is getting too much though. The way I

crave him is worsened by that night out, and for the last week at work, he's back to being a ghost. The few times I have spotted him, he's passed through the bar quickly, eyes trained on his phone, making fast, casual conversation with anyone but me. It's driving me crazy in all the best ways.

I need his attention.

While I'm waiting for him to come down for a lunch break so I can plan my moment to pounce, Will walks in.

"Joey, hey."

"Hey." I haven't seen him since he was carried out of the club, but at least today, he has more of a spring in his step. "How did you pull up?"

"Horribly." He's grinning.

"Let me guess—Keller nursed you back to health?"

Will hisses at me to be quiet as he glances around. "No, not … not exactly."

"Then why do you look one dog bone away from pissing yourself?"

"Fuck off, do not."

"Uh-huh." I run my eyes over him again. "You do look a lot happier than when I last saw you."

"Yeah, well, I'm normally happy. That was a rough day. Anyway, I wanted to say thanks for helping me through it, and, uh, sorry for being such a downer."

"You weren't."

"Kinda was."

I tuck my hands in the back pockets of my jeans. "You know, I meant what I said. About needing a friend. I know this sounds kinda preschool with coming right out and asking, but if you need anyone, that could be cool."

"I think I'll take you up on that offer."

"Nice." I step closer so it's only the counter between us.

"Now, tell me, did he rub your back while you threw your guts up? Tuck you in? Kiss you better?"

Will laughs. "Nothing that exciting. But he looked after me. I stayed in the spare room. Got some shirtless eye candy the next morning. So that helped."

"It always does. You could get that every morning if you moved in."

He hums, but he doesn't sound convinced. "If *he* actually offers, I might think about it. But he's a grown man. He doesn't want a roommate. Especially not one the same age as his son."

"Well, like you said, wait and see if he offers. That kind of thing is his call."

Will nods, staring off across the bar.

"You're hoping he offers, aren't you?"

"Desperately." His face contorts. "That sounds pathetic, doesn't it?"

The stairs behind the bar creak, and I know it can only be one person. "Yep, but speaking of desperate and pathetic, I'm going to go and be both of those things with my boss."

"Good luck."

"I'll need it." Because if I have to drape myself over his lap for his attention, I'm not professional enough to resist.

"Hey, before you run off, I need your number."

My gaze flicks to where Art's just appeared. "Okay, but I'm about to get real flirty, so go with it, okay?"

Will's face reddens. "Give me the best you've got."

I round the long counter and reach Will just as Art is halfway through the bar. My throaty laugh draws his attention, but I turn my focus completely on Will.

"I had a fun night too," I say, dropping my voice and running a hand up his chest.

Will's eyes widen, and I want to snigger at how shocked he looks, but I angle him away from Art so he doesn't give me away.

"Want my number? I'd like to do it again sometime."

Will smiles and pulls his phone from his pocket, looking uncertain, but at least the shock is melting away and being replaced by something close to amusement.

I punch my number in and hold the phone up between us. "Call me soon. Promise?"

Then Will surprises the hell out of me by leaning in and kissing my cheek. "Like I could stay away from a guy as hot as you."

Eh, he gets points for trying, at least, even though the delivery is off. Poor Will. If this is what he's like when he's actually flirting, there's no way in hell he'll ever score his best friend's dad. Dads are a whole new territory.

With the lunch rush not started yet, the room is still quiet enough that our voices carry, and the snarl on Art's face makes it clear he caught the gist of our conversation. He admitted he wants me; now I need him to take what he wants.

"Thanks," I mutter to Will, stepping away. "Let me know if I can ever return the favor."

"Will do."

He leaves, and I beeline for Art's table.

Even though needing time off is something us bartenders usually swap between ourselves once the schedule is out, sometimes I like to mix things up a bit and go to Art directly. It has the pros of both getting me one-on-one time and annoying the shit out of him. Two things I love more than anything else. Given the number of night shifts I have to switch around because of my night classes

—that he cannot know about since, as far as he's concerned, I already have my diploma—I've had a lot of opportunities.

"I have a favor," I announce as I join him.

"You always have a favor."

"But this time, it's important."

"And your cousin's wedding wasn't?"

I wave a hand. "*More* important."

He sighs, pretending to be bored when really, his eyes are locked on Will as he walks out the front door. "Out with it."

"I can't work next Wednesday but can make up for it Friday night."

"No." It's cute he tries when we both know he'll give in. He always does.

"But I have to take my girlfriend to this thing." Date with the girlfriend, meeting with my teacher, same thing, right? I'm pretty sure Art doesn't believe me, but I'm not about to tell him the real reason when it's covering the lie I told to get this job.

"What thing?"

"Well, it's a surprise, so …"

"I highly doubt I need to be kept in suspense purely because it's a surprise for her."

I grin, and his gaze drops to my mouth. "I'm taking her out to a movie."

"I know I'm prehistoric compared to you, but even I know movies have different session times."

"But this is a special showing. A throwback screening of her favorite movie. *Breakfast at Tiffany's.*" *Thank you, Hannah, for that little piece of information.*

"Uh-huh."

"So I have to change my shift, otherwise I'd be a horrible

boyfriend, and you're always telling us work-life balance is important."

"Yeah, make your work your life. There you go, balanced."

I pace around the table and drop my ass on the side of it. Right next to him. Even the air between us feels tight with tension. "You should get out more."

He sets his hands over his stomach and leans back in his chair to look up at me. "Oh, I get out plenty."

"I don't mean to hook up. I mean to have fun."

He snorts. "I have plenty of fun."

"What? With your divorced group? Remind me, where do you guys have your meetings again?"

"I happen to like it here."

It makes me wonder if he works because he enjoys it or if he's escaping from something. "The place will still run without you for one day."

"But it won't run without my bartenders. On their set shifts."

"Which is why I'm giving you plenty of notice for needing the day off."

"The roster's already out."

"Great thing I hear about being boss …" I lean down, way too close for it to look casual. "You can change whatever you want on the schedule."

He leans in to match me, and my whole body vibrates with his proximity. "I can also fire people too."

"Aww, you know just what to say to make a man swoon."

"Keep going and you'll find out just how serious I am."

I flick his ear, startling the intensity out of his face.

"You're the best. Really. My girlfriend is going to be so grateful."

"That I'm saving her from spending the day with you? I know."

"So, Friday?"

"Wednesday."

I smirk and wave a finger between us. "It's cute. How we always do this."

"At least one of us thinks so."

"You'll admit you find me adorable one day."

"Yeah," he agrees. "The day you actually show up for all of your scheduled shifts."

"You are just, like, so funny." I'm not even trying to flirt properly now.

"You're supposed to be using the day shifts to catch up on sleep."

I blink at his words, processing them. Turning them over because it kind of sounds like ... he really did swap them for me. "You *do* care."

"That you're not injuring my other employees? Of course."

"You moved my shifts around for me." Knowing that makes me feel like an asshole for needing to swap one now, but I can't help that my stupid teacher wanted me to check in for a stupid meeting.

Art grunts, and I know that no matter how hard I push, he'll never admit it. "How does your girlfriend feel about you flirting your way into other shifts?"

"If it's for her benefit, she's firmly pro-flirt."

"And what about you giving out your number to other men?"

I hold his gaze, letting my smile out slowly. "Why, Art. Were you eavesdropping?"

"You were practically shouting."

"That's dramatic."

"He was all but humping your leg."

I want to laugh. Really, really want to let it out at the thought of Will humping my leg. This jealous side of Art is so hot though, so somehow, I control myself. "If you'd rather I gave *you* my number instead, all you have to do is ask, snugglebutt."

"Call me snugglebutt again. I dare you."

"What are you gonna do, fire me?"

"You have no idea how I long for the day."

"Just edging yourself? I can help with that."

"You already do more than enough."

"That's right." I pretend to remember what he said, even though it's been on a constant loop in my brain. "You *want* me."

"And *your* body wants everything from me."

Okay, maybe I hadn't had total control when I said that, even though it's true. "Will you be here Friday night?"

"No."

"Pity. I was going to wear my sluttiest shorts. Just for you."

"Like those grandpa ones you were wearing the other night?"

I cluck him on the chin. "I guess you'll never know."

Then I walk away before we can go around again on the shift thing *or* I say more than I should. My brain might be fighting me on giving in to my urges with him, but when Art's around, my brain goes offline.

If it's offline, it can't fight me.

Problem solved.

And with the way it was pumping lust into my system at the mere sight of Art, it makes me think that I'm more ready than I thought. Regrets, no regrets. I owe it to myself to *try*.

Now I need to find the right moment.

12

ART

I NEED TO GO HOME. I *SHOULD* GO HOME. IT'S NEARING FIVE on a Friday, and sitting around in my office because the man I can't get off my brain is downstairs is as pathetic as I've ever been. The way he tempts me should be illegal.

My gaze drifts back to my security monitors, to the bar, where Joey is pulling drinks. He's so charismatic that people are drawn to him. Tip him big. Try to sleep with him.

I see you, I tell his image, not for the first time.

Damn … I'm screwed.

He says he's straight, he plays the part of a flirt, but I saw it in his eyes the other night. Curiosity. Want. My body burned having him that close.

But I won't make a move based on a hunch, and actually, given the clusterfuck I've gotten myself into, I doubt I'll ever make a move at all.

Ethics? Moi?

No one would believe it.

There's a light rap on my door, and my gaze flicks back to the security cameras. Joey is missing, and that was definitely his knock. I know his knock because he makes so many damn visits up here.

With a deep breath, I switch off the feed and wait.

A moment later, Joey cracks the door open, and his head appears in the gap. "You free, boss?"

"Would it matter if I wasn't?"

He gives me that smile I knew would come. Boyish, carefree. I watch as he steps inside and purposely closes the door behind himself.

"I was about to head off," I tell him. But I don't make a move, and by the way he looks at me, we both know it's a lie. "What do you want this time?"

"I'm on a break."

"Lucky I supply a break room, then, isn't it?"

Joey grins, and damn, I love that one. The one where he senses a challenge and it excites him. It excites me too. I can't stop picturing what that kind of grin tastes like. "Thought you might like my company. And to see my mega-slutty shorts up close."

My gaze immediately drops to said shorts. They have more tears than material, including a very tempting one near his groin. Thank fuck I keep the temperature constant in the bar, even though it's not overly cold out tonight.

"I approve."

"Thought you might." Joey's all smooth movements and steady gaze as he keeps coming closer. "I've been thinking about what you said."

"Which time?"

"At the club."

"I said a lot at the club." My heartbeat gets faster though.

Like I can sense something coming. "You're going to have to be specific."

"You said to let you know when my head and body are both on board. Good news, boss." Joey leans in. "I'm ready. And I have half an hour to kill."

My breath catches, threatens to suffocate me. The things he's saying are dangerous with a capital *D* because if he's serious, I plan to take him up on the offer. I'm done with the games. I can't keep running in circles for the guy, but I can't bring myself to stop either. I like flirting with him. I like that glimpse of possibility. What I don't like is the thought that none of it is as real on his end as it is on mine.

But the longer Joey looks at me like that, gaze never wavering, the less I'm about to hold back.

It's time to put an end to all of this shit. Maybe he's after more time off, or a raise, or some kind of promotion, I don't know, but what I do know is that tonight, I'm calling his bluff. We're both adults. We both claim to want this. So what would happen if I said yes?

"What do you plan to do with that half hour?" I ask.

"You."

I laugh at how simply he says it. "Me, huh?"

"Sure. If you'll let me."

I shrug and roll my chair back. "Ready when you are."

Joey's eyes widen, but I don't say a thing. Just sit there, waiting. Curious about what he's going to do next. All the possibilities flash through my mind, and I'd love for any one of them to come true. Joey has sufficiently wrapped me around his finger with no plans to let me go.

To my total surprise, Joey rounds the desk.

"Just stating," I say, "that there is absolutely no pressure on my end. You have my consent, but nothing that happens in here plays any part in your job."

"I know."

"So this isn't the type of situation where if you walk away, I'll fire you. Or if you suck my dick, I'll promote you. I don't play those games. In fact, if you suck my dick when you have no interest in sucking it, *then* I'll fire you."

Joey's eyes burn brighter, lips curling at the corners. "You want me to suck your dick?"

"I've wanted it since the day I hired you."

"You've got good taste."

"Or terrible taste, depending on how you look at it."

Joey laughs as he scrapes his hair back into a ponytail. The sight is so damn erotic my cock jumps in anticipation of what might be about to happen.

"Because I'm your employee?" Joey asks.

"Exactly."

"Why don't we pretend for tonight that I'm not?"

I snort. "Don't think it works that way."

Then Joey sets his hands on my thighs. Strong, veiny hands that slowly shift my legs open wider. "We're the ones making the rules," he says before slowly folding to his knees.

I never thought I'd see the day Joey Manning was on his knees in front of me. Fuck me, it's a view. Shrewd eyes, hard features, determination set into every angle. The slightest chunk of hair has fallen out of his knot, and this time, instead of ignoring it, I reach forward to tuck it behind his ear.

He leans into my touch like a love-starved kitten.

"You really want to do this?" I ask, voice low.

He doesn't answer, just reaches for my fly.

I suck in a breath, watching, waiting, dying to know if

he's going to chicken out or jump right in, and even I'm torn on which way I want this to go.

On one hand, all that flirting has given me a Pavlovian response to him.

On the other hand, him being straight would be a lot easier to believe if he actually stayed fucking straight.

The *ziiiiip* of my fly is loud enough that I can hear it over the beating in my ears. Joey sucks in a deep breath that makes his lungs expand, making him sound as nervous as I feel.

Which is wild.

Because I don't get nervous. Especially not over sex.

But there's one giant elephant between us, straining in his direction, and I'm just waiting to see if he's actually going to acknowledge it or not.

Am I calling his bluff? Is he calling mine?

It's the hottest game of chicken I've ever been involved with, and my dick's so hard it could chop wood. But the moment Joey curls his fingers into the waistband of my underwear, my hand slaps down over his.

His gaze snaps up to mine, and the uncertainty I was sure I could sense comes through loud and clear. Disappointment crashes around me, and I swallow hard, knowing this is right but wishing things could go literally any other way.

I'm almost shaking with want. His lips are right there. Parted, wet, like he's run his tongue over them, and the idea that they could be stretched around my cock right now is too much. I move his hand away.

"No," I say.

Joey's uncertainty disappears as his eyes narrow. "No?"

"You don't want this."

"Are you kidding me? Who the hell are you to tell me what I want?"

I push my chair back and stand, pulling my fly up with me as I turn my back on him. "It's all over your face. You're terrified."

"Yeah, because I've never sucked cock before. Not because I don't want to."

That gives me pause.

"You know what?" Joey bursts. Without turning to him, I can tell he's shoved to his feet. "Fuck you. All this time, you've been acting like I've been messing with *you*, but what about my feelings? Are you honestly that much of a dick that you've been playing with me to prove you could? Well, congrats, Art. You can land the straight boy. I hope you're feeling happy with yourself."

"You're pissed I said no?" I turn around with a frown. "There are no laws I have to have sex with you."

The son of a bitch actually rolls his eyes at me. "I don't need a lesson on consent, thanks. If you don't want to have sex with me, that's one thing. But you acting like you're saying no for *me*? Well, fuck you very much. I can speak for myself. You don't get to act like some kind of savior." He takes an angry step closer so his face is right next to mine. "I would have sucked your dick, and I would have loved every second of it."

He turns on his heel, making a beeline for the door, and I watch him as I round my desk, his words echoing in my head.

I'd stopped him because I thought it was right. I didn't want him to go through with this, regret it, and then … hate me. I didn't want Joey to hate me. Which is maybe the first time ever that I've acknowledged I actually give a shit about what he thinks.

I don't give a shit what anyone thinks. Except him.

I hate it. The fact that maybe I didn't stop him because *he* wasn't sure.

I stopped him because *I* wasn't.

"Wait," I say as his hand finds the door handle. My heart is beating out an erratic rhythm, and I'm off-balance enough that I need to rest my ass against my desk to stay standing. To stay in control. I inhale long and deep, grounding myself, reminding myself this is only sex.

And maybe sex with the annoying asshole will pop this swelling balloon of need once and for all.

I drop my voice, forcing all the conviction I can into the one word. "Stay."

13

JOEY

STAY. IT SLIPS DOWN MY SPINE LIKE ICE ON A HOT DAY. Chilling, pleasant, bringing goose bumps out across my skin. I'm still about a second away from walking out the door anyway, but I can't say I'm that proud.

Art had pissed me off when he'd acted like *I* was the one who didn't want it, when for the first time in my life, it was the most certain I'd been about anything. For once, Art was the one having second thoughts.

"What about your girlfriend?" he asks.

The question surprises me enough to face him. I shouldn't have. There's Art, in all his sexy fucking glory. Tall, lean, full lips, dark hair, and eyes so goddamn penetrating they could hit my prostate from across the room. That shivery, horny feeling passes over me, and I'm *craving* to kneel in front of him again. It isn't an urge I've had for anyone in my life, but all it took was one time to have me hooked.

He's still waiting for an answer, and I almost don't want to give it to him, but at this point, what do I have to lose?

"There is no girlfriend. I only said that to make you jealous."

His eyes flash, and then those pillowy lips quirk on one side. "Really?"

"Yeah, yeah, I'm sure you're thrilled."

"Thrilled doesn't cover it."

We lock eyes, and my next breath stutters out of me. The need is almost crippling. If he tells me to leave again, there's no way I'll be able to go downstairs and make out like everything is fine. Not after admitting that. Not after the way I've put myself out there for him, vulnerable to his rejection.

Art pops the top button on his dress pants.

The air between us is thick with tension, my pulse racing, the room deadly silent. I'm on edge, begging, begging, *begging* for him to move closer. To say something.

Instead, Art slooowly drags down his fly, then grips the edge of the desk on either side of his hips.

"A man never leaves my bed disappointed." He steps wider. "Enjoy."

Even though there's no bed in sight, I'm not about to stand around arguing semantics. I take my shot and hope like hell he doesn't reject me a second time.

My body is flooding with lust and adrenaline and a million other emotions that are threatening to crash down over me, but the one overriding it all is determination. I want this to be good. I want to enjoy it and for him to feel the same. I want this last year and a bit of sexual tension and flirting to pay off because it'd kill me for Art to walk away from here disappointed.

And given how much experience he's had, the odds aren't in my favor.

I kneel in front of him, dragging his pants down his powerful thighs as I go, and I'm immediately faced with his hard cock tenting his black boxer briefs. They're tight and cling to all the right places, and the sight of where the cotton hugs the top of his hairy legs is one of the most erotic things I've seen in my life. I'm almost cross-eyed at the image, and I have no idea how something so simple can be so fucking intimate, but I can't stop myself from touching. Both hands grip his thighs while my fingers sneak under the material. His skin is hot, and knowing it's *Art's* legs is threatening to overwhelm me.

Before I stop myself, I lean in and press my face to his groin.

Art's inhale is loud, and he shifts slightly, cock moving against my cheek, muscles bunching under my palms.

I can hardly believe this is happening.

I can hardly believe it hasn't happened before.

He clears his throat. "Even though I'm enjoying every second of this, you can't have long left on your break."

Ah, fuck.

Against every instinct, I'm going to have to be quick. I don't want to be back late and have someone come looking for me and find me with Art's cock in my mouth.

No need for all the staff to be jealous of me.

With that amusing thought, I pull down his boxer briefs and set his cock free.

I groan. Out loud. Not my finest moment, but I doubt it'll be the last time. His cock is … well, it's a cock. Different from mine, but the same in a lot of ways. He's long and thicker, which I'll be bitter about later, with an angry vein running up the underside and a dark purple, needy-looking head. I've never, ever thought about cocks and where they rank on the scale of sexy, but I can safely say with Art's right in my face, I can't ever remember being so turned on by something in my life.

Before I can think too hard about the whole situation, I wrap my lips around his head. A salty taste explodes across my tongue. He's already leaking precum, and somehow, I find that so goddamn hot. It's always been a massive turn-on with chicks as well, but I don't know if it's because this is my first dick, or because it's Art, or because he's my boss and I'm on a time limit, but my head is buzzing. I'm so checked out and turned on I wouldn't be surprised if I come in these ridiculous shorts I'm wearing.

"*Lindo.*"

It's only when I glance up at his raspy voice that I realize I'd closed my eyes. Tasting him. Savoring this moment. Art's gaze has darkened, and his stare has a heaviness to it that I'm not used to. I hold it and slowly suck more of him down.

His cock feels way too big for my mouth, and I'm barely halfway when I gain huge respect for all the deep-throaters out there because I have no goddamn clue how they do it.

"Use your hand," Art says.

I have no problem following orders. In fact, every time he gives me one, it only makes my cock harder. So that's new and kinda exciting. For him to be calling the shots while I do whatever I have to in order to please him.

My hand wraps around his silky-smooth erection, and I finally break his gaze. I work him over the way I love, jerking him off with my saliva while I lick and suck his head before diving down as far as I can go. Over and over until I gag, then back off again.

The sound of his ragged breathing and murmured Portuguese helps build my confidence. And not only have I discovered that I really, really love dick, but I'm actually having fun. It's a new level of flirting, to bring him close to the edge, then back off again, to tease him over and over, the way I've loved to do since we met, only this teasing isn't a game. It's for real, and there's only one way this ends. With him coming in my mouth.

My eyes roll back with that thought, and suddenly, there's nothing I want more than to feel him pulsing in my mouth. I stop teasing. Stop holding back. My cock is rock hard and begging to get in on the action, but I ignore it in favor of what Art needs.

I grunt as he pulls my bun out of its band with one hand before the other dives into my hair. He twists it around his fingers, pulling it until it prickles my scalp and makes my balls tight. Then he holds on as his hips give tiny thrusts.

"Yes, yes, Joey." His voice is husky. "*Tão bom. Tão perfeito.*"

Yes is a word I understand. I double down on my efforts, slurps filling the still room, Art's deepened breathing telling me I'm on the right track, the small bursts of precum like a promise of what he has in store.

I'm ready.

I want it.

I jerk him fast, and it's like every solo session I've ever had has been training for this moment. My jaw is aching, cheeks getting sore, neck needing to be stretched out, but I'm so consumed by his taste and the sounds he's making, the scent coming from his skin that I'm finding it hard to concentrate on anything at all.

Except Art.

Art's cock.

Art's cum.

Art's pleasure.

I'd do the entire last year over knowing I'd end up on my knees for him again.

This is addictive. Intoxicating. The way his cock passes again and again between my lips. Faster now. Pistoning in and out as he chases everything I have to give him.

My hand sneaks between his legs to curl around his tight balls, and it sets Art off.

"I'm coming," he gasps, body tensing, right before his dick twitches in my mouth, and spurt after spurt of cum hits my tongue.

I suck and swallow my way through it, chasing his release, and when he slumps back against his desk, hands freeing my hair, I run my tongue over him one more time to make sure I've gotten everything before letting him slip from my mouth.

He looks down at me.

I look up at him.

Something settles in my chest and feels *right*.

"Was that good?" I ask, a hint of insecurity leaking out.

Art holds out a hand, and I take it, letting him pull me to my feet. He tugs me closer until he can wrap his arms around me, and even though I'm still so horny that I'm hot all over, having him hold me like this sets off an explosion of nerves in my gut. "You have no idea." Then he looks right into my eyes as his hand slides into my shorts and closes around my cock.

His skin is callused—from what, I have no idea—and the roughness as he jerks me off, along with his eye contact, is too much. My legs are fucking *shaking*, and it's lucky he's holding on to me because at this point, he's the only reason I'm still upright.

"You're going to come," he says. "Then you're going to go back downstairs, tell no one what happened, and when your shift ends, you'll clock off and come straight back up here. Understand?"

I nod so fast I get dizzy.

"Good. Because I haven't had a taste of you yet." He leans in and bites down on my bottom lip at the same time as he pulls some kinda magic trick in my pants. He squeezes hard, twists his hand over the head, and then increases the pressure all the way down my shaft before releasing it again. All it takes is one more stroke and I'm done for. I collapse against him with a grunt, and Art doesn't stop touching me until he's milked out every last drop.

Right into my underwear.

He releases my lip with an evil grin.

"When I let you leave here tomorrow," he says, "all you'll be craving is more."

14

ART

I'M NOT A SLEEPOVER KINDA GUY. I HAVE MY FUN, I SAY MY thanks, then I'm a gentleman and escort my hookup to the door.

Unfortunately, the second I get my hands on Joey, that craving intensifies, and even coming in his mouth doesn't relieve it. All night, I'm on edge, anxiously waiting to see if he regrets what happened or if he comes back to me at closing.

And maybe I should have given him more credit because as soon as it hits 1:00 a.m., Joey walks straight into my office, flicks the lock, and strips out of his shorts without so much as a hello.

I fold my arms and lean against the doorway into the bedroom I have off my office, watching while he undresses. "Someone's in a hurry."

"Someone worked half a shift with dried cum in his pubes."

My head tips back on a laugh. "Did it remind you of me?"

"It reminded me that I'll need to get you back at some point." His shirt goes next.

I don't bother hiding how I check him out. "You assume you'll have the chance."

"Oh, I'll make sure I do." He drops his briefs, then straightens, running a hand through his shaggy hair. Holy fuck, that body. He's leaner than me, not quite concerningly thin, but his muscle is more obvious than I was expecting for someone who's never mentioned working out.

My curiosity goes into overdrive, but I push it down because I can't imagine he'd be impressed if I start grilling him on what he's eaten today. My cum doesn't count as a meal.

"Lean over my desk," I tell him.

"Why?" His eyes narrow. "Are you going to fuck me?"

"Would you let me?"

"Not sure yet."

"Then how about you lean over my desk and we'll see if we can't find an answer for you."

He takes a hesitant step closer, and I huff.

"I'm not going to fuck you. You'll be begging me to. But I won't."

He laughs, suddenly full of confidence as he crosses the room and leans over the wood. "I'm curious now."

And not at all shy. His ass isn't pointed my way, but as I move closer, rounding his body and bringing that sexy sight into view, Joey doesn't try to hide. His hole is on display, making my mouth water and my cock start to thicken. I might not be planning to fuck him tonight, but damn do I want to one day.

That kind of thinking only reminds me that ground rules need to be set.

"This is a one-night thing," I tell him. "Normally, I wouldn't even do that, but after how long you've edged me, I think I'm going to need it to get all this want out."

"I know what you mean." He glances back over his shoulder, and every time our eyes connect, I get this *zap* deep in my gut. It's addictive and feels incredible—which is why I immediately look away.

"One night, huh?" he asks.

"That's all I have to offer."

He grins. "I know who you are. I know casual's your style. But who's to say *you* won't be the one getting addicted to me?"

I run a hand down his back, mentally high-fiving myself when he arches into my touch. "I'm confident."

"Let's not forget you're the one who demanded I come back up here."

"And you came running like a lost puppy."

He snorts. "I've discovered a new toy. Sue me."

"I could, or … I could show you another one."

I palm Joey's ass cheeks, then kneel behind him and spread him wide. Leaning in, I lick a long stripe from his balls to his hole.

"What the *fuck*?"

My laugh is full of dark amusement. "Want me to stop?"

"I … I …"

I flick my tongue over his hole again.

"Fuck. Continue. Please. I think."

"Let me guess—never had your hole touched before?"

"Never."

I sneer. "You really are a straight boy. You've got three

seconds to tell me to stop, and after that, there's no going back."

"Do … do you like ass play?"

"On other men? It's my favorite. On me, occasionally, I crave it. I mostly top, though, because I like to give."

Joey twists to try and look at me again. "Isn't … isn't it the other way around? Like, the bottom's giving it up to get you off?"

I'm going to have a lot of fun educating him. "It's different for everyone, but for me, if I'm fucking a man, it's my job to make every inch of his body feel good. To make him beg for release. To turn him inside out and have him walk away completely sated." I suck my thumb into my mouth, then rub Joey's hole with it while I talk. "Topping for me isn't about getting off. I only get to do that when my partner is completely satisfied."

Joey shudders, fighting his body's natural instinct to withdraw from my touch. "And whe-when you bottom?"

That's a good question.

Instead of answering, I grab his hips to stop him from getting away and close my mouth over his opening. I lick and suck his hole and sink my teeth into his fleshy cheeks while I try to figure out what to tell him. Bottoming for me is different. There's more connection. The few times I've walked away from being dicked down by a hookup have left me feeling *off* the next day. It's not something I put myself through often, even if I crave it sometimes. The physical payoff isn't worth the mental toll I end up paying.

Joey's moans get louder as I double down on my efforts with my tongue, trying to loosen him up enough to penetrate him.

"A-Art." He's alternating between fighting my hold and

pushing back against my face. "It's … oh, holy shit. You're gonna kill me. Seriously. I'm so hard it goddamn hurts."

I swipe my tongue over him one more time before standing up behind him. He's gone to jelly again, panting and already sweaty. I love a man who doesn't hold back, and Joey doesn't try to hide how turned on he is.

I wrap my arms around him and pull him upright, my cock throbbing at the feel of his naked body pressed against my clothes.

Joey's head falls back against my shoulder. "That was …"

I hum because I know. Then I lift my pointer and middle fingers to his lips. "Suck."

"Why?"

"Because in order to play with your prostate, I have to shove these up your ass."

"But … but …"

I groan against his ear, pulling the lobe between my teeth. "If you don't want me to, say no, and I'll go back to using my tongue until you come. But if what you're about to say is worry or concern about me playing with your ass for reasons other than you don't want me to, I suggest you shut the fuck up and get my fingers nice and wet."

And like I'd noticed earlier, Joey's good at following orders. Every other interaction I've had with him, I never would have guessed, but the way he reacts so easily to my demands is fucking beautiful. His lips close over my fingers, and he sucks them like he was sucking my cock earlier. I give him a few seconds before pressing down on his tongue, and his mouth immediately floods with saliva.

"Perfect."

Joey tenses against me as my fingers trail along his crease before reaching his hole. I keep one arm around his chest, but his ass is clenched too tight for me to do anything. I tilt my head to press a kiss to his temple.

"I know it's different, but if you can't relax, I can't do any more. I'm not going to hurt you."

"I know. I just …"

"Do you not want me to?"

"I sucked on your fingers like a goddamn lollipop. Yes, I want it. We're just back to my body and brain being on different wavelengths that have apparently switched."

"I can work with that." His head being on board is the main thing. "Touch yourself. Slowly. Focus on getting to the edge."

He wraps his hand around himself, and I trail kisses down the side of his face until the rest of his body loosens. Then I get to work. Gently, slowly. I wait until he's ready before slipping my first finger inside. It's clear he's taken off guard by the intrusion, but he keeps on jerking off like I've directed, and I keep slowly fucking him with my finger. I take my time, stretch him out, let him sink back into that place where he's feeling good and loose, then press the second finger in. He fights it a little more this time, but I wait him out, letting him adjust—and it's a toss-up whether it's his ass or his mind holding him back. It's a different sensation, and sometimes it takes a minute to adjust. Sometimes it never happens.

Thankfully, it doesn't take long before Joey is pliant in my arms again, strokes getting faster. I fuck him with my fingers, getting harder and deeper with every whimper until I feel it.

"*Fuck, shit, damn, godshitting, holy fucks.*"

I almost crack up laughing, but there's nothing funny about the way Joey shudders and jerks off with purpose. He's pushing back onto my fingers, moaning and writhing in my arms, and it's the goddamn hottest thing I've seen in a long time. He's pinned against me, straining in my hold, hips thrusting back and forth between my fingers and his fist, and I get completely swept up in the sounds he's making. I kiss and lick along the column of his throat until I reach the dip of his shoulder. His skin is so soft and tempting and smells like *him*. My mouth closes over a spot, and I suck hard, determined to leave a mark.

"*Nrg*, Art."

He comes for the second time tonight, and a deep satisfaction settles in my chest. Dark and possessive and addictive. The feeling passes, but even when I remove my fingers, even when Joey slumps back against me and I brush his sweaty hair off his forehead and look into his lust-drunk eyes, I crave it again.

He turns in my arms and laughs weakly, lifting a hand to his neck. "Did you give me a hickey?"

"Yes."

"Little high school, isn't it, Art?"

"This is nothing like an inexperienced accidental bruise."

Surprise flickers over his face. "You did it on purpose."

"Yes."

"Why?"

"Because I want you to remember, at least for the next few days, every single thing about tonight. I want you to look at it and feel me behind you, my lips on your skin, and I want you to know that for tonight, you were mine."

He doesn't reply for a second, and my chest squeezes that maybe I've gone too far, but then that wild spark hits his eyes, and he leans in closer. "Tonight's not over yet. How many more reminders do you think you can give me?"

15

JOEY

IT'S STILL DARK WHEN MY ALARM GOES OFF. NEITHER OF US has had any sleep, and there's just enough light in here that I can make out Art blinking across from me. Given he's always at work, it makes sense he's converted what was probably a storage cupboard into a tiny bedroom, and for once, I'm grateful for his insane work hours. The downside is sneaking out of here before anyone shows up and sees me.

"I need to go."

"Probably," he mutters.

I got him naked somewhere around my third orgasm, and it was worth it. Art's peak masculinity. Long body, wide shoulders, beefy arms. His torso isn't muscular, but somehow, that makes him hotter. He has hair on his chest and stomach—there's no possible way to confuse him for a woman—and it's one of the things I enjoyed most.

"You never answered me, you know," I say.

"About what?"

"Bottoming."

His jaw ticks. "It's something I have to be in the mood for." His gorgeous dark-rimmed eyes lower to run over my body before he reaches out and runs a fingertip over a hickey he's left on my ribs.

I follow his gaze and stroke one of the little dark spots. "You really didn't want me to forget, did you?"

"You set me a challenge." His grin is wicked. "You knew what you were doing."

"Turns out I learned a thing or two over the last year."

"Maybe you'll learn a thing or two about blow jobs in the next one."

I laugh and pinch his arm. "You told me it was great."

"I'm not going to kill your spirit, am I?"

"Wow. Just when we were actually getting along, you went and made me hate you again."

He wraps his arm around my waist and pulls me closer. "What about in a year, we'll celebrate our hookup-i-versary with another blow job, and I can rate how much you've improved?"

"Depends," I say, trying not to focus on his lack of jealousy when it comes to me sucking off other guys. "Are you going to let me get some practice in before then?"

"I'm sure you'll have plenty of offers to help you out."

I pull away from him and flop onto my back, trying to keep my voice light. "Doesn't work like that for me."

"Why? Still straight?" His voice is heavy with derision and ... something else.

"I ..." I suck down a breath. "Am bi. I guess."

"You guess?"

"I dunno, Art. That's the whole problem. Before last night, I struggled to even say the word because I didn't feel worthy of it. Now … well, I've slept with a man. I fucking loved it. If you offered, I'd be back to do it again in a heart-beat, but …"

"But?"

"I don't get like this with guys."

"You don't?"

I feel like an idiot, having to explain this over and over. Some days, I wish it was black-and-white. Fifty-fifty. Men and women. I don't work like that though, and it's so complicated and, honestly, kinda stupid to get into all the time. "You're the first guy I've ever been with for a reason, okay? Can we leave it at that?"

"Sure." But I can tell he's not done. "But if you were one of my DMC guys, I'd tell you not to worry about putting yourself in a box. Step outside it, let your wings free. Trust them to take you where you need to go."

"And since I'm not one of your DMC guys?" I roll back to face him. "What would you tell *me*?"

"Stop putting so much pressure on yourself." The way his voice drops, almost to a whisper, makes it seem like he's talking about more than my sexuality.

"Sometimes we don't have a choice."

His eyebrows knot, but he doesn't say anything else.

I try to lighten the mood. "So … a year?"

"Well, that was to give you a performance review. If you're not going to be practicing this year, it might be even poorer than your first one, given you won't have the first-timer handicap."

"I'll take my chances."

"One night, Joey."

"But you fucked up and just offered me a second."

"In a year."

"I'll take it."

He eyes me. "And if you have a girlfriend at that point?"

"I'll dump her."

"Wow. Ruthless with this imaginary girlfriend."

"I'm going to regret telling you this since your ego is already out of control, but I would stay single to get to see your cock again. But you have to do the same. If you get a boyfriend, I'm not above cutting a bitch."

Art's laugh fills the room. "That's one thing neither of us will ever have to worry about."

"Good." I hold up my pinky finger between us. "Next year?" And yeah, I'd prefer we hooked up way sooner than that—I'll be working on it—but I just need to get Art to agree to a repeat. That's it for now. As soon as I know he's open to one, I can put in the work to make it happen.

Because last night, excuse the dramatics, was life changing.

Art eyes me. "Joey …"

"One year. Our fuckiversary."

"Ooh, that's better than hookup-i-versary. How am I supposed to say no to that now?"

"You don't." I shrug the shoulder I'm not lying on. "You give in."

And I have no clue of the thoughts running through his mind as he watches my pinky hovering between us, but whatever his doubts are, they lose.

He hooks his pinky with mine. "I'm too old for this."

"You also said you were too old to come for a third time last night, and I proved you wrong."

"Sure. That was *all* your doing."

I tackle him. "You really don't want to give me any kudos, do you?"

He rolls on top of me. "You were great. For a bi-ginner."

I shove him, and he shoves back, and we play fight to pin the other person. This is … a completely different side to Art, and I think I'm obsessed. No flirting or teasing or ridiculous comments, just him letting his walls down and enjoying himself. A small part of me tries to shrivel up at the thought that he's like this with all the men he hooks up with, but I push it away and remind myself that now, in this moment, it's me who gets this version of him.

Somehow, I wriggle out from under him and slam him back into the mattress, throwing all my weight against him. Then I duck my head and sink my teeth into his shoulder before making a split-second decision. I suck a quick mark onto his skin.

Art freezes, and I glance up at him, feeling smug.

"What was that?" he asks, looking sweetly perplexed.

"Your reminder. So next time you see me at work, you'll remember the time you had your tongue up my ass."

He smirks. "And how desperately you begged for it again."

I want to scoff and play it off, but … the man knows how to give a rim job. "It was a brand-new game. Can you blame me?"

"You were with the master. You didn't stand a chance."

I'm beginning to think I never did.

Saturday's my day off, so I leave Art's early—before anyone can arrive for work—and drive home drained, sore, covered in love bites, and happier than I've been in a really, really long time.

I almost wish I'd given in to him a year ago, but there's no way it would have been anywhere near the level last night was. You can call Art one hundred and one things and probably be right, but the one insult you can't hurl his way is that he's selfish in bed. Because he was right. He likes to give. And give. And *give.*

I'm pretty sure he drained me of cum for the next year at least.

I stumble inside at asscrack o'clock, noting Hannah's open bedroom door and *very fucking obviously* empty bed.

The happy vibes disappear, and I grab my phone to call her. The battery's low, and I cross my fingers that it holds out for long enough.

Her phone goes to voicemail, and then a message comes through a second later.

Hannah:
Finally home, huh? I'm fine. Sleeping. Maybe you should do the same.

Smart-ass. My phone dies before I can reply, so I stalk into my bedroom, plug it in, and sit on my bed, waiting for it to charge enough that I can angry-dial her again. She thinks she can stay out all night and reject my call like that? I mean, yeah, she's seventeen, and I was doing way worse at her age, but it's *because* I know what I was doing at her age that I'm mad. I'm already supporting both of my sisters; it would be just my luck to have to support an unplanned niece or nephew too.

My phone's taking *forever*, and after a night of sex and talking and more sex and some teasing, I'm beat. I lie back against my pillows, just for a second, just until my phone is back …

THE SORRY SUCKAS GROUP CHAT

Art: *Who's having dinner with me?*

Orson: *Can't tonight, I have plans with Ford.*

Griff: *Felix is in town, so we've got a family night planned.*

Art: *Payne?*

Payne: *But you didn't say "please."*

Art: *You're really going to abandon me in my time of need?*

Payne: *...*

Orson: *Need?*

Art: *I'm being dramatic. Obviously. I don't need you guys. But I know how you need me, so I'm just trying to make you feel wanted.*

Payne: *How generous of you.*

Orson: *National hero.*

Art: *When you make my memorial statue, I'd prefer to be honored naked.*

Payne: *Do the rest of us get a say?*

Orson: *I think we already know the answer to that.*

16

ART

I TAKE SUNDAY OFF WORK. NOT BECAUSE JOEY'S WORKING, but because people keep whining at me that I need to take days off, so here I am doing it. Mostly.

I might be working at home, and I might be searching through notes I've made for potential Nevele Ounces recipients. What was I thinking, choosing that name? It was a spur-of-the-moment thing, and now I'm stuck with it. It's either Nevele Ounces or me owning up to being the one throwing money around. I can't do it though. I've spent so long distancing myself from that person that he feels like a separate entity.

It's not enough to distract me from being tempted to go into work, just to check up on the place, but I keep my ass planted in this chair.

Sundays are busy. I wouldn't have a second to talk to him, even if I wanted to. And I don't want to.

We had sex. It was a long time coming, and so goddamn

worth the wait, but now I can add him to my "been there, done that" list and move on.

To other men.

Lots and lots of other men who don't have faded freckles or a cute line of small moles on their upper thigh. Men who know how to put in a hair tie properly or, better yet, don't need one at all. Men who don't work for me.

Men who aren't currently covered in marks I left on them.

God, he was a sight. I should have counted them. Were there ten? Twenty? Thirty? Every time he catches sight of them until they fade, he'll immediately think of me. My thumb runs over my shoulder again before I catch myself. No more thinking of Joey. And the way he shivers as he comes.

Somehow, I keep my ass in my seat until dinnertime, when I catch up with Payne. We go way back, having been through school together, and even though we lost contact for a few years while he lived in Boston, he's still the same guy I always knew.

Just older and, therefore, way cooler.

"Beau didn't want to come out?" I ask, taking the seat across from him.

"Nah, I dropped him over to see Marty and Lizzy on the way. He's deep in a book, so he's almost impossible to make sense of right now. I practically had to drag him out of there."

"And you didn't want to leave him home alone?" I guess.

Payne huffs. "I wanted to get through dinner without worrying about him. There are only so many times I can find him risking his life. He fell through the roof last week."

"Shit, is he okay?"

"Bruised all up his leg and ass cheek." Payne grins. "I've been looking after it for him."

"You tell Beau if he ever needs a hand while you're not there that Griff will be over in a second flat."

"Not you too."

Poor Payne. "It's fun. You're easy to rile up."

"I thought you were better than to go for low-hanging fruit."

"Have you *met* me? I literally have no standards. I'll go for the fruit that's rotting on the ground if I have to."

"Well, there's an image," he says. "And yet you won't go for Joey."

I shoot him a glare. "That was for the Beau comment, wasn't it?"

"Actually, that was because we've all got a bet running on how long it will take for you two to hook up. I've gotta say, you'd be doing me a favor to go for it in the next week."

I stare at him, but no matter how hard I stare, all those words won't make sense. "A *bet*?"

Payne lifts up his hands, but he doesn't look at all sorry. "They made me."

"I don't believe you."

"Good call."

I fix him with a look. "Out with it. What's the prize?"

"Winner gets free drinks at Killer Brew for the next year. All my money's being funneled into this park, so any savings are welcome."

"From now on, I'm charging you all double."

"As long as you hook up with Joey within the week, you can charge the others whatever you want."

"After everything I've done for you fuckers, and this is

how you repay me? Just for that, I'm going to be celibate for the next … month?"

Payne shakes his head.

"Two months?" Dear God, please don't let anyone have bet longer than that.

"Beau bet a year."

"*Beau's* in on it?"

"*Everyone's* in on it."

"Then fine." I cross my arms. "In that case, I'm taking a vow of celibacy, and you all are going to have to deal with my horny ass. You think I've got a big mouth now? Just wait until that mouth isn't getting any action. It won't only be Griff talking about how hot Beau is."

Payne face-plants on the table. "Maybe I'll let Beau keep doing dangerous shit. Then he might scar up his face, and the rest of you will leave us alone."

"Come on, Payne, you know looks aren't everything. Annoying you outweighs potential disfigurement."

"I'm so glad we're on the same page here. Serious note, how *is* the love life going?"

"It's active."

"*Love* life, not *sex* life."

I pretend to shudder. "All the same to me. I love to have sex."

"Art …"

"Had an all-night fuckathon last night, in fact."

"Sometimes it's like you don't hear people when they speak."

"He was amazing, I was amazing …"

"Like now, for example."

"Pity there won't be a repeat."

Payne ignores me and signals for the server while I thank

my lucky stars that I was able to steer us away from *that* conversation. Love life. Fuck me. They joke that I don't listen when they speak, but they're clearly returning the favor. How many times do I need to highlight that relationships and I don't mix? Why is settling down some kind of marker of success?

I have everything I could ever need, and it's not like I'm struggling to find someone to warm my bed at night. I don't want kids, so it's not like there's some imaginary biological clock I need to race, and I'm genuinely happy running my business, hanging out with my friends, and flirting up a storm with Joey.

With the adorable freckles and moles and cum-splattered abs.

I grunt, cursing that my thoughts are back there again.

But now that we've given in, *will* we still flirt? I've gotta admit that I'll miss it. I squirm in my seat, suddenly not feeling great about my decision not to go in today. What if the next time I see him, Joey has nothing for me? No flirty looks, no swapped shifts, no quips or banter or teasing.

I'm tempted to send out an email for overtime and kidnap my friends to make sure I have some there tomorrow night, just to see if he'll volunteer for it like he always does. But I can't spring something on everyone at the last minute, and as much as I might want to know what things mean going forward, I'm hit with a reminder of how he looked, skin pulled tight over muscle, deep rings under his eyes, and I hold off. Joey doesn't need any more overtime.

Payne drags his hand back through his longish hair. It's only long enough to hang around his ears, unlike Joey's jaw-length hair, but it still makes this odd sort of ache hit me.

My fingers run over my shoulder again, and I resign

myself to the fact that Joey has screwed me up for at least a week because every time I see that hickey, I'll think about him.

So I guess I have a fun week ahead of reliving the night, and *then* I can move on.

That shouldn't be so hard.

I'll see him tomorrow, let him know I'm fine with things staying the same between us, and everything will go back to how it was before we swapped bodily fluids.

Nothing needs to change.

"JOEY?" COURTNEY ASKS. "HE CALLED OFF SICK."

"What do you mean?"

She looks at me like she's trying to figure out if I'm joking. "He's not here. He wasn't yesterday either."

That motherfucker. I thank her and head for my office, trying to pretend like it means nothing while my stupid brain is calling me a big, fat liar.

There are three options here.

Either Joey's sick—unlikely since we were really fucking close the other night, and I'm feeling peachy—or he's using us sleeping together to do whatever the hell he wants around here, *or* he's avoiding me.

I have no idea which of those second two options would be worse.

Instead of torturing myself at my desk all day, I grab my keys, take the door at the back of the bar, and leave it behind for the brewery. Killer Brew looks like one enormous building at first glance, but the bar and market are separated from the brewery by a narrow walkway.

I don't have to spend much time back here since, over the last decade or so, we've got our brewing cycle down to an art form. Even though Dad retired early, he's always here talking our manager's ear off, and because of him constantly hovering, I do my best not to.

Houston is on the observation deck when I arrive, and the place looks like complete chaos, but I know better. We've started the sanitation cycle on one of the fermenters, so what looks like people everywhere is actually a well-oiled machine.

"Hey, Art," Houston says, patting me on the shoulder and immediately making me think of Joey again. "Come to check in on us?"

"Actually, I've come to work."

Houston chuckles. "Picked a good day for it."

"I know."

He eyes my clothes. "You want to do lab work?"

"Nope. I want to do that." I nod toward the sanitation equipment. It's the most important part of the process because of how easily bacteria can get into the beer.

Houston chuckles. "It's your brewery."

I thank him and head down onto the work floor. Houston and I worked here together in our twenties, just like my niblings will if they ever want to take over Killer Brew. It's hard, hot, dirty work most of the time, and I know every step of the process.

Thankfully, I'm here early enough to get scrubbing and hope the grit work will get the agitation out of my system.

And it does for the most part, but when I leave there that afternoon, sore and sweaty, my annoyance from earlier comes rushing back. It lasts all through my shower and increases when I can't even jerk off because every time I try, all I can think about is Joey. This issue was fine before we'd had sex, but now it's becoming a pain in the ass.

Once I'm dry and dressed, I pace my living room for a couple of minutes and then decide *fuck it*.

Maybe it's not professional of me to be checking in on a sick employee, but I'm not going there as his boss. I'm going there because I need to give this anxious uncertainty a rest. I'm used to being laid-back, so when I'm not, I don't know how to handle it.

I drive to Joey's house, and even though I know I should turn my car around, once my mind is set on something, that's it. He lives in a quiet part of town, all tiny single-story houses that have been converted from the short-stay accommodation setup when the Kilborough Penitentiary was in its heyday.

I pull up out the front of his address and push down the sinking feeling when I arrive. The small strip of grass out the front is overgrown, threatening to climb over the front steps and porch, two panels of the picket fence are missing, and the front room has a sheet pinned up in place of curtains.

It's all cosmetic, I remind myself. Nothing a little love can't fix.

Still, I know the markings of someone struggling, and my red flags are waving.

The mailbox is overflowing with letters, but when I pause to grab them and take them inside, I find a stack of reminder notices.

What the hell is going on?

With what I pay him *and* his second job, things shouldn't be this bad.

I change my mind about delivering the letters to him and

leave them where they are, then cautiously make my way to the front door.

I knock, and it opens almost immediately, revealing a tall, thin girl with Joey's features. Her bright smile immediately drops when she sees me.

She points. "Art, right?"

"Yes." I'm about to ask about Joey when a car pulls up behind me, and her smile reappears.

"He's in bed sick, see ya!" She ducks around me and heads for the car, leaving the front door wide open.

And me standing there wondering what the hell to do now.

I cautiously take a step inside, wanting to warn the silly girl about how easy it would be to rob the place, only it looks like someone already has.

There's a couch, a small TV propped up on a crate, and a tiny two-seater table that's seen better days pushed into the corner.

I almost feel like I should leave and pretend I was never here because I get the feeling Joey wouldn't be happy with me seeing this. He might joke and act carefree, but I'm starting to realize that maybe that's exactly what it is. An act.

I quietly close the front door behind me and step further into the house. It's dark and depressing, no windows left open, and what smells like burned cheese lingers in the air.

This isn't good. If I was Joey, I'd probably want to spend as much time as possible out of the house as well.

There's an open door off the living area, showing a bedroom, and two closed ones down a short hall that leads to a laundry room. The first is a tiny bathroom, so the second must be where Joey is.

I knock softly, and when no one answers, I nudge the door open a slit.

My chest stutters at the sight of him sleeping, soft features relaxed, one lean arm flung over his head. He's kicked off the comforter, and even from here, I can tell his shirt and hair are damp with sweat. I back the hell out of there as quickly and silently as I can.

I know I need to leave, but I can't stop the clawing need that comes over me to *do* something.

He'd never accept my help though. I might not know a lot about him, but I know that.

I want to feel relieved that he's not avoiding me, but him being sick doesn't exactly fill me with the warm fuzzies.

My feet gravitate toward the kitchen to at least drop him in some Tylenol, but there's nothing there. No food either, and the bathroom is equally as bare.

Yeah, this doesn't work for me.

Before I can talk myself out of it, I swipe his keys from the counter and leave, promising myself that I'll make a quick run to the grocery store, and that's it.

Absolutely nothing else.

17

JOEY

I'M STILL DRAINED AS HELL TUESDAY MORNING WHEN I wake up, smelling like roadkill and in desperate need of a shower. The first thing I see when I open my eyes is a bottle of water and some Tylenol on my nightstand, and I thank the universe Hannah was aware enough to duck out for some.

I down them, willing the drugs to kick in and do their thing before I try to climb out of bed. I'm torn on whether my need to shower or eat is stronger, and then I'm going to have to make some calls because I have no idea if I rang in for work, and it would be just my luck to get sick and fired all in the same day.

Art would be fine—he's got more than enough employees—but I feel terrible for letting Freddy down when he should have more than just me around to help him.

I force myself up, and it's beyond tempting to pull the covers back up and suffocate myself. I'm immediately hit with my constant worries about bills, work, and school, and I have no idea when it's all going to end. It's bleak when I wish the fever would take over again so I don't have to think about any of it.

I stumble to my feet, grab the first clothes I pull from the clean washing basket, and stagger to the bathroom, hitting the wall a few times on the way. Fuck, I'm dizzy, but while the break from my worries was great, the break from my income will only be making everything worse. I need to get back to it.

I take a leak, then sit on the floor of my shower because standing too long under the hot water makes my head spin. I'm probably getting filthier than anything by sitting here, but I ignore the potential bacteria and relax into the steam, loosening up my muscles.

The haze around my brain slowly clears, and when I look down, all I can see are angry bruises all over my pale skin. For the first time in days, I smile.

Some of the smaller ones have already started to fade, but I sit there and look at them all anyway, getting butterflies over the memory. I wish that night never had to end.

Hannah's obviously picked me up a new shower gel, and the smell immediately reminds me of whatever the hell Art uses. I marvel at the coincidence, pouring out way too much and coating myself in it.

I climb out of the shower, dry off, then stand there and give myself a quiet moment to inspect the marks covering my back and ass too. I look like a fucking mess, but there isn't a single part of me that regrets it. I only hope Art feels the same.

And that once I've given him some time to process, he's easier to get into bed next time. Yeah, that night has taken the desperate edge off, but every time I remember his deep voice in my ear, his rough hands, the way he expertly worked me over until I was powerless to stop myself from coming my brains out, the need hits hard all over again.

I thought work was torture before? I let out a weak laugh. Oh, this shit is going to be impossible.

You know. If I still have a job there.

I get dressed and head to the kitchen for coffee, only when I step out of the hall, I come to a complete stop.

What ... *what*?

It takes me a second to realize I'm still in the same house.

"Is this still a fever dream?" I mutter, hand combing through my damp hair in shock. "What the ..."

First, the windows are open. With *curtains* hanging beside them and glass so clean I can see out of them. The TV is sitting on a low, shiny white cabinet, our table and chairs have been replaced with something that *also* looks new, and there's a rug and goddamn *cushions* on the couch.

I'm too scared to move in case I break this hallucination and abruptly find myself back in reality.

Slowly, I take my first step. Nothing changes. Then another.

"What in the fucking hell ..."

The weirdness only increases when I open the fridge and find it full. The cupboard too. Container after container of pastries that have clearly been homemade and then a whole variety of dishes in the freezer.

I scramble for my phone and call Hannah, but she does that frustrating thing where she immediately hangs up on me.

Hannah: *I'm in class*
Me: *Did you do this?*

Hannah: *Do what?*

Me: *The house, obviously. Where did all this shit come from?*

Hannah: *Oh, I just assumed you did.*

Me: *I've been sick.*

Hannah: ***shrug emoji***

Teenagers. I pull up Amelia's number and call her instead.

"Hey, Joey, I'm getting ready for class, can I call you after?"

"No, actually. I'm kinda freaking out."

Unlike Hannah, Amelia stops what she's doing. "Why? What happened?"

"Did you order a bunch of shit for the house?"

"What are you talking about?"

"Furniture and … and food."

"No …" Her tone turns cautious. "What's happened?"

I grab a container of what looks like tarts from the fridge and open it. They smell goddamn heavenly, and I bite right into it before answering. *Holy shit.* "Holy shit."

"Holy shit *what*? Joey, are you high?"

"I might be."

At her stunned silence, I laugh.

"Sorry, I've been sick the last few days, and I've just woken up to someone having Mary fucking Poppins-ed the house, and there's food everywhere, and now I'm kinda spinning out, but this tart tastes amazing."

"I am so confused …"

"So you *didn't* do all of this?"

"No. Listen … is everything okay at home? I've tried calling Hannah a few times, but she's always busy, and now

... I've gotta be honest. All this talk about furniture and food ..."

"We're fine," I say, immediately shutting down her worries.

"I know that me losing that meals scholarship was a hit, but I've applied for a whole bunch of other ones, and if you need me to pick up a part-time job, or—"

"No. I told you, I've got everything covered."

"If ... if you're sure."

"Promise. I love you. Now, get to class."

"Love you too."

We hang up, and even though I'm more confused than ever, I push the curiosity aside. I make a coffee and take the container of tarts over to the new table, where I demolish every single one of them.

I'M STILL FEELING LIKE DOGSHIT WHEN MY PAY HITS MY account later. Instead of relief at having money again, all it does is remind me of all the things I have to pay for. The wad of bills waiting in the mailbox, rent, car repayments. I'm tempted to close out of my banking app and pretend like none of it exists.

Unfortunately, denial is not the magical solution to make everything go away. Go figure. A good chunk of my money goes straight to Amelia so she doesn't realize we're anything but fine; then, once I've taken out rent, I have enough to scrape together for the bare minimum of repayments.

I sigh as I transfer Amelia money for board and food, then grab my keys and head out. Only when I reach the mailbox to eenie-meanie-miney-mo my utilities, there's nothing there. I open the lid to make doubly sure, and nope. Not one overdue notice to be found.

I stand there staring, like they'll somehow show up if I wait long enough, but I'm so fucking confused. Hannah wouldn't have taken them inside. Firstly, the place is so damn clean I would have spotted them immediately, but second, she's reached a point where she doesn't see anything she doesn't want to.

This prickling awareness creeps down the back of my neck. Whoever fixed up my house has done something with those bills, and if it's what I think they've done …

I jog back inside, grab an old bill from the drawer, and dial the number listed. My gut is a riot of nerves while I wait on hold, trying not to hope but way too past that point, so if I'm wrong, I'll probably cry.

I'm not a crier. I'm a fixer. But that's how hard it will hit.

Only when the woman on the other end answers, she says the words that make me want to kiss her.

"It looks like a payment was made this morning. Actually, the overdue amounts have been settled, with the next three cycles covered in advance."

I'm in so much shock I barely remember to thank her before hanging up the phone. With excitement thrumming through my veins, I pull out another bill and another. All with the same result.

And when I call through to my Realtor's office and speak with the property manager, she informs me that my rent is paid up to the end of our lease.

I sink to the floor and just sit there. In the middle of my kitchen. Trying to process this light, almost panicky feeling coming over me. I have an overwhelming need to laugh, but

I'm still too exhausted to do much more than let out a shocked little "huh."

That's … that's everything. It's all covered. For another year.

A whole year.

Is this what freedom feels like?

I grab another container of pastries from the cupboard and wolf down the lot, and then on a whim, I call back my property manager and ask the one question burning through me.

"Who paid the money? Did they give a name?"

It's like I can hear her smirk down the line. "He did. Nevele Ounces."

18

ART

I'M DETERMINED TO LEAVE KILLER BREW BEFORE JOEY shows up for his shift, but whether on purpose or by accident —I'm still having the debate with myself—he's already behind the bar when I'm walking down the stairs.

My footsteps slow, ears strained to pick up the conversation happening below. It's not something I should be listening to, not something I even want to hear, which is why I'd planned to duck out early.

"You got Ounced," Mitch says, and I try not to cringe at the expression. Apparently, Joey feels the same way.

"Don't put it like that. You're taking the magic out of it."

"What else would you call it?"

"Just some bastard taking pity on me. And I've gotta say, pity never felt so good."

"I dunno," Courtney muses. "You don't feel a bit creeped out? Some person coming into your home while you were out of it and doing whatever the fuck they wanted to it?"

And this is one of the many, many reasons I don't let it be known who I am. Everyone has an opinion, and there are sure to be people out there who claim I'm doing this for myself or who try to twist my actions. Try to make out like I want credit or am playing the role of a hero.

Which is complete bullshit.

People like Joey, who are doing everything in their power to get by and it's still not enough? Those people are fighters. They're strong and stubborn. They're the types of people others should look up to. Not people like me whose only contribution to life is money.

I keep walking, missing the rest of their conversation on purpose. I don't want to know if Joey is creeped out by what I did; I don't want to know if he feels like a charity case, which a lot of people do. I stand by what I did. If you offer someone help, they're a lot less likely to take it because some asshole somewhere tried to make people feel like having pride was a virtue.

I say screw that. Life is hard enough. If you can get help, get it.

But until people will do that for themselves, I'll keep giving help without being asked. Without being thanked or credited. Without a single person in the world knowing that it's me.

I take comfort in the knowledge I'm helping people sleep easier at night.

I've almost made it all the way to the door when Joey's husky voice calls out to me.

"Art, a minute?"

Tension immediately tries to take over, but I shake it off and turn to see him crossing the bar toward me. And fucking hell. He's wearing a loose tank top that shows off way too much of his arms, his ribs, his neck and collarbones. And every inch of that skin is covered in marks left by my mouth.

"Looks like you've been up to some fun."

Joey stretches his arms over his head, slowly twisting from one side to the other before letting them drop again. "Best night of my life, actually."

"You look like a cheater."

"I never cheated on anyone."

"Not even your supposed girlfriend?" I taunt, leaning in with a cocky grin. "I meant the cat. Fitting, with the way you were purring in my hands the other night."

The glimmer of … I want to say arousal, but I'm not totally sold on that, fills his eyes. "I would have described it more as screaming."

"That was the other fifty percent of the time. I'm a man of many talents."

"I'll say." Joey crosses his arms, drawing my attention back, yet again, to the marks there. It probably isn't healthy how much seeing them fills me with want. He wears them well. No embarrassment, no shame, just a complete advertisement of what he's done and, from the looks of the way he's eyeing me, what he *wants* to do again.

Time to shut this down. Repeats are all well and good. Having a companion cock to play with works for me a lot of the time because it's little effort, the lines are clear, and you learn what the other man likes.

But Joey … repeats with Joey are dangerous.

Because of the way he's looking at me and not at all because of the way I'm looking at him.

"So …" he begins.

"I'm running late. I'll see you later."

"Art."

"Joey."

"*Artur*."

I lift an eyebrow at him using my full name. "Was there something you wanted?"

It's the wrong thing to ask.

Joey steps closer, just that edge too close to be an employee talking to his boss. My gaze snags on those faded freckles under his eyes, and I remember what they taste like. "You know what I want."

"Skin that doesn't bruise so easily?"

"A boss who's not a smart-ass, maybe."

"Better talk to Freddy about that one. We both know it's a useless wish with me."

"When can we do it again?" he asks, bold as fuck and playing on all the confidence I love in a man.

"You really think you've got what it takes to master the art of raging erections?"

"Raging? Please. Giving yourself a bit of credit there, don't you think?"

"We both know I'm no slouch in that department."

"Maybe I'm misremembering." Joey taps his stubbled chin. "Guess you'll have to refresh my memory."

The bastard actually gets a laugh out of me. I hate that. Being unable to act like I'm not affected by him. "Nice try. But shouldn't you be working?"

"I'll get there."

That little seed of worry that he's using me threatens to take hold again. "I've gotta spread my loving around. There's a reason you're begging for more. I'm addictive. I get it. But I've granted you a repeat in a year, and ..." I lean in. "After twelve months of replaying our night together over and over, you're going to be desperate for me by then." I straighten and give him a two-finger mock salute. "Laters, Joey."

I should have known it wouldn't be that easy.

"I wasn't the only one purring that night." Joey blows me a kiss. "Wait the twelve months … if you can."

Then he spins on his heel and walks back toward the bar, giving me an entirely inappropriate and irresistible view of his denim-covered ass.

As much as I hate to admit it, I might have a harder time resisting him than I thought. It was easy, at first, to ignore the way he brings me alive with want, because so far as I knew, he was straight. Straight guys are easy to disregard, no matter how good-looking they are.

Now that I know he's available and interested in more, he's putting me in a bad position. The kind of position where I need to be a big boy and show some fucking maturity for once in my life instead of letting my dick take the wheel.

The problem is that the rest of me never learned how to drive. I have a head brain and a heart brain and a dick brain, and only one of those can be powered on at once. There's no room for emotion when you can be getting laid, and there's no room for horny-fun-times when my business hat comes on, but …

Someone's clearly messing with my wires because Joey's short-circuiting all three.

As much as I dick around and have fun, I'm a practical guy. An itch needs to be scratched, you get a stick. A problem pops up, you find the solution. It's part of what prompted Nevele Ounces in the first place.

Someone needed help, I had the means to help. Whether it's money or grunt work or through my extensive business contacts, there's no problem too big.

Joey needs some financial breathing room? It's his.

Griff needs repairs done? They happen.

Payne's dick of an ex won't sign the divorce papers? I have a lawyer friend pay him a visit.

Nothing is too big or too much. Nothing requires angst and confusion and whining about boy troubles.

Nothing except Joey, apparently.

Because like he's a worked-up rattlesnake, I know I shouldn't touch.

And damn do I want to go back there again anyway.

19

JOEY

I STEP OUT OF THE CONVENIENCE STORE, SHOULDERS strained after all the heavy lifting from this morning, and stretch my arms over my head. The tight pull, the slightly painful relief, I lean into it and then let out a long breath as I drop my arms again.

This last week has been mind-blowing. Working and knowing that whatever I earn, I bank. Instead of using the opportunity to take a breather, I'm throwing myself into things harder than ever.

Work, study, supporting my sisters. I feel like I've jumped on a treadmill with renewed energy, using the next year to sprint for my life.

This could be the only chance I have to actively try and get ahead, and you can bet your ass I'm going to take it.

"Joey?"

I swing around at Art's voice, and my face immediately breaks into a grin. "Boss man. You're out early."

He gestures toward the two kids beside him. "School drop-off. What are *you* doing here?"

"Just finished work."

Surprise takes over his face. "You're still working here?"

"Sure am." I eye him. "Why?"

"The gossips at work say you came into some money recently." I swear his teeth are grinding. "So shouldn't you be taking it easy? No more falling asleep on the job?"

"Actually, I feel better than ever." I'd throw out the point that the only sleeping I'll be doing at work will be the type encouraged by him, but even I know to keep it clean with kids around.

Art glances down at the girl beside him. "Take your brother inside and pick a treat. I'll be right behind you."

"A su-sugar one?" the boy asks. Both of them have wild, dark hair and piercing eyes that are exactly like Art's.

"Why not?" Art gives a resigned sigh, but there's a spark of something fond in the way he watches both kids run inside.

The fondness disappears when his gaze snaps back to me. "Why aren't you taking this opportunity for what it is?"

Definitely not what I was expecting him to come out with. When he sent the kids inside, I'd been hoping there'd be more flirting coming my way, but instead, Art looks annoyed.

I frown. "I *am* taking it. What else do you think I'm doing here?"

"Working yourself into the ground. Again."

"Rich coming from a man who doesn't leave work."

"I know my limits."

"And I know mine."

Art runs a hand over his face. "I really don't think you do."

His whole attitude is pissing me off, so I step closer, wanting to railroad whatever this is. "And that's the problem with you. You think you know what everyone else wants. But I *do* know my limits. At work ... and in the bedroom."

"Don't go there."

"Why not?" I pout. "I thought it was important information to know."

"The only importan—"

"Tio Artur?" His niece pokes her head out of the shop. "You're taking forever."

Art nods to her and throws a look my way. "I have to go."

He walks into the shop, and I know this is where I should scramble, but ... I don't wanna. I don't work today or have to go in for classes, so other than some research, I'm in the clear this morning. And this morning, I want to spend time with my boss.

And let him yell at me for overworking myself, apparently.

Who knew care could be so hot?

I lean back against the wall, hands in my pockets, and wait. It only takes a few minutes for them to step back out of the store, Art's nephew over his shoulder and his niece laughing beside him.

"The sugar monster will eat you whooole ..." Art's words trail off when he spots me. "Still here?"

"It just so happens I'm heading in the same direction as the school."

"Isn't that your car over there?" He points at my shit box.

"Nope. Never seen it before."

And like a petulant child, Art rolls his eyes. I love that I can bring so much annoyance out in him.

I hold out my hand to his niece. "We started out on the wrong foot. I'm Joey. Your uncle's friend."

Her gaze cuts to Art, and she holds up a hand to cover her mouth, but I catch the question loud and clear. "Is he a stranger?"

"No, he's safe." Then he tacks on, "For you."

I love the idea that he finds me dangerous.

"I'm Alice," she says, shaking my hand. "And my brother is Gus. What were you doing that day you were watching him through the shelves?"

"I wasn't watching Gus," I tell her again. Maybe this time, she'll hear me since we're not surrounded by hysteria.

"He was watching *me*," Art says, smug grin in place.

"Oh." Alice scrunches up her face. "Are you boyfriends?"

"No," Art answers at the same time I say, "Maybe."

"Joey's what adults like to call a pain in the rear end."

"Isn't it pain in the ass?" she asks.

Art looks like he wants to die. "Swear again and I'll tell your mother."

"You wouldn't."

"Don't test me."

Her little face turns evil. "Traitor."

Art shrugs. "Is that supposed to hurt?"

"Do you *like* being a traitor?"

Touché.

Meanwhile, Gus is standing there, chomping on his candy bar, watching me. Neither of them is paying him attention, and I appreciate a kid who takes advantage of the situation.

"Taste good?" I ask.

"Yup."

"What flavor did you get?"

"Just chocola-late."

"My favorite too."

"Can you give me a piggyback?"

"Sure can."

"What?" Alice interrupts. "He's already eating his chocolate? That's not fair. I want my chocolate."

Art lets out a long exhale through his nose. "You're not having anything with that attitude."

She does the same exhale thing he did and says in a robotic voice, "It's not fair if Gus gets chocolate and a piggyback ride and I don't."

"Life's not fair."

"Especially for girls. Mom says the only way to make it fair is to speak up."

I already love her. "How old are you?"

"Eight."

"Wow. You're a smart one."

"I know."

I wave my hand toward her, smiling angelically Art's way. "You going to say no to that and be on the side of the patriarchy?" I crouch down, and Gus doesn't hesitate to climb onto my back. His fingers and face are covered in chocolate, which I guess I'll be wearing soon too.

"Down with the patriarchy." Art laughs and crouches down so Alice can throw her arms around his neck. He stands with a grunt, and we fall into step with each other.

"Thank you for this wonderful idea," he says.

"I'm choosing to ignore that sarcasm."

"Ignore it all you like; that doesn't mean it's not there." He huffs. "I'm too old for this."

"Please. You're not fooling anyone with that 'too old' shi … stuff."

"That was a close one."

"I don't spend much time around kids. I'm learning as I go."

"You're good at that."

"Ah." I nudge him with my elbow. "So you admit I'm good."

"Don't remember ever saying otherwise."

The fact he isn't trying to deny what happened or that he enjoyed it is a nice feeling. We're quiet as we walk down the street, and it's the kind of quiet that's heavy with unasked questions. We've never really seen each other outside of work, let alone just taken a walk together with his niblings in tow. I'm being presumptuous, but Art hasn't told me to back off, so I'm going to keep pushing, little by little, until the quiet isn't filled with questions but with comfort.

I'll wear him down into liking my company if it's the last thing I do.

"So why are you doing school drop-off?" I ask, wanting to find out everything I can about him.

"I wanted to. My sister is doing it solo, and I love these two little brats, so I try to have them as much as I can."

"You're a brat," Alice throws back.

"I agree with her."

"If I'm a brat, what does that make you?" Art asks me.

"A *very* good boy."

And maybe stirring him up isn't the way to get him to like me, but it's too fun to resist. I want that Art who's fun and flirty, who doesn't hold back and is careful about whatever he says. That Art is the one that most people get to see, but there's always a hesitance from him when I'm around, and I hate it. He's too serious. It's not him. And we both know it.

I start bouncing Gus up and down as we get closer to the school, pretending to be a pony. "Favorite thing to do with your niblings?" I ask him.

"Cook."

"What do you cook?"

"Food."

"Do you ever answer questions with more than one word?"

"Occasionally."

I glance over to see him fighting a smile.

"Do you think I'm charming?" I ask.

"No."

"Was that a lie?"

One-half of the smile breaks free. "Maybe."

"Most ridiculous thing you've ever done?"

He snorts. "You."

We meet eyes, and like that, the tension is broken. Both of us snigger all the way to the gate, where we set the kids down. They both give Art a hug and hurried "thanks, bye" before disappearing inside. He watches them go, but I get the feeling it's only so he doesn't have to face me.

"On a scale of one to ten, how much do you hate me?"

"My back? A ten. In general ..." He finally glances at me, eyes running from my hair all the way to my feet. It shivers awareness through me. "A seventeen, at least."

"What are the chances I can get that number down?"

"Minimal."

I step closer, shoulder to shoulder, tipping my head back

enough to say by his ear, "What are the chances you want me to?"

"Higher than I'd like."

"You know I'm going to be a total pain in the ass about this, right?"

"So, business as usual?" He grins, turning to cuff my shoulder with a heavy hand. "Life is full of challenges. I've never met one I couldn't face."

"Those are fighting words."

"I'm not scared of stepping into the ring."

"Is that what you want?" I ask. "To go one-on-one with me?"

"Been there, done that. You'd have to be pretty special for me to be interested in round two."

I tug the collar of his button-up. "Let's both remember you said that. Because I have the feeling it's going to come back to bite you in the ass very soon."

Then Art completely surprises me by reaching up and tucking my loose strands of hair behind my ear. His warm hand hovers there, sending heat across my jaw and down my neck. I want to lean into his touch, but it's gone too quickly.

"I'll see you at work tomorrow."

"Ah. Actually. About that."

Art straightens, immediately putting distance between us. "What?"

"I need to do the night shift. If that's okay." Stupid professor and her stupid feedback on my stupid essay. I have to rewrite almost the whole thing. I feel horrible asking, especially when Art's whole body fills with tension.

But he just nods once. "I'll adjust the schedule."

Then he turns on his heel and leaves.

Sending any progress we'd made rapidly down the drain.

20

ART

"YOU DIDN'T NEED TO DO ALL THIS," PAYNE SAYS, SWAYING slightly on his feet. "Who cares about forty-one?"

"Who doesn't? Whether it's sixteen or twenty-one or forty-one. Why shouldn't we marvel in another year on this glorious earth?" Besides, if there's an excuse to throw a party, I'll take it. People think it's because I love to get loose, but really, I don't drink a lot at these things. It's a bigger high to stand back and watch all these men getting out of the house and enjoying themselves.

Payne blinks at me for a moment. "I'm getting another drink."

He staggers away, and I turn to where Mack is watching him.

"Pity he was off the market so fast."

"I think things worked out exactly how they were supposed to." I fling an arm around Mack's shoulders. "Life has a funny way of doing that."

"When does mine start to work out?"

"When it's supposed to."

"Well, life certainly is dragging her feet on me."

I snigger. "Who says life's a she?"

"True. With how much mine is in shambles, it can only be run by a man."

"I resent that." I wave a hand over the party. "Look at everything I've been able to accomplish."

Orson laughs as he reaches us. "With the number of parties you throw, I'd be worried if you didn't have it down to an art form by now."

Speaking of art forms, my gaze strays to where Joey is at the bar. Lean muscles, faded bruises, and hopefully smelling like me. The way he did yesterday.

I didn't appreciate Joey inviting himself into my morning with the niblings. At all. It was too … domestic. My time with them is sacred, and the last thing I want is them being subjected to any and every guy I'm sticking my dick into.

Or *did* stick my dick into. Past tense. With any luck, never to be repeated.

"I don't think you've ever given this much focus to a thing in your life," Orson says, waving a hand in front of my face.

I slap it away. "You're a complete shit-stirrer with no idea what you're talking about."

"So you're *not* staring at Joey?"

"Nope."

"And you don't want to sleep with him?"

That question grates on me. "Never." Again.

"You're lying," Mack says, turning to Orson. "He's lying, right? Art wants to sleep with everyone."

"Except Griff. But yeah, basically. So he's *definitely* lying."

I drain my drink, flip them off, and take a swift exit from *that* conversation. Payne's birthday party was a surprise one since I knew he wouldn't show up if he'd be walking into a night of attention. Luckily, his brother is only too happy to see Payne embarrassed—that's the kind of sibling bond I can get behind.

Some of the DMC guys are here, along with their partners and a few of the people Payne and I went to school with. It's a fun night, but I've only had the one drink, and I'm sipping my second one.

That idiot bartender of mine shouldn't be here.

I paid off *everything* for him. Why is he still working at Freddy's? And why, for the love of my sanity, is he still swapping out his shifts?

To say I'm pissed is putting it lightly.

The days of being Zen about whatever happens between Joey and me are gone. We slept together, and now he's back to his same old tricks. Asking to move his schedule around at his whim and flirting up a storm with the drunk chicks in the bar. I should have known better.

I almost want to sleep with him again, just to prove I can.

If he's going to get what he wants out of me anyway, why shouldn't I use him the same way?

That thought turns my stomach. I scrub a hand over my face as I try to center myself in this room full of my friends. Yet another party, which I usually love, and somehow I feel … misplaced.

Me.

Artur de Almeida, the man who's comfortable anywhere

with anyone. The man who can charm his way into any man's pants.

Apparently, even the straight ones.

I cut my eyes back toward the bar, but Joey has left serving drinks and is making his way around the party, collecting empty glasses.

Ah, fucksticks.

I dive into a conversation with Griff and his boyfriend, Heath.

"I'm *just* saying, there is always more we can do at Halloween," Heath says.

Griff rubs his chin. "But we already sell out in October. Do we need to—"

"Whoa, whoa, whoa …" I lift my hands. "What the hell are you talking about work stuff for? At my party? Nope. Forbidden. If I can't trust you two to talk about sex, who around here will?"

"Barney and Leif?" Griff suggests.

"They're traveling, so not here, so not able to turn on my ear holes. You two, spill. What crazy sexcapades have you been up to lately?"

Griff chuckles. "What kind of men do you take us for?"

"The horny kind. And you're always horny, so don't try to deny it."

"Wasn't gonna."

"Might be my favorite thing about you," Heath tells him. "Well, that and the way you blush."

"Fuck you very much, I don't blush."

"Sure. Of course not. Definitely not blushing right now."

It amuses me when Griff slaps his hands over his cheeks. "For that, you're not getting any tonight."

I snort. "Even I don't believe that. Heath's known you most of your life. You really think that will work?"

"I can hold out. For one night …"

Heath leans forward and sets an evil hand on the top of Griff's thigh. "If you take me into the bathrooms, I'll suck you off here and now."

I hold up both hands. "Not while I'm within hearing range. If you're busted for indecent exposure, I don't want to be implicated. Also, I'll be tempted to listen at the door."

"Pity." Griff shrugs. "We might have invited you to watch."

And at any other time in my life, I would have dragged them into the bathroom myself. But first, Griff is a grade A shit-stirrer who doesn't mean a thing he says, and second … I scoff and don't even let myself think of the second option.

"No response." Heath tilts his head. "Where's Art? Our friend who sees any dick as an offering to the gods."

"It's true. The gods bathe in the jizz of my prospects. It's their fountain of eternal youth."

"Well, that's certainly not accurate," Beau says, joining us with a very drunk Payne hanging off his arm. Payne collapses into one of the chairs, and Beau takes the space next to him, pulling his boyfriend's head into his lap to run his fingers through his hair.

I grunt. "You two are disgusting."

"Says the man talking about cum baths."

"They're very popular in Portugal."

"More bullshit."

"Excuse you, sir, I am an expert."

"So, we agree. You're an expert in bullshit."

I turn to Payne. "I don't think I like your boyfriend very much."

Payne lurches drunkenly to his feet. "Say that to my face. Numbnuts." Then raises his fists to a decorative vase.

I lean around him to see Beau's amused expression. "You're the one who will have to deal with him in the morning."

"You say that like it's a threat, but it's really not. He's clingy when he's hungover."

"That sounds like torture."

"Only if you're allergic to affection."

"Which Art is," Griff points out.

"Unless it's Joey you're talking about," Orson says, and lucky me. More of my friends here to give me shit.

"Don't start."

And like his name summoned him, Joey's ass hits the arm of the couch right next to me. "Who's talking about Joey? Art? I know, he's obsessed, right?"

And *finally*, these bastards think to show a shred of loyalty by keeping their mouths shut.

Well, except Payne, but he's on another world to the rest of us.

"You two should fuck," he says with all the class of, well, me.

My gaze shoots up to meet Joey's.

He winks. I hate that I find it sexy. "Ideas for next time." Then he leans over me, filling my nose with the smell of my soap, and collects my half-full glass. "Empty? Too bad. You'll have to come and see me if you want another one. After your friend, we've cut it down to one drink per person."

"I'm not done with that one yet."

The smart-ass blows me a kiss before leaving.

My friends are still silent. Which, yay? They've learned

how to keep their mouths closed, but this isn't a good kind of silence. This is a—

"*Next time?*" Orson demands.

Ah, fucksticks, I was hoping they missed that. "Oh, look at that, I need a drink."

Only when I go to make a getaway, Griff pulls me back down into my seat. "Yeah, nice try. Explain."

"Explain what?"

"How you hooked up with Joey and somehow kept quiet about it."

"I'll have you know I don't tell you about everyone I sleep with."

"Yeah, you do." Orson looks way too happy about this. "Last time you were out, you were in the group chat while you were *inside* the guy."

I huff. "That was like … New Year's."

"He's right," Griff exclaims like somehow I don't know these things. "You've been very quiet about your sex life since then."

"See?" I point at him. "I can be a gentleman."

"Or—and this is the most likely option—you haven't actually hooked up with anyone since then."

Ho. Ly. Shit. I cast my mind back, trying to picture when the last time was that I messaged someone for a quickie. That I went out and scored a sloppy blow job in a back room. I *tried*, and then Joey showed up and cockblocked me.

Before that?

"Do you think he's gone into shock?" Heath asks idly while the others watch me closely.

I shake my head. "You don't know what you're talking about."

"I guess Payne wins the bet," Beau says. "I thought this would be more of a slow burn."

"Yeah," I say, reminded of what Payne told me. "Fuck you all very much for *that*."

"Okay. To wrap up." Orson claps his hands together. "Our captain of cummage is on a dry spell and has only slept with one man, who also happens to be the man he's been obsessing over for at least a year, then didn't bother to tell his besties about it."

Griff hums. "I smell fuckery in the air."

And then Beau very unhelpfully adds, "Or the commitment is catching."

I push to my feet—successfully this time. "You're all incredibly unpleasant company who are making way too many assumptions. I hope you all look forward to the group chat tonight, where I'll be coming to you live from another man's colon. Excuse me."

"Be sure to tell Joey we say hi," Heath calls as I walk away.

I want to disown every one of them.

21

JOEY

I watch Art walk down the hall toward his office and debate going after him. The night has slowed down, and Court has everything under control, so I slink around the back, make sure no one is paying me attention, and follow him down the hall.

He's barely closed the door behind him when I push it open, step inside, and shut it again.

He whirls around at the noise.

"Hey, hottie."

"Joey."

"Are we really gonna do the name thing again?"

"Leaving wasn't an invitation for you to follow me, you know."

"I love that even you don't sound sure about that."

He huffs. "Why does everyone assume they know what I'm thinking tonight?"

"Because you're not even trying to hide it."

I watch greedily as Art flops back into the small couch that sits in front of a bookshelf. His long arm rests along the back of it, and I'm already picturing crossing the room and curling into that spot when he says, "Get out."

Still playing the game, I see. "Do you actually want that?"

"Since you're so sure you can read my mind, you tell me."

"You don't want to know the answer."

"I think you're the one of us living in denial."

That actually makes my head fall back on a laugh. *I'm* living in denial? I'm not the one of us running away from this thing at every opportunity I get. Art might be used to being pursued by men, but I'm not used to being the one doing the pursuing. The least he could do is take it easy on me.

He drops the act, exasperation melting from his face before my eyes. "What do you want?"

I pout at him. I'm not cute enough to pull it off properly, but at least it softens him. A little. Okay, maybe that's only my imagination, but whatever it takes to get through this next part, I'll lean into hard.

My steps close the distance between us as I reach for my collar and pull it to the side. "They're fading."

"Your brain cells?"

"My sexy marks."

The way his eyes run along my neck makes me think he agrees. "I can still see them."

He's trying to keep his voice level, but I sense a hitch. A weakness.

It pushes me to slide into the space next to him, the seat

too small for there to be any room between us. "I need your help."

"My help, huh? I'm sure I'm not the only man capable of giving you a hickey."

"No, but you are the only man capable of giving me a hickey *from you.*"

"Ah, so we're stating the obvious? Like how you don't actually *need* a hickey from me."

He hasn't moved away though. In fact, I swear he's inched closer, just a little. With a deep breath and every inch of courage I can manage, I throw my leg over his thighs and straddle him.

Art blinks at me in shock, even as his hands close around my hips. I want to swoon at the touch, the possessive hold, but I also don't want to draw attention to it and have him back off.

"I do though," I tell him, hooking my index finger into the gap between the top two buttons of his shirt. His chest hair is rough, and he smells like candy, and those goddamn steady, dark-rimmed, disarming eyes are making me forget how to think. I offer my neck to him like I'm offering up a buffet to a vampire. "Please …"

"Joey …"

"Only if you want to." I shift to lessen the pressure my jeans are putting on my cock. "Because I really, really want you to."

"Joey, you don't give me a chance."

"Not true. I've given you plenty of chances to tell me to fuck off."

"And I have."

"Like you mean it." We lock eyes, and the intensity in

his stare makes me swallow thickly. Makes my breathing shatter. Restart. Break apart all over again.

Then he leans in.

Instead of the immense pressure I'm expecting, his soft lips brush my skin in a kiss. A curl of pleasure travels from my neck, through my chest, and deep into my belly. It's warm and welcome. The kind of feeling I want to bottle up and keep forever. My hand grips a fist around his shirt.

Art runs a long line of kisses down to my shoulder, and then he closes his lips over my skin and sucks. Hard. Quick. He pulls off in seconds before he starts again. And again. Shivers race through me, and the moan that builds in my chest is way out of my control, but fuck it, I want him to know what he does to me.

Which I'm beginning to suspect is way too much.

Always too much.

He never leaves my mind, and sitting here, with him, is giving me the kind of peace I haven't had in … I can't remember *ever* feeling like this.

Art's cock thickens under my ass, prompting a whole new race of excited thoughts. Dirty thoughts. Thoughts about what his friend suggested. About this position, but naked and impaled on his cock.

It's not like I've never thought about it before, but it's never, *never* gotten me this turned on.

"Oh my god," I rasp.

And my words seem to whack sense into him because he pulls away.

"No," I whine. "Keep going."

He chuckles, and the sound warms me. "Correct me if I'm wrong, but you have a job to be doing."

And that's about the only thing that can break through

this lust. Remembering that I've ditched Courtney and left her to pick up my slack.

"Dammit."

He hums, stroking a hand down my back. "She'll come looking for you if you don't get that sexy ass back out there."

"If I say that I don't care and my sexy ass wants you, is that enough to make you forget about it?" I'm only joking though. Despite what Art probably thinks about me, I *am* a team player. When my dick's not in charge.

"Your ass wants me?"

"Desperately." I don't mean to sound like a breathy dickhead, but too late now.

His attention is pinned on my lips, hand on my back hovering dangerously close to the ass that wants him very, very much.

He inches forward, nose tracing my scruffy jaw. "How desperate for me are you?"

"Let's check the gauge." I take his free hand and settle it over the bulge in my pants. "That's a hard ten."

He squeezes my cock, and I swear I almost black out. "A very hard ten."

"A very hard ten that's very hard to argue with?"

I know I'm pushing my luck, but he's so close. Hovering right on the edge. I can see the way he wants to give in and say fuck it all and let me in again. I can feel it in every heartbeat beneath his shirt, in every heavy breath, in the way his whole body is coiled tight.

His lips reach my ear. "Your desperate little hole is going to have to wait. You're going to go out there and show off my marks to everyone, and once the party is over and the place is cleaned up, you're going to stay behind and finish what you started." He flexes his hips, cock flush against my ass.

"Only one problem with that plan, boss man. Your marks are under my shirt."

Reading my mind, he nudges my jaw up, then latches onto my throat. He's expert level at love bites because, like the others, it only takes a few seconds for him to get results.

"That better?" he asks.

He has no idea.

"And, Joey?"

"Yeah?"

"I'm going to make you pay for telling my friends we've slept together. I'm the one who does the teasing, not the other way around."

"Trust me when I say that you've got the teasing thing down pat."

His laugh is deep and filthy. "Your poor little hole isn't going to know what hit it."

WITH THAT OMINOUS PROMISE, ART SENDS ME ON MY WAY. I'm too keyed up to work or do much more than think about what the hell I've gotten myself into, and I've reached the point where I don't think I care much. I've sucked the man off; who cares if I bend over for him and take his cock up the ass? Who cares if I *want* to? It's no one's business but ours, and yeah, it goes against everything I've been raised to think. It calls into question some of my thoughts on masculinity and who does the fucking and all of those other things that just *are*, but I'm happy for them to take a back seat.

I haven't overthought a single thing in my chase of him, and I don't want to start now. So far, my cock's perfectly in control of the situation, and I have no desire to try and take over.

Even if it means I'm getting fucked tonight.

Jesus. The excitement that hits my gut at that thought is almost too much. Art naked. Art behind me. Art walking me through it, as considerate and attentive as he was last time. Seeing that side of him pushed buttons I didn't know I had. Who knew the hookup king, the eternal flirt, the man who vowed never to settle down for anyone could be so sweet in the bedroom.

As hot as it all was, deep down, in the very heart of everything we did together, I could tell his number one aim was to make sure I was comfortable.

He made it almost too easy.

And as I prepare to take another step out of my comfort zone tonight, there isn't a single part of me nervous about it because I *know* that Art will make sure I'm comfortable with it all again.

I mean, I *am* slightly shitting myself about, you know, *actually* shitting myself, but I've done anal with women before, and it's never been an issue, so I guess I'm about to find out how I compare in that department. A ridiculous sort of laugh threatens to leave me, but I catch it just in time.

"You, uh, run into a cupboard or whatever back there?" Court asks, side-eying me.

"Yeah, we were …" The bottle conveniently on the end of the counter behind her is in prime position to support my lie. I swipe it up. "Running low on rum."

I can tell she's still suspicious. My hickey isn't exactly incognito.

"Looks painful."

Nowhere near the most painful thing I'll be doing tonight. Hopefully. My gaze flicks to Art again, as though I'm checking he hasn't snuck out, but he's still with his friends, still smiling and talking smack. "It was worth it."

She's struggling to keep a straight face. "For the over-time pay, right?"

"What else would I be talking about?"

Courtney's dark eyes slide slowly from me to Art and back again. "Can't think of a thing."

I wouldn't confirm it even if she did call me out on being alone with Art and coming back with a hickey, even though I know she isn't going to say anything. She doesn't even challenge my assertions I've always made about being straight, and I love her for it.

I just don't have time to be appreciative of it right now.

There's no room for anything else but the one thing taking over my mind.

How much fucking longer until this party ends?

22

ART

MY FRIENDS ARE SO GODDAMN ANNOYING. DON'T THESE alcoholics ever turn off?

Mack is dancing on a table, Keller's *still* doing shots because apparently he's immune to alcohol, Payne is passed out on the floor while Beau rapidly types away on his phone, and Griff and Heath are all but dry humping on my couch.

The rest of the guys are behaving somewhat normally, but it's two in the morning, and they're all still here.

Now that I've decided I'm going to fuck Joey, I'm going to fuck him, and all these so-called friends are being the cockblock to end all cockblocks.

I'm getting frustrated, pacing, haven't touched a lick of alcohol since I left my office hard up and fuse lit. I haven't been able to keep my eyes off Joey all night. Which is obviously different from before my office when I … was also staring at him like a creep.

Only this time, I'm creeping with the full knowledge I can do something about it.

And that little smirk he's wearing is driving me out of my mind.

"Okay!" I shove Keller's shots out of the way and climb up onto my bar. "Payne, I love you. Happy birthday. Embrace life to its fullest and whatever, but it's time for all of you to get the fuck out."

There's a short silence, followed by some laughter and catcalls. Griff hollers something at me, and Payne sways as he sits up, then lets out a massive thump as he drops to the floor again. Beau grabs a cushion for his head.

And not one single person makes the move to leave.

Fuck this.

I jump down, jog down the stairs to where the main bar area is still busy, and go for the fire alarm.

Is it dramatic and over-the-top?

My dick says no, and he's never been wrong a day in his life.

I pull the alarm with zero regrets and cringe as the shrieking hits my ears. It floods the bar with so much noise it might as well be a physical assault, and I watch as patrons lurch from their chairs and hurry to cover their ears, looking around in confusion. My bar manager, Lisa, jumps into action, ordering an evacuation, and that clawing need inside me starts to settle when my friends leave one by one.

Joey's one of the last down the stairs, and as soon as he's within arm's reach, I tug him around the corner from the people lingering and draw him in close.

It only takes him a second. "*You* did this?"

"Well, duh. Smart, huh?"

Instead of the grudging respect for my plan that I expect, he face-palms. "I guess you forgot about—"

The sound of a siren builds over the alarm, and the smug pride I'd felt at my plan dies a quick death. "Well, fuck."

"I thought you were smart."

"*I* am." I gesture to my crotch. "But he's only operating with one brain cell."

With reluctance, I pull away and head back over to switch off the alarm. Through the large front windows, it looks like most people are making their way down the street and into cars, except for the staff still lingering by the doors.

"I want it on record that this is all your ass's fault," I grumble, then run a hand down my face as the flashing red lights light up the bar.

Well, I've hit peak dickhead level, haven't I?

It takes way longer than I want it to for me to be able to convince Rodney and his team that it was a small kitchen fire we quickly got under control. Thankfully, the kitchen closed up at eleven, so there's no one around to corroborate my story, and after a walk-through of the area, Rodney's satisfied there's no risk of it restarting in another part of the building. You know. Because there isn't even a lingering smell of smoke.

"Should we come in and start cleanup?" Lisa asks.

Given I've wasted half an hour on my stupid fucking evacuation, I decline. "I'll pay you all for the rest of your shift. Go home. You, uh, deserve it. For your quick work."

And Nevele Ounces will be making a decent donation to the fire department tomorrow, thanks to my dumb ass wasting resources.

The second the door closes and locks, I swing around to find Joey. It doesn't look like he's in the bar, and I swear if he's headed home with the others, I'm going to sob into my regrets, which basically encompasses every part of tonight.

After checking to see if he hid out in the storage area around back, I climb the stairs, fingers crossed that he's waiting for me in my office.

Only when I reach the mezzanine, I don't have to look far. There, framed by the huge mullioned windows, is Joey, wearing nothing but a shit-eating grin.

"Looks like I'm not the only one who was desperate."

I match his smirk, stalking closer as I undo the buttons on my shirt. His cock is flushed and standing straight upright, but it doesn't hold my attention.

Surprisingly.

Instead, my gaze keeps returning to his face.

"You sure about this?"

Joey clears his throat, but his voice still comes out husky. "Yeah. I am."

I nod, tossing my shirt over the back of the couch and reaching down to remove my belt. As certain as he seems, I'm still sensing hesitance or *something* coming from him. I pop the button on my pants and take a seat on the couch. Then I pat the space next to me.

Joey, being the little shit that he is, ignores my invitation and takes a seat in my lap. Again.

"Comfortable there, are you?"

"Best seat in the house."

I smile and reach up to tuck his hair behind his ear. My fingers linger there, eyes taking in that breathtaking face, before I lean in and kiss him. Just a skim of lips. A distraction. Something to take his mind off what's coming.

"You look breathtaking there, by the way."

"So you agree that we should do this more often?"

I groan. "You don't let up, do you?"

"Well, I have a fuckiversary rating to work toward. It's really unfair of you not to let me study."

It is. It's so, so unfair and cruel of me. I shouldn't let Joey suffer like this. I should be a good, kind mentor of gay sex and sleep with him at every opportunity. Bill Gates was dedicated to his craft; why shouldn't I be?

But like every other time I've thought of going after Joey again, that warning simmering in my blood tells me not to. Promises that giving in will wreck me.

"This isn't a conversation I can have when I'm horny. One brain cell, remember?"

"Fine." Joey cups my face and kisses me this time. It's harder than mine was, lingers, once, twice, three times. Like he's testing the kiss and whether to go deeper. I'm dying for him to. Wanting nothing more than to dive in with no regrets. Get in, get off, get out. It's how I've always run my life. But I also want him to get comfortable, so that means no rushing. We have the whole night. Because there's something about night that makes it feel like this isn't happening.

That it exists separate from real life.

"I almost forgot," he whispers before ducking down and sinking his teeth into my shoulder.

Yesss. The mark he left was almost gone, and it thrills me more than it should at the thought of having it back again. Another whole week with Joey carved into my skin. The bite turns from a dull burn to a sharp sting before he pulls away.

My chuckle surrounds us. "You good now?"

"Every time I see you, all I'll be able to picture is that under your shirts."

"Good."

I flip us so quickly Joey doesn't see it coming. Then I lay

his naked form along my couch before climbing over the top of him. My fingers skim his nipple before running down his side. "Why am I so attracted to you?"

He laughs. "Now, that's what a man wants to hear when he's about to be fucked."

The response frustrates me, but I don't know how to tell him that's not what I mean. Joey's hot. Conventionally attractive. Being attracted to him is a no-brainer, but *this* attracted? This burning need to have him. To make him feel good. To make him want me and no one else. I've never felt possessive over anyone, but when I look at him, it's there. Just simmering beneath the surface, the need to reach out, take hold, and never release him again.

I shut that shit down faster than final call.

"Do you want me to tell you how sexy you are?" I tease.

"Wouldn't hurt."

"That I love your pretty little nipples."

"They appreciate it."

"That your cock makes my mouth water."

"It *is* tasty."

"That the way your hair never stays in its band drives me out of my mind."

His gaze sharpens. "Noted."

Instead of worrying about what he plans to do with that information, I reach behind his head and let his hair out.

"Perfect length to pull as I fuck you."

He shudders visibly beneath me. "So get to it."

"Open up, *meu lutador*." The endearment catches me by surprise as I slide my fingers over Joey's lips, and before he can comment on it, I fill his mouth with two digits. "Give them a good suck. Get them nice and wet so I don't hurt you."

His obedience is incredible. His lips wrap around my fingers, and he sucks like his life depends on it. Spit coats my fingers as he licks and sucks, and it's such a complete throwback to when it was my cock in his mouth that the little soldier gives a good kick.

Joey's eyes light up, telling me he felt it.

"What can I say?" I kiss his jaw. "Your mouth was made to be filled."

He pulls off. "So was my ass."

"I'll be the judge of that." I reach down to get started prepping, but then when I run my gaze over his body and look up to find him still watching me, that warning feeling hits again. I change my mind.

"Turn over. Grab the armrest and point that sexy ass my way."

Again with the obedience. This flirty, confident, stubborn man giving me whatever I want, because he's getting what he wants. Again, concern over him using me tries to take hold, but I shake it off. If he is, it's too late to stress about that now.

I can be pissed with myself over it tomorrow, after a night of mind-melting orgasms, rather than pissed off with myself now, with no way to take the edge off.

"Open your legs more."

Joey's knees shift as wide as the couch will allow, giving me the perfect view of his hole. I got a good look at it when I rimmed him last time, and it's just as hot as I remember.

I run my fingers over it, causing him to twitch away.

"Relax."

"You know, I'd say that it's easy enough to say when you're not the one doing it, but unlike when *I've* said that to women, you actually have been in my position."

And for some reason, hearing him talk about sex with other people just plain pisses me off. "Well, next time you put it up some chick's ass, you'll know what you're talking about too," I say dryly.

Joey chuckles as I rub his hole. "Think she'll peg me if I ask sweetly?"

"I think you'll never find someone to fuck you the way I will."

"Well, that settles it, then." He glances over his shoulder, cocky expression in place. "You're going to have to keep doing it."

I spank him. Hard. "Behave, or I won't do it a first time."

"Yeah, right." He grits through the sharp pain, arching his back, putting himself further on display for me. "I'm sure you could resist me like this."

I hate that he's correct about that. There isn't a single queer man in the world who could walk away from Joey bent over for them like this.

I press a finger to his hole again, massaging it and softening it until I'm able to slip a finger in there. My handprint is blooming deliciously on his cheek, and I wonder if he'll let me mark his ass up before he leaves too.

"Ooh, feels weird," Joey says, rocking back onto me.

"And that's only one little finger. You haven't felt anything yet."

"Gimme another."

"I'll tell you when you're ready for more." And while he might be already, I'm not giving him the satisfaction of being right. I'm also not going to rush him after that initial hesitation. I'm making this good for him. I'm making sure he enjoys it. And maybe bottoming turns out not to be his thing after this, but it won't be for lack of trying.

"That's it, Joey," I murmur, getting a second finger in on the action. It's tighter this time, both fingers being squeezed by his hole, and the feel of them being sucked into his body makes my cock throb. I take my time—this is foreplay for me as much as it is for him because I can't stop my eyes from tracking every line in his body. The arch of his back. The curve of his ribs. The way his shoulder blades flex as I brush over the nerves in his ass. Drawing out his pleasure. Teasing him. Working him up and making him forget about the pain.

My third finger makes him tense up again, but I wait him out, wanting to reach around and touch his cock but wanting to get him hard over the thought of ass play and nothing else. To get him there faster, I lean down and flick my tongue over his stretched entrance.

"Argh, you know my weakness." His words are all garbled, but I catch them. Let them burn through me as I spit on my fingers while I fuck him with them.

I wait until he's taking them easier, until he's pushing back and his cock is at full mast, balls jumping in his sac every time I hit that right spot.

Then I pull them out without warning.

Joey lets out a grunt of protest.

"Relax …" I tell him. "You're ready for the main event."

23

JOEY

THE SUDDEN EMPTINESS MAKES ME WANT TO SOB, ESPECIALLY when Art stands from behind me and runs his fingers through my hair. I turn to look up at him. His fly is parted, cotton-brief-covered cock poking through the gap, and I scowl that he isn't even naked yet.

"This main event has a hell of an intermission."

I get the deep, sexy chuckle I'm hoping for. "I want you on the other side of the room, bent over that cabinet in front of the window. I'm going to get lube and a condom, and I don't want anything to hold me up from being inside you."

The confident way he always talks about sex does it for me. I'm no prude myself, and most of the chicks I've been with have been sex positive, but not like Art. He doesn't play coy. He says exactly what he wants and the way he wants it. It means I don't have to guess or fumble around; I just do what he tells me and trust him to make it feel good.

And from the one, *almost* two, times we've been together? He's more than earned that trust.

Art knows sex.

And some stupid part of me has decided it's not happy with that.

It wants more.

I remind myself that with a man like Art, we're taking baby steps here.

He leaves to get the supplies, and I do exactly as I've been told, like a good little solider. I bend over the cabinet, trying not to focus on how it's the perfect height to be fucked over, and definitely trying not to focus on the fact Art clearly knows it.

I'm well aware of his history, and it has no place in our present.

His footsteps give him away, and I don't turn to look when he gets back. I wait, gazing out at the mountains and up to where the Kilborough Penitentiary stands. It's darkened now, closed to tourists, and while I can see a world beyond the window, there's no one around to witness the things Art is about to do to me.

His presence warms the backs of my thighs before his hands run down my back. Those skin-melting calluses bring my nerve endings alive, and I lean into his touch, craving more. Reminding myself to be grateful this is happening again while knowing it won't be enough.

"You okay?" he asks, and the simple question solidifies the comforting vibes I was getting from him earlier. He might have a reputation for loving sex, but it's a two-way street with him.

No wonder so many men keep on coming back for more.

My dumb ass included.

But it's hard to be bitter about that when he drags the head of his cock along my crease.

"Please do it," I beg.

"I love a man who remembers his manners."

He presses his cock to my hole and pushes forward. There's pressure—a lot of pressure—and a split second of panic and regret before Art's tip slips inside me. I expect him to keep pushing, but he stills, hands holding a death grip on my ass cheeks, so I can't even push back.

I'm not sold that I want to though. It's overwhelming and straight-up weird, this feeling of being split open. I want to be a pro at this, to ride Art like he's never been ridden and leave him wanting more, but for right now … I can't even move.

It's not that it hurts, really, though there's a slight pressure; it's more that my brain has jumped on the *nope* train and isn't willing to budge.

"I'm not giving you more until you're relaxed," he warns.

"I'm trying."

"Talk to me, *meu lutador*. Tell me what you feel."

And I might not have any clue what that word means, but it sends a thrill through me like last time.

"I don't … have words …"

"Do you want me to stop?"

"Hell no. But my stupid body doesn't know if it wants you to keep going either."

"Does it hurt?"

I shake my head.

"Are you scared of me going further?"

"A … a little. Not scared," I hurry to clarify. "More … apprehensive."

"Then we'll stay like this until you're ready." And in the slowest movement ever, allowing me to feel every shift, Art drags his cock out and then presses the tip back in again.

Over and over, he slowly fucks me with the head of his cock, never pressing deeper, getting me used to the feeling of him entering me over and over. Blood pumps into my dick again, and where I was tense and unsure before, those feelings are rapidly being overrun by need. I need him to keep going.

His grip bites into my ass, spreading my cheeks as he builds up speed but still keeps things frustratingly shallow. He's barely penetrating me, but somehow, that feels so much more intimate than if he'd slammed home. Like a nudge, a kiss, a brush, stimulating the nerves around my stretched opening, and the heavy breathing behind me clues me in that Art isn't unaffected by this.

"Think you could get off like this?" I ask.

"Easily. This view I have will live rent-free in my mind for a long, long time."

"With all those other men?"

He chuckles, pausing inside me just enough to drive me out of my skin, and leans forward to kiss the back of my neck. "Joey … you are incomparable."

Ah, fuck. Apparently, that's all I need to hear because insecurities be damned, this is the greatest moment of my life. With Art occupied, I press onto him, slowly, steadily, and he waits me out, giving me the freedom to take him at my own pace. Some of those feelings of being unsure threaten to take over again, but all I need to remember is how good it felt when only Art's tip was moving inside me for my body to want more.

It feels like an eternity before my ass makes contact with

his hips, and as soon as I'm impaled on him, Art grabs the front of my thighs and flexes forward, pressing himself even deeper.

It's … it's …

Goddamn perfect. His large, rough hands, his coarse pubes rubbing against my ass, the deep stretch, his nose pressed into the dip between my neck and shoulder.

I reach down for his arms and pull them up around me.

"Fuck me like this."

He freezes.

Then lets out a long breath. "Okay."

He barely pulls out with each thrust, just holds me tight against him and flexes his hips in a way that presses him in deep. Over and over, brushing that magic spot, filling me completely. I lean my head against his head, hold my hands against his hands, back to his front, thighs almost bracketed by his.

I've never felt so consumed.

And my cock has never been so angrily neglected.

Art keeps testing me, thrusts getting longer, faster, harder. Each one fills me completely and makes me think that I can't take any more. But I do. I want it. Crave it. Knowing this is Art, after over a year of banter-filled foreplay, of flirting and teasing and steering us toward this point, only makes every movement, every touch more intense.

His arms around me loosen, hands skimming up and down my sides, along my arms, up my back, one hand burying in my hair. Gripping hard. *Pulling.*

"*O teu cabelo vai ser a minha morte.*"

I tremble against him, completely at his mercy, neck arched backward, exposed, for him to suck more bruises into my skin. His thumb brushes my nipples, teeth graze my shoulder, grunts fill my ear, and before I know what I'm doing, I'm pushing back onto him, matching Art's pace thrust for thrust. We're both sweaty. Both close. Both desperately trying to hold out.

But playing chicken with my cock only works for so long before I'm giving in and wrapping my hand around it. I've never been this desperate in my life. Never driven this mad with need.

Art's hands have found a home on my hips as he slams into me, and I alternate between pushing back and fucking my fist.

I'm leaking, balls tight, and even though I wasn't sure at first, I never want this to end. Never want to be parted from him.

I feel so filthy and raw and vulnerable to be connected to him like this. It's different, for so many reasons, but the biggest one isn't what's happening physically, but all the shit going on inside me.

I try to ignore it. Try to push it down. But it builds right alongside my orgasm until I can't take it anymore. Art's nailing that spot that's making my body sing, that's making my cock swell and beg for relief. And when it hits, my orgasm sizzles along my spine, burns in my groin, and my whole body tenses up as I finally, *finally* come.

Waves roll over me, one closely followed by the next, as Art gives a few more hard, erratic thrusts before he goes tense too.

I have no idea if I can actually feel him twitching in my ass or if it's all my imagination, but almost as soon as it's over, I want to feel it again.

Instead, he slips out, and I try not to complain.

Apparently, my whine does the same job though.

Art hums, deliciously low, and pulls me upright so I'm pressed back against him.

He doesn't say anything, just holds me there, and while my orgasm gave me physical relief, that dumb feeling inside of me grows.

"I don't want to go home," I say.

Art's lips press to the skin behind my ear. "Then don't."

THE SORRY SUCKAS GROUP CHAT

Art: *Joey says hey ;)*

24

ART

I CAN'T GET ENOUGH OF MY FINGERS ON HIS SKIN. MAPPING out the grooves between muscle and tendon and bones. The tiny moles, his light body hair. The almost-healed scratch on his arm. And my bruises.

It's not only that they turn me on; it's something deeper, something *more* than that. I've given guys hickeys before during sex, but I've never once had one back, and once the high was over, I had no interest in looking at them again.

When it comes to Joey, I can't stop looking. Touching. Kissing. He's filling the well inside of me that I never knew existed. It's an emotion I'm not used to, and I'm not even sure I want to get used to it. Feeling claimy over someone, feeling like I can never let them go, that I'll lose my ever-loving mind seeing them with someone else ... it's not me.

I desperately want to cling to the guy I am.

I *like* that guy.

But ... I'm starting to worry that I like Joey more.

"Okay," Joey says, voice scratchy. "You know we'll probably have to sleep at some point tonight, yeah?"

"Sleep is overrated."

"Says the guy who keeps whining that I don't get enough."

He's got me there. "You should catch up with sleep so you *don't* have to do it when you're with me."

I should know what the sly smile is before he speaks, but my mind is blank of anything but how good he feels.

"For someone who doesn't want this to keep happening, you keep slipping. That makes me think that realistically, you know you want to fuck my brains out again."

"I like sex," I hedge. "You're offering it up on a platter."

He hums, eyes narrowing on me. "You could get it from anywhere though. Platter and all. You know what people in this town think of you."

"That I'm an easy son of a bitch."

Joey snorts. "That you're a catch. Any single, queer man would be happy to land you. In fact, I've heard a few guys in here, plotting on how to lock you down. You better be careful, Mr. de Almeida. You're a hunted man."

"That so?" I lightly kiss along his neck. "Tell me that's not the reason you wanted to get me into bed so badly."

"Nah, that was all pure selfishness. I knew you'd be good in bed, and I wanted to see what all the fuss was for myself."

"And now that I've proven myself?"

His eyes drop, scraping my stubble, my neck, then back up to my lips. "Inconclusive."

"If you can't tell that I'm a grade A fuck by now, then there's no hope for you."

"I've always admired confidence in an old man."

I smirk and slide a finger along his crack and into his loose hole. Joey gasps, and something like pride fills my chest.

"Sounds like this old man's still got it."

"Fine." He wriggles in so our chests are pressed together. "You're amazing. The hype has been proven."

"Perfect."

Joey's sigh brushes my lips. "I don't want to go to sleep yet."

"You're the one who said we needed to."

"Yeah, but … what if you keep being a stubborn butthead and we don't get to do this again? I should enjoy it, right?"

I know what he's asking. I know he wants me to give in and make plans for us to hook up as often as we can, but the thought of that … risky. So risky.

What if we do and I get hooked?

What if we do and I *don't* get hooked and have to somehow tell him it's over?

I'm a wimp at hurting people, and given my history, it only makes sense to assume that anything we start will crash and burn.

"Tell me about your husband," he says.

I blink my thoughts away. "What?"

"Well, you were married, hence the whole DMC thing. Who was your husband? What was he like?"

"Honestly … it's a struggle to remember. I don't think about him much. We were dating a short while, got swept up in the passing of same-sex marriage, got hitched, and then very quickly got divorced again."

"Why'd you get divorced?"

"Because we were young and dumb. We never should have been married in the first place, but promising forever to someone you barely know hardly ever works, and in our case, it *really* didn't work."

"Lucky bastard doesn't know what he was throwing away," Joey murmurs.

I'm not sure if he's expecting me to hear or respond or what, so I keep my mouth shut.

"Do you ever see him?"

"Nah, I wouldn't even know where he lives anymore. It wasn't some huge breakup—we just worked out that we were idiots and moved on."

"Fair enough."

"What about you?" I ask, morbidly fascinated. "Any girl-friends steal your heart?"

His laugh is hollow. "None of them ever tried. They'd have to, you know, want to stick around for that."

"Why don't they stick around?"

"Because I work a lot and have my two sisters relying on me. Most people don't like to come second in rela-tionships."

"Wow, you're really selling me on seeing you again," I tease. "You're telling me that all those women you pick up in the bar aren't dying for a second date?"

"What women?" he asks, confirming what I've always suspected.

"The ones you walk out at night."

Joey props his head on his hand and gives me a soft smile. "I was making sure they had a safe ride home. Since working here, there's only one person I've been interested in."

"Oh yeah?"

He laughs. "You're not even going to pretend to be humble and ask who?"

I run my hand from his pecs to his half-hard cock. "Nah, because then you'd be forced to lie."

"Ask me." He leans in a little.

"Fine." My lips brush his. "Who is the only person you've been interested in for … over a year now?"

"You. And I wish as much as you do that it'd stop."

25

JOEY

I HAVE NO IDEA HOW ART TAKES THAT, BUT IT'S THE TRUTH. I'm feeling things for him that are *big* kinds of feelings, and without a guarantee of anything more, the weight of that emotion is going to crush me. In the morning, I'll go home, shower, and get to moving on with my life, all the while remembering how he held me.

Like I'm important.

Like he can't get enough.

"I remember you," he says, voice dropped low. "From when we were younger."

"What ..."

"I'd see you around sometimes. Nothing creepy—my parents would just be like, 'oh, the Manning boy is here, go say hi,' and of course, I was a teenage shithead who was too cool to hang out with kids, so I didn't."

"How old were you?"

He shrugs. "I can kinda remember hearing about a baby.

Then a flash of you at, like … five? And again when you were almost in high school."

"I don't remember you at all."

"Not surprising since you're like nine or ten years younger than me. There's one moment I remember clearer than others. I'm not sure where we were. Caroline Blakely's holiday party, maybe? You must have been about six? Seven? And these older kids kept trying to get you to steal some of the presents. So you did. Opened every single one of them."

I flinch as the memory comes back to me. Trying to impress those guys had ended up with me locked in my room for the rest of the night. My parents didn't like me drawing attention to them.

"Great memory," I say dryly.

"I think it stuck with me so much because I heard my mom say that if you got your own presents, you wouldn't have been tempted by them. I'd never even thought of that. *Everyone* gets presents at Christmas. The idea that someone might not …"

This sinking feeling of helplessness falls over me. I didn't know that people knew about that. That they'd gone around pitying me before I'd been old enough to take my sisters and leave. As a small kid, you think your parents have it all figured out. You trust them and think they're the greatest.

The real loss of childhood innocence is figuring out all that's a lie.

"I don't think we're pillow talking right," I say.

Art laughs. "Maybe, but that moment had a pretty big impact on me. Later that week, I snuck treats into those older kids' pockets at Freddy's, and when he caught them, he made them all stand there as he called their parents. I watched from the same aisle you used to spy on me."

Art did what? I'm struggling to find words as it sinks in that even before we knew each other, Art was protecting me. His heart is too big. Too good.

"You're incredible," I say, letting out too much all over again. I clear my throat. "Tell me about your parents. Were they from Portugal?"

An affectionate smile lifts one corner of his lips. "My grandparents were. They came to Boston, hated how busy it was there, and moved further and further out until they hit Kilborough. It was really small, not like it is today. Mostly people running farms or working at the prison. Mom's parents lived in Portugal their whole lives, but they sent Mom here for college. She and Dad met … and here I am."

"And thank fuck for all that."

"Hear, hear."

He chuckles, and we fall into a thoughtful silence. The love that fills his voice when he talks about family makes it so hard to believe he doesn't want that for himself. If he says he doesn't, then I believe him, but all of his love going to waste feels like a crime.

"You really don't want to get married again?"

I expect him to deny it immediately, like he does with his friends, so his hesitation feels bigger than it is. "No. I don't think so. All I know is that I wish I never had to begin with because getting married is the kind of thing you do with a one-of-a-kind type of person." He looks like he wants to say more, so I'm surprised when he asks, "What about you?"

"I don't think about it."

"Why?"

"Because life is shit and hard enough as it is, without adding another pressure on top of it."

"Isn't marriage supposed to be about finding a partner though?"

"Is it?"

"That's what it seems like with my parents."

"Well, either they were the lucky ones, or people suck at finding their partner. Fifty percent of marriages end in divorce and all that."

"Ah." He grins. "So what you're telling me is that because I've done it once and failed, the odds are in my favor."

"Something like that." I eye him. "But last I checked, you have to actually date someone and get to know them before you start a shared life. Since that's something you'll never do …"

I'm fishing for information, trying to push him into giving me the tiniest bit of hope. Just a glimpse. Just something to show me that he's open to the idea.

"Damn." Art pretends to grimace. "I guess I'll have to be content weighing the odds in someone else's favor."

Not the answer I was looking for.

And it's my fault for constantly wanting more than Art. He's never hinted at a desire to settle down—he's actually done the complete opposite. He's made it clear, right from the start, that he's not down for that kind of fairy-tale ending.

Which should be a good thing because I wasn't lying when I said it sounds like a lot of work.

Only when it comes to Art, he makes me want to put in the effort.

26

ART

ANOTHER ALL-NIGHT FUCKFEST, ANOTHER SLEEPOVER, another morning of Joey trying to convince me this should happen again before he slips out the door. And even though my mouth says no, I think it's all reflex by this point. He's clearly not straight, he's clearly not unaffected, and the excuses I've been surrounding myself with are wearing thin.

I'm staring down the barrel of a decision that could change my life forever.

Continue leading the bachelor life.

Or give in and see where this thing takes me.

The terrifying thing is that one of those choices feels like pulling the trigger on a one-way trip to pain ... yet it feels like the only real option anyway.

Every time I even try to contemplate ending things —*really* ending things and not just denying him because seeing Joey fight for me turns me on—it makes something shrivel up inside me.

It could be my heart, but I like to joke I don't have one of those.

If I end up in a relationship, *Christ*, if I end up hurt, people will know it's all bullshit. I don't know how to be anyone other than the man who jokes around about sex and gets his dick out for anyone at any time.

It's just past dawn, and I'm already craving a day in the brewery. Hard work and manual labor to get me through. I'm itching to move, keep my body occupied so that my mind can't take over. I could hit the gym or make plans to go out dancing. I could go and bake with my niblings or go for a hike in the mountains or see what I could find out around town about people who might need my help.

Instead, I lie in bed, looking out the window, staring at the sky and wondering what Joey is doing right now. It's the weekend, so I know he didn't go to Freddy's. Does that mean he's at home? Does he like what I did to the place? I hate not being able to ask him about these things, but then that just adds an extra layer of confusion to this … *situationship* we have.

What I did as a concerned donor is one thing; paying off every little thing for the guy I'm starting to build feelings for is another area entirely. What would Joey think if he found out it was me? Would he care? Would he think I overstepped? These are questions I've never needed to worry about when I give the way I give. But starting this … *something* with somebody I've given a lot of money to opens up the kind of moral dilemmas I haven't considered before.

People are tricky, layered, and unpredictable. I can hope all I like that he'll take my generosity in the way I want it to be taken, but there's no guarantee of that. I could keep it a secret from him, never reveal the truth, but even though I know shit all about relationships, I've picked up enough to know you should never start one on a lie.

I roll out of bed and stretch my arms high over my head, feeling each pop and strain of my muscles as they loosen from a night of hard fucking.

That itching feeling hasn't left me. I'm almost bursting at the seams. A small part of me needs to talk about this, but I wouldn't even know where to start or who I could bring it up with. That's one thing about playing this set part all these years. People know me one way, the way I've always been. Twenty-five years of cementing this persona have led me to a very awkward position. I'm always telling my men that change equals growth and growth is good, and look at me here, not able to take my own advice.

I'm a hypocrite.

Joey doesn't deserve a guy who's all wishy-washy about him. Joey deserves the type of man who'll claim him, who'll be proud to be by his side. In my head, I can see myself being that man. I figure that has to mean something, considering I've never seen myself that way before. Never even wanted to.

And now, this loose-haired, cocky-attitude bartender has torn down everything I thought I knew about myself with a few pretty words and a fearless attitude.

But the more I see of Joey, the more I realize he's exactly like me. He puts on a confident smile when he feels most displaced. He acts careless when he has the weight of the world on his shoulders. He pretends like absolutely nothing affects him when really, he's driven, ambitious, and working toward something that I haven't been able to put my finger on yet. Joey creates the character he wants the rest of the world to see, but unfortunately for him, I've been doing the same thing for far longer, and he's making it too easy for me to read his cards.

I'm onto you now, Joey.

And with every glimpse he shows me, I only want to see more.

And isn't that fucking peachy?

Two options. Two gun barrels. One choice is safe. Easy. It should be a no-brainer. Stay away. Avoid him. Give myself time to remember who I am.

Or pull the trigger.

Maybe a grenade would be better imagery, given the way Joey is sure to blow my world up.

———

AVOID AND IGNORE, IT IS.

Or at least, that's what I think my plan is going to be. Apparently, Joey has other plans.

On my usual Sunday morning at the market, picking up groceries for the week, Joey is there doing the same. He doesn't give me more than a nod and a good morning, and I can't figure out if he's respecting my wishes over keeping this thing low-key or if he's just pissing me off with his nonchalance.

That afternoon, when I stop to fill my car up, he's already at the gas pump as I pull in. He flicks me a wave before he leaves.

He picks up extra shifts that week, so his name is all over my schedule and his image is all over my CCTV; he's at Freddy's when I get there with the niblings to pick out their treat. Sure, maybe I'm earlier than usual, and he's not finished yet, but even when I ask him what he's *still* doing working here, he just says he likes it before disappearing out back.

I'm grinding my teeth as I watch him walk away before I catch on to what I'm doing.

"I want a piggyback ride!" Gus all but yells.

And even though I'm irritated with Joey, I dig deep for my most patient uncle voice. "I can't give you one and not your sister, so no piggyback rides today."

"I don't want one from you." And before I can stop him, Gus runs off.

Fuck.

Alice shakes her head. "He's out of control."

"Stop being judgy," I throw her way before heading to the end of the aisle where her brother disappeared. Before I can get panicky about losing sight of him though, Joey walks out of the back room with Gus on his back.

"Ready to go?" he asks.

I narrow my eyes at him. "Walking with us, are you?"

"Can't deny Gus his piggyback ride."

While last time, I didn't want Joey anywhere near me or my niblings, this time, I have to fake exasperation before heading to the checkout to pay.

Alice climbs onto my back as soon as we're outside, and we head for the school. Something warm and unstable is rocketing through my gut, giving a leap each time our arms bump together or Joey points out something to Gus.

"Birdies!" Gus shrieks, and Joey takes off running after them.

"Your friend is being weird," Alice says.

"Why?"

"He's not talking to you. Aren't you friends anymore?"

Jesus. When even an eight-year-old can pick up on the

tension, at least I know it's not all in my mind. "We were never friends," I say.

"Didn't look that way to *meee*."

"Are you being nosy again?"

"Asking questions isn't nosy. Mamã says it's how we learn."

"Well, there's nothing you need to learn about when it comes to Joey." I glare after him as he jogs down the street, Gus bouncing on his back. That unsettled itching is coming back, making me want to run after them.

Why am I fighting this?

The question hits me so fast and hard I actually stop walking for a second.

"Alice?" I ask.

"Yeah?"

I can't believe I'm about to ask the advice of a child. "What do you do when you get a crush on someone in your class?"

She squeaks into my shoulder, reminding me of the kid she was before she started doing all this growing up. "I don't like anyone."

"But if you did?"

She giggles. "I'd kiss them."

"And if they ran away?"

"Then I'd never talk to them again and find someone else to like. But Mamã says I'm too young to kiss boys."

"Your mom's right. Though she should probably go over consent with you too."

"What's consent?"

Yeah … this is not my wheelhouse. "Your mãe can have that talk."

But at the end of the day, Alice is approaching things

from a kid's point of view. A simple one. One where you break down all the what-ifs and forget the consequences and ask yourself, "What do I wanna do?" and right now, I want to run after Joey.

So I do.

I break into a jog, gaining on where they've slowed down, and as we pull up beside them, I shoulder check him.

Joey veers off to the side for a fraction of a second before he recorrects and throws his shoulder into mine.

Alice shrieks and kicks her feet out at them, just missing, before Gus throws the branch he's holding at us.

"You've done it now," Joey warns, tightening his hold on Gus's legs.

Then they come barreling toward us. We sidestep them and nudge Joey off-balance, but he retaliates by throwing his weight backward and clipping me with Gus's backpack.

For the rest of the short walk, we attempt to dodge and shove and overtake each other, to the point Alice and Gus are in tears laughing, and the smile across my face feels unbreakable. We're careful not to be too rough and injure the kids, but if there's one thing I've learned about my niblings, it's that they're hardy fuckers, and a little thing like a bump or scratch isn't going to get in the way of them having fun.

I'm almost disappointed to reach the gate and have Alice slide from my back.

Gus turns his tear-streaked, grinning face up at Joey. "Did we win?"

"Yeah, buddy." He holds up his hand for a high five, which Gus slaps before turning and bolting for the school.

"You didn't win, we did!" Alice shouts, running after him.

I wave toward where they've disappeared. "Okay, bye?"

Joey claps me on the shoulder. "They have a new favorite. Try not to take it so hard."

Then he turns and goes to cross the road.

"Whoa." I'm grabbing his arm before I can stop myself. "Where are you going?"

"Ah … home?" His brown eyebrows bunch up in confusion.

"Let's hang out."

He stares at me for a second. "I … I can't."

"You don't work until tonight."

"You know my schedule by heart, huh?" Unfortunately, he doesn't give me the usual teasing tone that I'm just realizing … I *miss*.

I still haven't changed his schedule back from the daily rotation because while he's getting up at who knows what hour to start at the convenience store, I can't justify going back to having him work late.

"Only because you were supposed to work today, and you swapped. Again." And this time, he didn't bother asking me to do it. Technically, he's not supposed to. Joey's following the rules by swapping with the other bartenders instead of asking me to change it, but … I don't like it.

"Yeah, I have plans today, sorry."

I let go of his arm like I've been burned. "Right. Okay."

His smile is too friendly. Too … platonic. "See you later, then."

I almost laugh at myself as I watch him walk away, but it's not because I'm amused. It's because I'm an idiot.

Those two choices I thought I had?

Turns out they were never mine to make.

BITCHIN' BACHELORS GROUP CHAT

Art: *What does it mean when a guy's avoiding you?*

Keller: *Wait ... is this—is this relationship advice? Has the day come?*

Art: *The day hasn't come, but I sure have. Hey-oh!*

Carlton: *You set him up for that one.*

Keller: *He never disappoints.*

Mack: *Awwww is Joey avoiding you? Need us to talk to him?*

Art: *Shit no. This isn't high school.*

Keller: *You sure about that? We're literally in a group chat, gossiping about a boy. How much more high school can you get?*

Carlton: *Technically we're not gossiping about anyone ... yet.*

Mack: *Yeah, Art! Spill!*

Art: *You know what? Forget I said anything.*

27

JOEY

I'M PLAYING A DANGEROUS GAME.

Acting indifferent toward Art is nearly impossible. Every time I see him, my default is to flirt, to get under his skin. Only I've tried that for well over a year, and he still won't agree to lean into this chemistry we have.

He's being a stubborn idiot. So now I'm being a ridiculous idiot and trying to show him how things would be without me around. And either I'm the dumbest person alive for even contemplating it or a fucking genius.

It'll kill me if it's not the second option, and that's not even my pride talking.

It's all these *emotions*.

Because what started as fun, what started as a burning need that I had to extinguish, has become an inferno. I want sex, all the sex, but I also want more waking up beside him, more murmured conversations before the day starts, more soft kisses and kind words, more of him taking control and making me feel … right.

He takes the stress out of everything. I need that.

I'm not ready to walk away.

But if there's one thing I know about Art, it's that he likes a challenge.

And so far, my plan is getting results.

Art has never, ever asked me to hang out.

It almost killed me to turn him down, and if I didn't have studying I needed to do, I wouldn't have. I would have thrown my whole plan, dignity, and brain out the window and followed him wherever the hell he asked me to.

Sex? Sure.

Work? Yes, sir.

Manual labor? Sign me up.

I've never been more grateful for an upcoming assessment before.

When I get to work that night, I have to acknowledge that I'm going to need to look at slowing down. It goes against everything I've worked at for years. Downtime doesn't suit me, but neither does getting so sick I'm basically comatose for days. The thing is, my bank account *finally* has money in it. My fridge is stocked. The bills that come in are all green, showing that glorious little negative number, letting me know I'm in advance.

I've done a budget and started allocating money to things weekly so that I can try to keep in advance as much as possible. I'm making my car repayments on time. Once rent hits again, I'll be back on struggle street, but for now, I'm breathing. I'm getting ahead. And I'm trying to get through my coursework as fast as possible so I can nail down an actual career path before money becomes an issue again.

And since I can't walk away from school and Art pays way too much for a lowly bartending job, it means Freddy's is the thing that will need to go. Problem is, I like Freddy. I like talking to the morning customers and seeing Art with his niblings once a week.

Until I can walk away from that, I'm going to have to keep on dealing with the exhaustion.

"Hey, Joey," Will says, taking a seat at the bar. "Why are you thinking so hard?"

I laugh and pull his usual drink for him. Since that night we went out, we've caught up once or twice for lunch, and I actually think I'm making a friend. A real friend. It's exciting stuff.

I hand over his beer and tap my nose. "You know who."

Will glances around like he's looking for Art. "He here?"

"I haven't seen him, but I only just started." Images of him being upstairs with someone else haunt me. If he is, I only have myself to blame. "What about you?" I ask. "Not often you're drinking through the week."

He gives me a cheeky grin and lifts his glass. "Technically, I didn't order this."

"But it hasn't stopped you from drinking it. Funny that."

"Hey, when a cute bartender buys me a drink, I'm not going to be ungrateful."

"Oh, is that how we're playing it?"

Will tips his drink toward me. "I'm flattered, really, and—"

"Bartenders aren't allowed to buy patrons drinks," Art says, appearing out of nowhere. My gut gives a violent flip, and it takes all my willpower not to immediately smile. He throws down some bills in front of Will. "There. On me." Then Art glares my way. "You know better."

"So I can't buy hot men drinks, but you can?" I throw back at him.

"This is my bar, *meu lutador*. I can do what I like."

"Mu … luta …?" Will tries to echo, watching Art as he storms away.

I'm as confused as he is. "He's called me it a few times when we're together. No idea what it means."

"Have you looked it up?"

"I wouldn't even know how to spell it."

Will pulls out his phone and starts searching for a bunch of iterations of the words. As I watch him, I'm torn. I want to know what Art's saying to me, to understand, but at the same time … the level of affection in his tone when he says it is translation enough. Whatever it is, it's for him and me—and well, whoever else he calls that, I guess—but the point is I don't want Will to be the one to tell me.

I cover his phone with my hand. "Knowing Art, it's probably not a good thing, so just leave it."

"I dunno, that looked like jealousy to me," he says, glancing around as though he's checking Art isn't still within earshot. Knowing Art, he probably has this whole bar rigged up with mics so he can eavesdrop on everyone.

To be on the safe side, I shrug. "I don't think Art has the capacity for jealousy. That kind of thing requires actual emotions being involved."

Will sighs. "I wish I didn't have the capacity for jealousy."

"Still got it bad?"

"I dunno if it's worse because I know I can't have him, because he's exactly my type, or because he's just so fucking nice to me all the time, but I'm gonna explode if I don't say something to him soon."

"You're going to tell him?" From every conversation we've had so far, I never, not in a million years, would have picked Will as having the balls to do that.

"No," he says, confirming my suspicions. "But it's so hard to keep it in."

I can't imagine what the guy is going through. Things are rough as it is with Art and not knowing whether there's enough interest there to go further, but in a choice between getting the chance to sleep with him and not getting that chance, I'm going to jump at the sex.

There's nothing Will's said about Keller that makes me think there's interest there. I just hope I'm wrong.

"How long until Molly leaves?"

"Pretty soon."

"And …"

Will's tan cheeks darken. "I'm moving into Keller's. Reluctantly. And only until I find a place I can afford on my own."

"It sucks Hannah isn't leaving for college until August, otherwise, I would have been up for a roommate."

Will perks up. "Would you though?"

"Want a roommate?" It wasn't something I'd considered, but … having a second person to contribute financially would be a huge load off my shoulders. "That actually sounds incredible."

"Yeah?" Will's eyes are wide. "August. That's only four months away. I can totally do that."

"You sure can." I'm talking out of my ass, trying to be encouraging, but while Will might be relieved to have the option, he has no clue how much of a relief it is to me as well. We shake on it, and I laugh. "For that, I'm definitely buying you a drink. Screw whatever boss man has to say."

"Actually, I need to head out. I'm cooking dinner for Molly and Keller tonight and just thought I'd stop in and say hey."

"Well, I'm glad you did."

"Me too. I'm so relieved I could kiss you."

I actually consider letting him. Just for a second. Because if buying him a drink could prompt Art to descend, I could only imagine what *that* would do. Fortunately for Will, I'm a good enough friend to not drag him into our games.

He leaves, and I get started on the after-work rush. It's not busy, more a steady flow of people, giving me a chance to chat and joke around. It's the part of the job I enjoy most.

"The Coca-Cola lines are running low," I tell Courtney when we have a lull. "I'm going to go and change it over."

She waves me away, and I head for the stock cupboard where all of our lines are hooked up. I've just finished changing it over when a prickling creeps along my neck and down my spine. I don't need to look up to know exactly who's standing there, watching me.

"Come to help?" I ask, trying not to let him in on how happy I am that he followed me down here. It only confirms my theory that he watches me on those monitors of his, and that thought turns me on more than it should.

When I stand and whirl around, he's way closer than I expected, and he immediately steps in, cutting off the distance between us.

"What was all that out there?" he demands.

"All what?"

"With Will. The flirting. The holding hands."

Yep, *definitely* watching me. "I don't know what you're talking about. I also don't think bosses are supposed to accost their staff in supply closets."

His eyes narrow. "Want me to walk away?" he asks dryly. "Just tell me. Tell me you're done with me and not interested, and I'll never bother you again. Ever."

The words twist my stomach. "Like you could resist."

His lips twitch, and he goes to step backward, but my hands catch his waist before I can control them.

"Apparently, you're the one with trouble resisting," he notes.

This time, when he moves closer, he presses his whole body to mine. "Let me be perfectly fucking clear." He grabs my jaw, tilting my head up to meet his eye. "You wanted to catch me? Well, congratulations, you've succeeded. But now you have to pay the price of my attention, and you're going to get it. Because I'm not done with you, and until I am, you're mine. No other men. No other women. Just me."

I let out a shivery exhale, tilting my face until our mouths are a breath apart. "Same goes for you, stud." I grab his erection through his pants. "This is for me and only me."

Art laughs, the kind of indulgent laugh that creases his eyes. "Joke's on you. That traitor has been yours for months."

"What an awesome wingman. Should I thank him?"

"Later." Art's lips brush mine before he takes a swift step back. "My one rule is no fooling around during work hours."

"That's fair."

"Good. Now, get your sexy ass away from me before I break it."

I leave, half jogging down the hall to get back out there, still trying to process the fact that Art … asked me to be exclusive. Kind of. For sexual purposes only.

The optimist in me won't stop picturing how I can turn that into more.

28

ART

JOEY JOINS ME UPSTAIRS WHEN HIS SHIFT ENDS. WE GO straight into my bedroom, where Joey immediately makes himself at home. He kicks off his shoes and pulls his shirt over his head, but before he can reach for his pants, I stop him.

"So impatient." I chuckle into his neck, wrapping my arms around him from behind and stilling his hands with mine. "Where's the fire?"

"You're the one who pulls fire alarms, remember?"

"But I'm not the one scrambling to strip off like it's an Olympic race." The hurry he's in confuses me because even though we enjoy a bit of banter and teasing, when it comes to sex, we usually take our time.

"Isn't this what you want?" he asks, craning his head around to see me. It's dark in here, with only a single lamp in the corner, but I catch a glimpse of something I bet he's not expecting me to see.

Nerves.

Not nerves like last time where he wasn't sure about being fucked and how it all worked, but nerves over me. *I'm making him nervous.*

Joey.

I'd laugh if I didn't find it so … disappointing.

And it's not him I'm disappointed in. It's me. I thought I'd made it clear earlier that I want this to keep happening. He doesn't need to be worried about me being scared off or whatever the hell is happening here.

"No," I answer, and I think it surprises us both.

Getting off is something I love to do. It's no secret. I'm the sex guy. But despite having the reputation of Mr. Cheap and Nasty, I like to think I'm a good guy to the people I hook up with. I look out for them; I'm considerate. I want the guy I'm with to feel wanted and cared for. To have the illusion of affection, even while we fuck like rabbits.

I never, ever want to make someone feel even the slightest bit uncomfortable with what we're doing.

"What do you mean?"

I take Joey's hand, then walk over to sit on the side of the bed and pull him to stand between my legs. He still smells like me, and while I miss the bergamot, there's something primal about pressing my nose to the soft skin of his stomach and being surrounded by my scent.

"You smell good," I say.

He shifts. "Yeah … it kinda smells like you, actually."

"I noticed."

"So, you don't want to have sex?"

I suck a mark into his side. "I don't recall saying that."

"You said that's not what we're here for."

"No, I said I didn't want to rush. This body is mine to enjoy." I grin up at him. "So let me enjoy it."

He lets out a relieved laugh, sliding his hand through my hair. "You're ... not what I expected."

"Oh, yeah? What did you expect?"

"A player."

"Well, I've always been that."

"Yeah, but ..." He pauses to think, and I give him the time. "I pictured you as the type to fuck and run."

"Are you into stereotyping people?"

He scoffs. "Do you forget I've worked downstairs for over a year now? I see the men come in, and I see them leave again. Some of the others even have bets on how long it will take. Apparently, your record is forty minutes."

Well, that's a fun piece of information. I never realized how invested my staff were in my sex life. Which, considering I know everything around here, is unsettling. "You ever won the bet?"

"No, I don't play along."

"Why?"

"*Really*?" With two fingers on my chin, he turns my face toward him. "I tried to pretend those other men didn't exist."

"Why?"

This time, he rolls his eyes at me. "Because I was insanely jealous of them. I wanted to be the one up here with you, and I thought I'd never have the chance."

Hearing that shouldn't make me feel as warm as it does. "I never knew."

"I made it pretty fucking clear."

"No, what you made pretty fucking clear was how you were straight and flirting with me to get ahead. Which I overheard you telling Courtney more than once."

Joey's whole face falls. "Ah."

"Yep."

With a sigh, he grips my shoulders and straddles my lap. "You didn't like that."

I give him a dry look. "Would you have?"

"Nah, that was shitty of me." But even with his words, there's a smile trying to lift his lips. "Wanna know why I said it?"

"Dying to."

"Two reasons. First, I honestly never thought I'd be with a guy. I've had weird little crushes before, but nothing like how badly I wanted you. And second ..."

I wait as he swallows and meets my eye.

"I was saving myself the embarrassment of when you inevitably turned me down. If I pretended to them—and myself—that it was all a game, I could try to hide from the disappointment."

"Why the fuck did you think I'd turn you down? I'm not known for being picky, and while looks aren't everything, all of this"—I wave a hand over him—"does it for me. Bad."

"So you're saying if I'd pulled my head out of my ass, we would have been hooking up sooner?"

"Maybe, but like I tell my friends, time means nothing. Age means nothing. There's no expiry date on life experiences; you'll get them when you're ready for them. Maybe if we'd hooked up back then, we wouldn't have been ready for it."

"Ready for what?"

That's a heavy question. A question that requires me to put all the swimming thoughts and feelings I'm having into a sentence that makes sense. It's beyond me. I'm not convinced there are words that encompass everything happening between us, and trying to explain what's going on in my head only cheapens it. "To be knocked clean off our feet."

Before Joey can reply and push for more than I'm ready to give, I pop the button on his jeans and reach inside them to pull out his cock. He's soft, but it only takes a few seconds of my thumb massaging his tip before his cock plumps in my hand.

"I love turning you on," I tell him.

"Why?"

"Because knowing you feel good makes me feel good. I'm the one who gets to touch you, the one who gets to bring all these delicious feelings out in you. The one who gets to build up the pressure in your pretty cock until you're begging me. The one who gets to give you exquisite relief. And the fact that it's you and it's me just does something to me. Something I can't put my finger on. Chemical or mental or physical … whatever it is, you've got me goddamn addicted. I've been so, so careful never to get addicted before." I spit into my hand and wrap it around him again.

"Art …" His deep, husky tone makes my hand tighten around him.

"Yes?"

"Don't hurt me."

"Hurt you? It's the opposite, *meu lutador*. I want to make you feel good."

I draw Joey into a kiss, unable to believe how much doing only this drives me wild. I'm learning his taste, the feel of his soft lips and rough stubble, the way his hair slides so perfectly smooth through my fingers. The way his tongue fights for dominance, his teeth clash with mine when he's getting too turned on, his fingers curl into my shirt and hold on for dear life.

I let go of his leaking cock and pull back.

"Stand up."

He doesn't question me, and it warms me to my soul.

I lean in and wrap my lips around his cock as I slide his pants down his legs. He thrusts into my mouth lazily while he tries to remove the jeans from his ankles, and once he's free, I release him and stand too.

"Undress me."

Again, no argument. He just does. Fingers and cotton skimming my sensitive skin as he removes my shirt. Knuckles grazing my cock as he removes my belt and lowers my fly. I'm already so hard for him, but he ignores my needy dick and lowers to his knees. Slowly, teasingly, he pushes my pants from my hips, down my thighs, until they're loose enough to fall to the floor. My briefs are next. Another slow tease. Fingertips grazing erotic zones. And me, trying to control my breathing instead of following my urge to fuck his face already.

When we're both naked, I take Joey's hand and help him to his feet. Then I wrap an arm around his waist and lower him onto the bed.

With his body crushed beneath mine, I'm able to feel him everywhere. Skin and hair and precum. Rock-hard, silky-smooth shaft, pebbled nipples, steady, hot hands rested on my lower back.

When I went and got myself addicted to him, I really went all the way. I'm noticing all the details I wouldn't normally, appreciating and reveling in every scent and sound and touch.

I can't stop kissing him, all of him, any part of him

within reach, and I just don't want to. The freckles under his eyes, his nipples, the line of moles on his thigh. Maybe it was the buildup that makes this thing so intense between us, but I get the feeling it's all Joey. Joey and my dumb body telling me that I want him. All of him.

"You gonna fuck me again?" he asks.

"Nah, *meu querido*. I thought you could fuck me."

"What?"

I grin down at him. "If you want to."

"Hell yes I do. Are you sure?"

"What do you think I was doing up here while I waited?"

Joey whines. "*Damn*, that's hot."

I laugh into his mouth, kissing him again, as I move to straddle his waist. His hard cock drags a line of precum over my ass cheek, and I blindly reach under the pillow for the condom I stashed there earlier. I break our kiss long enough to tear the packet open with my teeth and pull out the rubber.

"Sneaky."

I'm about to point out to him that this isn't my first rodeo, but after hearing about how the other men made him jealous, I keep it to myself. I don't want anything to ruin us being together, and if that means pretending I'm a mother-fucking virgin for him, I'll do it.

I roll the condom down his cock and position myself over him. Our kiss slows as I lower myself onto his dick.

Joey lets out a long groan, and I keep going until I'm fully seated.

"Is … is this okay? For you?" he asks, barely sounding coherent.

"What do you mean?"

"You said you mostly top. You don't like bottoming much."

I shift on top of him, loving the stretch and sting and the way his cock is filling me up. "I also told you I crave it sometimes. And since I fucked you, this is all I've been able to think about."

"How do you want it?"

"Hard. Give me everything you've got."

Joey crashes our mouths together as he shifts beneath me. Every movement lights me up inside, and when he's finally in position, he gives me what I want. He bucks up into me, matching my pace, bringing our bodies together hard and fast. My fists are curled into the pillow beside his head, trying to steady myself, trying to make sure we don't fall off-balance and end up with someone hurt. Joey knows what he's doing though. His grip on me is tight and possessive, and I never imagined I'd want to be possessed, but when it comes to him, I'm quickly learning I want everything he can give me.

It's terrifying and almost too much. I'm not a feelings guy. Only it turns out that maybe I am, because when Joey flips us over and pushes back inside me, I feel it. In my chest. This pressure to be closer. To need more.

He kisses me and holds me close, making me want to swoon for him. It's a complete contrast to the pounding he's giving my hole, and I love the two sides. The two experiences. Close and affectionate versus fast and filthy.

"Tell me you're close to coming," he begs.

"I'm close. Just keep going."

It's not even a lie. My cock hurts, my balls tingle, and I refuse to touch myself and give my cock a moment's relief. I keep letting the pressure build. Keep focusing on the way Joey is nudging my prostate and making it sing. Every brush, every bump, zaps of pleasure hit my balls and have me rocking beneath him. My cock is desperate to get in on the action, seeking out friction, getting the occasional brush from Joey's stomach, but I'm fighting it. Desperately. Clinging.

I always lose. Every time I try to come untouched, I always give in or walk away disappointed. But I want this. I want to have this with him, even if he doesn't realize. Even if my balls are screaming at me to surrender. Even if my cock is angry and swollen and all it would take is one stroke for it to be all over.

Joey grunts, each one louder than the one before, signaling he's getting close. That loose chunk of hair is stuck to the side of his face with sweat, and before I can give in and touch myself, I yank out his elastic and bury my fingers in the strands. His thrusts get harder, deeper. I pull my thighs up, and *zing*. He pegs my prostate perfectly, and I let go. My cock throbs as it unloads, spilling one heck of a load onto my gut, and I can barely believe I finally got there.

Joey lets out a curse. "So. Tight." His groan is full of relief, and he gives a final small thrust before stilling inside me.

He flops down, and I wrap him up in my arms, trying to pin a name to the way I'm feeling.

It's beyond happy. It's beyond satisfied.

I'm just a man with a wrecked hole, holding a man I care about, completely fucking content in this world.

29

JOEY

FOR SOMEONE WHO WOULDN'T EVEN COMMIT TO A REPEAT when we started hooking up, Art's becoming surprisingly needy. Every afternoon after work, I sneak upstairs, where we make each other come and then hang out in bed, talking about the most random shit. It's nothing serious or deep, but the conversation never stops.

He asks me ridiculous questions like how the hell socks with sandals are back, whether he can buy my cock a bow tie for its birthday to end the night with a fancy fuck, and whether I think marshmallows belong in a salad. And I make him sing the alphabet backward, list the steps in the brewing process so I can fall asleep to his voice, and make him promise I can wax his chest one day, just for a bit of fun.

He's left me covered in so many hickeys Freddy asked if I'd been in a fight.

Sure. With Art's mouth.

I'm working on getting the shelves stocked when a

familiar little voice comes from beside me. "Can I work here when-when I'm big?"

I glance down to find Gus's big eyes gazing up at me. "If you want to."

"If I do, I can eat candy bars e-every day."

"Or you could be a candy bar taste-tester."

"What do they do?"

"Eat them first and make sure they taste good."

Gus's big eyes fly wide. "That's a-a job?"

"Probably."

Alice cries out to him from the other aisle, and I glance up to spot Art, but it's not him who appears with her. The woman with Alice looks like Art, only with finer features and more lines around her mouth and eyes.

"Hey, Joey," Alice says.

I throw her a wave, and the woman eyes me.

"Joey?"

"He's Tio's boyfriend," Alice fills in.

"Friend," I hurry to correct, then point at her. "Which you know."

She smiles angelically. "That's your story. Tio Artur told me he's lonely sometimes, but he also said he's not lonely with you."

Art said that?

Sure, we're fucking and spending time together, which is great, but that really hits. Him admitting to someone else that what we have makes his life that little bit better.

The pride washing through me takes me by surprise.

"I didn't know Art was seeing anyone." The woman holds out her hand. "Mariana. His sister."

"Oh." I hurry to shake her hand. "Nice to meet you. And he's not. I mean, *we're* not. You know."

Her eyes narrow, looking *so* much like her brother. They don't need X-ray glasses with a look like that. "How do you two know each other?"

"I work at Killer Brew."

"Huh." Her lips tighten in the corners, and I know what she's probably thinking. Him hanging out with his employees isn't the most professional thing in the world, but he never used his position over me or treated me any differently.

"And they-they give us piggyback rides to school." Gus launches himself at my back, and I hurry to half catch him, half steady myself from crashing into the shelves.

"Some days, yeah," I agree weakly. "It was totally unplanned the first time, but now he brings them in once a week. That's it though." I have no idea how Mariana feels about me hanging out with her kids when this is obviously the first she's heard about me, so I give her the most gentle, nonthreatening look I can manage.

She *is* Art's sister though, and I should know by now not to underestimate a de Almeida.

"I don't want to know what you two do on the *other* days." A sly expression crosses her face.

"Puzzles. And Scrabble. All PG wholesome fun."

There is nothing about her expression that says she believes me.

"Yeah, I've heard all about my brother. Frequently. Unfortunately. But it's only just occurring to me that I haven't heard his name mentioned in a while."

My cheeks grow hot at what she's implying. Art told me it's been months since he slept around, and this is basically confirmation he wasn't messing with me. "That's a fun piece of trivia."

She hums, looking me over. "Do you cook?"

I'm thrown by the random question. "I try." I don't, but I want to win points here.

"Art's looking after these two at my place tomorrow." Her growing smile puts me on guard. "You should help him."

"Yes," Alice hisses. "You have to."

"P-please, Joey, please?" Gus begs.

"Why do I get the feeling I've been set up?"

"You wouldn't say no and disappoint my children, would you?" Mariana asks.

"Ah, well, it's Saturday. So I *do* have the day free."

"Free to spend with my brother."

"I'll check with him first, and *if* he says yes—"

"No," Mariana cuts me off. "Don't tell him. Let me surprise him. Just come over at eleven. I'll write down my address."

I wave a finger between us. "You are aware of how weird this is coming across, right?"

"Yep."

"Just making sure."

"Tomorrow. Eleven. Art will get a kick out of it."

"I'm not so sure."

"I know you have no reason to believe me, but I'm not going to set you up for awkwardness."

"Then what are you doing?"

She shrugs. "Forcing my brother's hand."

"Into …"

"Dating someone. Finding his man. Settling down."

"You did hear the part where I said we're friends."

Mariana snorts. "Yeah, I heard you lying through your teeth."

"How do you know it was a lie?"

"Easy." She nods toward her kids. "Them. Art is super protective of his niblings. If he's bringing them here to spend time with you, he's testing you."

"Testing me?"

"To see how you are with them. They're arguably the most precious things in his life. He doesn't share them with just anyone."

I look at Alice and Gus, filled with a newfound appreciation for the little hurricanes. "You think?" The question slips out before I can think it through, and I immediately regret it.

"Tomorrow." Mariana leans in a little. "Don't make me have to live through hearing about any more of my brother's, uh, *adventures*."

"He's very anti-relationship," I point out.

"No, he isn't. He's very anti-*pointless* relationships. That's why he never puts in the effort."

Mariana leaves with the kids giggling behind her, waving and calling that they'll see me tomorrow. It already feels like a mistake, but if Art's annoyed with me being there, I'll tell him Mariana forced me into it under threats of much, much bodily pain, and then I'll bolt.

Solid, mature plan, if I say so myself.

Freddy hands over the address Mariana left with him as I clock out to leave, and I punch it into my phone to look up. It's not far, which is perfect. Easy fleeing distance is a must.

When I get home, Hannah's still there getting ready for school. She's dyed her hair black and has an arm full of bands and an ear full of piercings, but she's smiling for the first time in a while.

"You look happy," I comment.

"It happens sometimes."

I laugh. "Not usually when I'm around."

Hannah straightens and eyes me. "What?"

Well, I might as well come out with it. "You're always snappy with me these days."

"*Urg*, it's not you. It's …" She huffs and drops her bag onto the couch. "This year has sucked. For all of us."

The thing is, a month or so ago, I might have agreed with her. "It's only a rough patch."

"Can it be called that when everything keeps getting worse?" she throws back.

"Like what?"

"Like … like *everything*. I only scraped a pass in my exams, I'm in the same clothes I was wearing junior year, I'm about to graduate and go off to college, and all I keep thinking about is how you'll be here. By yourself. With no one to look out for you. Amelia left us, and I'm going next, and then what? Who will make sure you eat? Who'll check over your coursework? Who's going to be here, making sure you're doing something other than working and studying?" Hannah plants her hands on her hips.

I blink at her. "You're worried … about me?"

"Obviously. You're working yourself into the ground. Sometimes it's like *I'm* the parent around here. You're out of control."

I must be in some kind of alternate universe. "*Me*? You're the one constantly going out all the time."

"To *study* group. To stop myself from failing."

"Wait. You weren't out killing your liver and tempting teen pregnancy?"

She screws up her face. "Please. With the mom and dad we had? I know what a condom is, Joey."

I cringe because that word should never come out of my

sister's mouth. Ever. Though, I have to concede it's better than a baby coming out of her hoo-hah.

"Rewind a minute, because all year, I've thought you were on a one-way track to bad choices."

"Eww, why?"

"The attitude, the suddenly alt-goth look, you never wanting to talk to me …"

"Haven't you always taught me not to judge someone by how they look? Hypocrite, much?"

"Ha. See? There." I point her way. "Attitude."

"Yeah, because this year you've been behaving like a big fucking baby. It's frustrating."

"Have not."

"Have too. You wouldn't let me get a job to help you. You keep treating me like a kid. You're never around. And it's so blindingly obvious you're struggling, but the patriarchy's got you good."

Oh *lawd*. "What does the patriarchy have to do with this?"

"It's convinced you that you have to be in charge and should never ask for help or talk about your issues."

I'm so ready to fight her on being a dumb teen, but … actually, I think she's right on that one.

I drop down beside her bag. "Maybe you have a point."

"Ah, yeah." She perches on the arm beside me. "I have a lot of great points if you'd bother to hear any of them."

"Oh yeah? Like what?" My eyes fall closed.

"You should bang your boss."

"What?" My eyes shoot open again as I jerk upright. "Where the hell did that come from?"

She waves a hand around her. "If he did all this for us, he wants some eggplant action."

My brain short-circuits at discussing Art with a second person today. "You are so off base ..."

"Right ... because every guy Marie Kondo's their friends' houses and throws a bunch of money their way." Hannah rolls her eyes, turning her attention to her nails.

"Art didn't do this."

"Ah, yeah he did."

"Ah, *no he didn't.* Nevele Ounces did."

"Who the fuck is Nevele Ounces?" Hannah screws her whole face up.

"That's the point. No one knows."

"Okay, well, it was either some imaginary Peter Pan wannabe, or it was your very hot—for an old guy—boss who was here checking up on you."

"Art was here?"

"Yes." She's looking at me like I've grown a second head. "Why are you struggling with this?"

"Because ... because ... it's *Art.*"

"What? He doesn't do nice things for people?"

"No, it's not that." I think of everything I've ever heard about Nevele Ounces doing. He's reached almost mythical status for the people who know about him, and the thought it could be *Art* doing that? There's no way.

No one knows who Nevele Ounces is, and Art is definitely the kind of loudmouth who'd take credit for his do-gooding. Taking away all of my stress? I'd never hear the end of him being my hero.

"Look, if you don't identify that way, it's cool, but—"

"I do."

She blinks at me. "Umm ... okay."

"I like him. Too much."

"Is this ... are you coming out? Because I was joking

about the banging the boss thing, but I'm totally here for you if you do."

For the first time in a while, I smile at her, surprisingly overwhelmed with how much her support means. "Thanks."

"Of course." She waves her hand toward the rest of the house. "I didn't do this, and you didn't do this, so …"

There's no fucking way.

"Just trust me," I tell Hannah. "Whoever did all this, it wasn't Art."

It's clear from her expression that she doesn't believe me.

I give her an evil grin. "But that doesn't mean I won't take your advice anyway."

Her groan lingers long after she walks out the door.

30

ART

"You all have fuuuun," Mariana sings as she leaves, and there's something in my sister's voice that has me on high alert. I swing around to ask her what she means by *that* tone, but the door's already slammed behind her.

Alice and Gus are watching me from down the hall, faces bunched against the mischief they're so clearly holding in.

I point at them. "Spill."

Alice clasps her hands in front of her in a demure way that is definitely *not* Alice. "It's the new costume we got you. *Very* pretty."

Relief sweeps through me. A princess dress I can deal with. If Mariana thinks a little thing like that is going to panic me, she doesn't know me well at all.

"Okay, take me to it." I hold out my hands, and they grab on, pulling me down the hall to their playroom. They're giggling a ridiculous amount, considering we play dress-up all the damn time, and I'm racking my brain, trying to figure out what could be so bad, when we reach where the costume dress is hanging up. There are two bags.

"What's all this?"

"Thi-this one's for—"

"Next time!" Alice practically screams, cutting Gus off. He starts laughing his head off, and that same suspicious feeling from earlier sets in again.

"What's going on?"

"Nothing. We're dressing up and baking, and you're taking too long. I want pastéis de nata."

"Fine ..." I look from Alice and back to Gus, waiting for one of them to break, but neither does. Looks like I have no option but to get into the dress and get on with my day. Whatever ... *thing* is going on here, I'm going to have to be patient for it.

Today, I get to be Cinderella, complete with giant blue dress that is going to make baking a safety hazard. I'll have to make sure I don't let them in the kitchen while I'm using the oven.

"And the tiara," Alice says.

"But I'm not true royalty."

She clears her throat and lifts the crown higher. There's no point arguing because it'll be going on anyway.

I tuck it into my hair and curtsy. "Better?"

"You look beau-beautiful, Tio Artur," Gus calls from where he's lying on the floor with his legs up the wall and a hat over his face.

"That's Princess Arty to you, toad."

He laughs, and the doorbell sounds through the house. Because of course it does.

I turn to Alice. "Ten bucks for you to get the door."

"Are you embarrassed?"

Well, there's a question I don't wanna answer. Embarrassed? No. More that I don't want my sex god rating to be severely diminished from running around in a dress. Sure, there are some guys who'll get off on that, but it's not my kink, and I'd hate to get their hopes up. On the other hand … I'm always lecturing them on clothes being genderless and telling Gus he can wear dresses if he wants to. Kids are too young to understand that just because I don't *want* to doesn't mean it's not because it isn't okay.

Well, well, Art. Look who's putting his money where his mouth is.

"Twenty?" I try without answering her.

She crosses her arms. "Mom says we can't answer the door to strangers."

And there's no arguing with that.

I hike up my skirt and make my way back down the hall, reminding myself that I've never cared what anyone thinks before, so why start now?

My bravado lasts right up until I open the front door.

And find Joey standing there.

He blinks at me. Slowly lowers his eyes, then brings them back up again. "A-Art?"

I cross my arms and lean against the doorjamb. "That's Princess Art to you too."

Joey grins and sweeps into a bow, detangling one of my hands. "Your Majesty." His lips brush my knuckles, and I have to admit, it's not bad.

"What are you doing here?"

"Your sister requested I come and help a fair maiden."

"I might be in a dress, but I'm anything but fair. You remember that." Now the initial shock of seeing him is gone, I take a moment to check him out. He looks as good as ever.

I keep waiting for this attraction to him to die down, but the fucking thing hasn't lessened at all. In fact, my chest is ballooning, and I'm overtaken by the strongest urge to pull him inside and kiss him. Not even a filthy kiss either because the kids are around, but just a … kiss. A nice one. Because I wanna.

Before I can follow that thought through, Gus comes barreling down the hall.

"Come get dressed!"

As fast as he appeared, he and Joey disappear again. I close the door behind me and find Alice standing silently.

"I saw that," she says.

"What?"

"So romantic …" Then she starts giggling and making kissing noises, and it takes real effort to remind myself why I love these kids.

"Come on." I take her hand and pull her down the hall. "I'm assuming this is what all the secrecy was about earlier?"

"Yep. Did we surprise you?"

"Very. You were super sneaky. I hope you have a villain costume in there to wear today."

"Actually, I'm Princess Jasmine, and Gus is my tiger."

"And Joey?" I ask, thinking of the other bag that I'll have to chew Mariana out for later.

"Come and see!"

When we reach the living room, Gus is waiting, and the door to the playroom is closed. I adjust the annoying skirt—because seriously, what the hell were these costume designers thinking?—and wait. Cooking in this thing is going to be a pain in the ass.

The door clicks, opens, and when Joey steps out … I

forgive them. I forgive every one of my traitorous family because Joey is Prince fucking Charming, and somehow, I have to keep things PG around here with him wearing all *that*.

Sorry, costume designers. Sorry, Mariana. You all got this thing very, very right.

The pants are tight, the shirt is loose, and he's got a jacket thrown over his arm.

"It's way too hot for this," he complains.

"I'll turn up the air."

"You're generous," he deadpans. "Wish *I'd* gotten the dress."

I laugh and adjust the AC, then head into the kitchen to start pulling everything we need out.

"How did my sister rope you into this?" I call across the space.

Joey airplanes Gus onto one of the kitchen stools, and Alice climbs up beside her brother.

"I met her in Freddy's, and these two told her I was your boyfriend."

"And I bet you didn't correct her." Which, surprisingly, I don't mind.

"Only a million times, but I don't think it made a difference."

The brief flicker of elation dies. Apparently, him not claiming me is a *disappointing* thing, which … I probably should look into a little more. Especially since it doesn't surprise me that Mariana didn't believe it, but it does surprise me that I don't actually care that she didn't. Keeping up an image with my friends is one thing, but Mariana could always see through me. I'll bet she's thrilled at the thought of me settling down. Not that I am. Even if I am only sleeping with the one man for the foreseeable future. It's still fun. Just a different kind of fun.

"What are you doing?" Gus asks.

Joey shushes him. "Looks like your uncle is thinking. Don't interrupt. It's hard work when you're a grown-up."

I smother my impulse to flip him off.

"But I want to cook pastéis de nata." Gus moans.

"What?"

"Tarts," Alice tells Joey.

I refocus on grabbing the ingredients and setting them out on the countertop. We've made pastéis de nata so many times before that I mostly let the two of them take over and only worry about the hot stuff. It's sweet watching the way they talk Joey through it. He's also a worse cook than a five-year-old, so I make a mental note to never accept if he invites me over for dinner one night.

Not that he would because we don't do things like that. The disappointment makes me wonder *why* we don't do things like that. Sure, the sex is great, and I'm always down for more, but taking him out, holding his hand, having someone to laugh and flirt with while we eat ... it sounds pretty wonderful.

My friends and their happiness flash through my mind. The guys who have found partners: Payne, Griff, Orson ... I loved that. For them. It isn't something I ever thought I'd buy into myself. Who needs monogamy?

Turns out it's not a need with me.

It's a want.

And I want Joey in it with me.

As a ... boyfriend? I guess that's what I'm implying.

I glance up at Joey, at his cute concentration line and the way he's listening to Alice so intently. The flour is smudged over his faded freckles, and that ever-present chunk of hair has slipped free of his knot.

The word "boyfriend" settles over me, and this deep click resounds through me, like I've unlocked something I never knew I wanted.

But how the fuck does someone even bring up that kind of conversation?

I try to relax into the day, owning my part as Cinderella and really playing up the princess card. *Oh no, the kitchen is a mess? Servants! Grab a rag!*

"Who knew the great Art de Almeida was worried about getting his hands dirty," Joey murmurs beside me while the kids argue about who gets the TV first. The pastéis de nata are already in the oven, and the smell is making my mouth water.

"We both know I'm okay with getting very, *very* dirty."

"I think I'm having memory loss. You might need to remind me. Tonight."

I latch onto the opening like a starved man. "Dinner."

"What?"

"I'll, uh, pick you up. Take you out to dinner."

A disbelieving smile curls his lips. "Like a date?"

"I guess you can call it that. If you want to."

"Oh, I want to."

"Well, good. You do that."

"Fully intend to." He glances at my niblings over his shoulder. "Tio Artur is finally taking me out on a date."

That sets them off. Everything from *ooohs* to asking if we're going to kiss to calling us boyfriends. I shake my head, happy swelling in my chest ever present, and pin him with a look.

"Well, you've done it now."

"Just saying, I expect you to pull out all the stops tonight, princess. Really romance me. Make me feel special and want to stick around."

"Who says I want you to stick around?"

Joey creeps into my personal space, only stopping when his chest brushes mine, and the Prince Charming costume is really, *really* doing it for me.

"It doesn't need to be said when it's obvious. And you might as well have a neon sign."

"Saying?"

"Saying that you want me. As more than a hookup or a booty call. You just—"

"Want you."

"Exactly."

I nod. "And you want me."

Joey's expression softens, and he whispers, "It's not a game anymore."

THE SORRY SUCKAS GROUP CHAT

Art sends a photo.

Payne: *Nooooo!*

Griff: *Is that?*

Orson: *I never thought I'd see the day Art de Almeida was ... adorable?*

Payne: *Or in a dress.*

Art: *I can pull it off, right?*

Payne: *As long as you think so.*

Griff: *Joey looks hot as fuck, though.*

Art: *Doesn't he?*

Orson: *Ummm are we just glossing over the fact JOEY IS COOKING WITH HIS NIBLINGS?!*

Payne: *I was, yeah.*

Orson: *Offense! All of the offense! Where was our invite?*

Art: *Tbf I didn't invite him, either. My sister was playing matchmaker.*

Payne: *Clearly worked.*

Art: *Well, you can see him. How do I say no to all that?*

Griff: *Hubba hubba.*

Art: *I will end you.*

Payne: *Now you know how I feel.*

Orson: *Okay, offense aside … are you guys, like, in a relationship?*

Art: *Better sit down for this one.*

Griff: *Already on the toilet.*

Payne: *Fuck me.*

Art: *We're going on … a date.*

Orson: *Gaassssssppppppp!*

Griff: *Shit.*

Payne: *Fuck me two times.*

Art: *Too late for that, Payne-y boy. I could be officially off the market.*

Orson: *Wow, I'm so happy for you.*

Griff: *Your manwhore days are over.*

Payne: *I can hear the men of Kilborough sobbing from here.*

Art: *Yeah, well, I dunno how he's taking it all yet. So we'll see.*

Orson: *Uncertainty looks good on you.*

Art: *Fuck uncertainty, I'm pulling out the big guns.*

Payne: *Wow. Do you mean …*

Griff: *Are you …*

Orson: *He's going to see it?*

Art: *Yup. And I'll tell you a secret, guys. I'm nervous as fuck.*

31

JOEY

THE. TARTS.

I haven't been able to stop thinking about them since Art pulled them out of the oven earlier. Golden and sweet and perfect.

I *know* those tarts.

Because I ate two whole containers full of them.

Was Hannah right? Is Art Nevele fucking Ounces?

The rational part of me wants to deny it because the idea is outlandish, but … am I going to stick my head in the sand like that? Hannah saw him at our place. He left tarts exactly the same as these ones. Homemade too. Not something he would have bought from the store.

What are the possibilities that Art left a bunch of food for me and Nevele Ounces came along and paid shit off?

Two separate do-gooders?

I run my hand through my hair, which I've just spent the last few minutes getting right. Art will be here to pick me up for our date soon, and I'd hoped that by the time I saw him again, I'd know where I stand on the whole thing. On one hand, I feel like I'm supposed to be all grateful, and I am. Mostly. I think.

It's just … There's the nagging little voice in my head asking if the only reason Art's giving me the time of day is because he sees me as some kind of charity case. He's given me a great job, doesn't get pissy about being flexible, and *now* has literally paid off every damn thing I owed … My gut turns over itself again, spilling out a feeling that is suspiciously like guilt.

No matter how many times I remind myself that I didn't ask for this, that Art can do whatever he wants with his time and money, it doesn't help. I feel like, well, a loser. A man who can't even look after himself, and if Art *is* responsible for everything that I suspect he is, that means he knows that about me. How the hell can he be interested in a man who'll never be able to support him the way he supports them?

I'm self-sabotaging. Already. Over a relationship that's barely even started.

The knock on the door makes me swallow my nerves and halt my freak-out where it stands. I've waited too damn long for this date, and I'm not about to ruin it by asking questions I might not want to know the answer to.

"Joey, superhot boss man is here," Hannah calls, and I catch Art's muffled laugh.

No need to stroke his inflated ego. I head out into the living room and know exactly what she means about super-hot. That man is suuuuper fucking hot.

Dark gray slacks, heavy watch, black button-up open and showing off a glimpse of brown chest and dark hair.

"My eyes are up here."

And when I meet said eyes, they're right above the cockiest smirk I think he's ever worn.

"You guys might be dressed, but this feels pornographic," Hannah says, covering her face. "I'm out." And she hurries into her bedroom and slams the door.

Thank fuck.

I close the few feet separating me from Art and press up into a searing kiss. After a morning of being restrained, I've needed this. Badly. Especially when he grabs my ass with both hands and squeezes. His soft groan almost has me suggesting we cut this date short and skip to the end-of-night festivities. It's only my curiosity that stops the words from coming.

"I've missed having my hands on you," he says, voice gravelly and deep.

"It hasn't even been a whole day."

"I know. You're a real problem."

"If you thought I was going to be anything less than trouble when you met me, you're not a good judge of character."

"And that's exactly what got my attention in the first place." He squeezes my ass one more time before stepping away. "Let's go."

"I didn't get the memo about dressing up," I say. At least my faded jeans don't have rips in them though. "Maybe I should change?"

"Nope, you look perfect."

"I do?"

"Trust me." Art slings a big arm around my shoulders and directs me to the door.

"Where are we going?"

"I was going to tell you, but now I don't think that I will."

"Art …"

He laughs. "Springfield. I've got a picnic, and they're doing a … Shakespeare in the park type of thing."

"Shakespeare?" Yikes. I left school for a reason. Not that I'd tell him that.

"Yeah, yeah, I hear the skepticism in your tone. Where's the trust?"

"Immediately revoked when you tell me we're going to watch Shakespeare."

"Ye of little faith."

"Oh, no. I already don't understand you."

He slaps my ass and opens the car door for me so I can climb in. It throws me for a second as that's normally something I'd do, but I sort of love the reversal. Being the one who's taken care of for a change.

He sets the radio on low as we drive.

"Do you like the theatre?" I ask.

Art shrugs. "I like anything that makes me laugh."

"And *Shakespeare* makes you laugh?"

"It's already worth it just from how much it's thrown you. Don't tell me you're one of those people who buys into the myth about Shakespeare being boring."

"It can't be a myth if it's true."

"He was a potty mouth who made up words and kills off basically everyone."

"If you say so."

"You'll see." His smug confidence actually has me curious. I can safely say there's no one else on earth I'd trust when they say Shakespeare is *fun* than him.

So I guess we're doing this.

The outdoor amphitheater is filled with families, and Art spreads out a large blanket slightly away from people. He's got a fuck ton of food, and even though I know this date was a spur-of-the-moment thing, it's all so organized and smooth that I never would have guessed if he didn't blurt the invitation out at me today.

"So, do this with lots of guys, huh?" I tease, ignoring the jealous streak.

"Nope. I don't date."

"Then what do you call this?"

He lies down on the blanket and pats the spot beside him. "Okay, I *didn't* date. Better?"

"But you do now?"

"Yes."

"With me?" I'm grinning hard, and I love the way he eyes it like I might bite him.

"Looks like it."

I don't push more than that, just start pulling out the food and setting it down in front of us. Then I lie down beside him. Art wraps his arm around my waist and kisses my neck, and we somehow fall into a disgustingly sweet bubble of feeding each other and play fighting.

Until the show starts.

I'm really dreading telling Art about how much I hate this whole date idea and wonder if I can sneakily fall asleep when his voice reaches my ear.

"These little assholes are the witches," he says. "They're idiots with magic and a chip on their shoulder and so petty they'll curse someone just for looking at them wrong. We like them."

"I'm confident Shakespeare never wrote that."

"That's the thing. It's all open to interpretation."

And Art's interpretation is … wild. Everything from Macbeth killing his father to fuck his mother—I don't know if he's shitting me with what's happening or trying to get a reaction out of me, but I'm confident this was never taught in school.

He talks through the whole thing, and I've gotta say, Art's way of teaching the play should be built into the high school curriculum.

"Who would have thought you were a Shakespeare man," I tease.

"I'll have you know I'm cultured as fuck."

At some point during the play, Art sits up, and my head ends up in his lap. It's comfortable, and I'm so relaxed I don't want to move, even though people are already starting to pack up around us.

"How was that?"

"Not the worst thing I've ever sat through."

"See? Broaden your experiences, and you'll only be mildly disappointed!"

"That should be a bumper sticker."

"Ooooh, new business idea for when the Killer Brew goes under."

"You think that would ever happen?"

"Nah. It makes too much money."

I'm not at all surprised with how busy it gets in there. "Do you like it?"

"Working there?"

"Yeah."

He's quiet for a moment. "Yes. It's maybe not the thing I dreamed about as a kid, but I'm privileged. All the money I'd ever need, a job I like, employees who not only show up but put out …"

"You better not have meant that plural that just fell out."

"Who's to say?"

I thump his leg, and he laughs.

"Fine. *One* employee."

"That's better."

He drags his fingers through my hair. "What about you? What would you be doing if you chose any job in the world?"

"The sad thing is that I've always known it wasn't a possibility, so I never even bothered to dream."

"What do you mean?"

I sigh. "Well, you know how when you push someone, they can tell you that thing they got starry-eyed over as a kid? I can't. Not even if I really think about it. I don't have a dream beyond not hating what I do and being able to afford to pay my bills."

"That shouldn't be such a high bar to reach."

I think about everything Nevele Ounces did for me and let it sink in. Really let it impact me. And while I'm lying there, looking up into the face of the man who gave me so much freedom, I can't hold my guilt against him. It's my issue. "It shouldn't," I agree. "But it is for a lot of people."

"Can I ask why you always knew you couldn't have dreams?"

I break eye contact. "My parents were bad people. Well, I suppose they didn't start out that way, but unfortunately, substance abuse is more addictive than looking after your own kids. They went between being too high to notice us to lashing out when they couldn't get a fix. So I took my sisters one day and left. They've never even tried to find us."

I understand that addiction isn't something to be ashamed of and get that it can sneak up on people, that coping in this hard world isn't easy. But as a child of two addicts, it always brings me down that I was never enough to make them *try* to recover.

"Would you want them to?"

"I …" My chest hurts when I think about them. "No. My emotions try to trick me into wanting that, but I know if they came here, everything would end up so much worse."

"Fair enough."

"Can we please stop talking about depressing things now?"

"Of course. But so you know, it doesn't bother me. I like knowing whatever you want to share."

"And you're not judging me for being a poor little son of a junkie?" I try to inject humor into my tone because it's how I deal with the past. Talk about it like it was funny, a party joke. Something that never happened to me.

"I get the feeling you judge yourself enough."

"Somebody thinks they're smart."

He smiles and leans down to press a kiss to my forehead. "Let's go."

"The night's over already?" I whine.

He laughs and stands, then helps me to my feet. "Nope. You're staying with me tonight."

I check the time. "The bar's still going to be busy though. People will definitely see us together."

He cocks his head and studies me. "Would that bother you?"

"Fuck no. I don't give a shit who knows."

"Good." He tucks my hair back behind my ear. "But we're not going to the bar."

"So where are we—"

"My place. I want you to spend the night."

The way my heart swells at those words catches me off guard. "Who knew you even had a place," I joke. "Everyone thinks you live at work."

"I know. There are only a handful of people who've ever been in my space."

"And … you want one of those people to be me?"

Art's stare grazes my face, forehead to chin, and when our eyes meet, vulnerability gazes back at me. "I do."

My fingers slide through his. "Whenever you're ready, then."

32

ART

WELL, LOOK AT ME GETTING ALL EMBARRASSED AND nervous. I sicken myself, honestly. I'm scrambling to hold on to any shred of confidence that I usually have, but every time I glimpse Joey, every time I picture him in my house, in my bed, a mosh pit starts in my gut and makes me want to hurl.

The greatest part of it all is that it's in a *good way* though. I want to hurl in a good way. I feel sick in a good way.

Like I've just looked over the side of a mountain, bungee cord attached, knowing that this is how survival of the fittest weeds out the weak links.

And I'm gonna jump anyway.

As we pass by the large house I grew up in, where my parents still live with *their* parents, Joey turns to me in surprise.

"You live with your folks?"

"Not exactly."

Confusion lines his brow, but I don't address it because he'll see soon enough. Mariana moved out first, and when it came time for me to go, I ... couldn't. My grandma and grandpa needed a lot of help, which my parents were adamant about doing themselves, only they really, really couldn't.

So I lied. Told them it didn't feel right to be away from home, and I had my home built on their property. It's surrounded by high walls and gardens and blends in so completely that no one knows it's here, but it's only a short walk up to the main house, where I can check on everyone.

When I pull up behind the block, into a parking space under a large magnolia, we're both thrown into shadow.

"So ..." Joey starts.

My lips twitch, but I climb out, then round the car to open his door.

"I thought we were going to your house," he says gently as he joins me on the dark footpath.

"We are."

"Do you live in this tree?"

This time, he gets a laugh. "No. I ... built this place. To be close to family. Only a handful of people have ever been here, and that includes my sister and niblings."

"Is there a reason?"

"I'm not sure you'd understand."

"Well, I definitely won't if I don't know what it is. If you tell me though, I can at least try to."

I think for a moment, sorting through the words. "I share a lot of myself. With everyone. I don't just mean my slutty ways either. Killer Brew, the parties, the DMC. I'm there for my family and friends. I fuck around, I help out if people need it. The majority of my life is an open book. And when you live that way, it can get exhausting. Even for an extro-vert like me. So … I've made these little pockets in my life. Things I can enjoy solo. This house is one of those things." Nevele Ounces is another.

"I get that. Thanks for trusting me."

And until he says it, I hadn't realized how much I needed for him to understand. To know that bringing him here wasn't a whim or some way to try and charm him out of his pants yet again.

My heart is in my throat as I take his hand, lead him down a short, narrow alley, and unlock my gate. I'm so private about my space that while my parents know it's here, they've never visited. I go to them. My niblings have the occasional sleepover, and Mariana has only ever been here to drop them off. I let Orson stay with me while he was getting back on his feet, and … that's everyone.

Until now.

My cottage is all one room. Kitchen to the left, bedroom to the right, living space in the center. My bathroom is behind a large wall that my bed is set into, but it doesn't have a door. There's no need for privacy when I'm the only one who lives here.

"Can I be honest?" Joey asks.

"Of course."

"This is the complete opposite of what I'd been expecting."

"What were you expecting?"

He thinks as he looks around. "A bachelor pad. Some-thing that screams money."

I watch as Joey walks over to my couch and runs his fingers over the old patchwork blanket. "My gran made that."

"I figured." He points to a rainbow pot with a struggling fern in it. "And that?"

"Alice painted it when she was five."

Joey laughs, moving through the space. He pauses to look at the photos on my wall, the artwork plastered all over my fridge, the dragon plaster figures on the windowsill that I made with Alice and Gus, before Gus broke the wing off his and we ended up sticking it back on upside down.

And as Joey takes in all of the little moments my house is filled with, that nervousness increases. That urge to be defensive. To point out that these things make me happy, and why shouldn't I have those reminders around?

Joey circles back to me and, without saying anything, closes his hand over the back of my neck and draws me into a soft kiss. "I see you, Artur de Almeida. You can hide who you are from everyone else, but I see it."

I swallow thickly. "And who am I?"

"You're the guardian people don't expect."

I chuckle, trying to play off how his words hit. "Guardian? You think a lot more of me than I deserve."

"I think that's what you want people to think. I think you're always there for your sister." He waves a hand toward the main house. "And your parents and your friends. You never point it out or draw attention; you do it in a way where they barely notice your presence, but they would if they didn't have it anymore."

"Joey, you're overestimating me."

"I think people are so used to you giving and solving their problems and being their rock that it goes overlooked. I think you want people to buy into this ridiculous playboy image you love so much because it means they don't look so hard at the other stuff. And you're *so good* at the other stuff.

You don't throw all those parties for yourself, do you? You're not the one who needs to be social. Who needs a reason to be around people. You're *always* around people, unlike your friends. You give them that community they need. I didn't notice at first. The schedule change, the extra hours, the CCTV. You don't follow me outside when I walk people out because you're jealous, do you, Art?"

I frown.

"You told me, and I didn't listen. Duty of care. You're everybody's protector, and no one ever knows."

My face has gotten hot, and when I go to shift away, Joey pulls me in tighter. "Clearly, my cum has made you think I'm better than I am."

Joey's eyes narrow. "Donations to Alice and Gus's school. Tommy's daughter's braces. The payment plans at the garage that disappeared, according to Courtney. My house. My bills. The food."

Each word sinks lead into my stomach, even as he grips me tighter.

"I *know* who you are."

"How …"

"You're not as sneaky as you think you are."

"I could deny it."

"You could, but I wouldn't believe you."

"Well, fuck."

Nevele Ounces has been mine. My safety. Joey's just stripped me bare and left me reeling.

Joey laughs, breaking the tension and dragging me over to my bed. He grabs the stuffed teddy in the middle and lifts it my way.

I unstick my throat and croak, "It matches Gus's. We made them together."

He sets it on the nightstand, facing away, which I take to mean he has fun things planned for later. Joey kicks off his shoes and flops down on his back, then pats the space beside him.

"You're wearing too many clothes," I point out.

"I'm wearing exactly how many clothes I need to be for us to finish this conversation. Any less, and you'll get distracted. I know you too well already."

I groan because he really does. I don't know when that happened, but I guess I'm in it now. Following his lead, I kick off my shoes, then go one step further and shove out of my pants before crawling up beside him.

"If you think you can distract me with those thighs, you're wrong."

"Believe it or not, I know you too, *meu lutador*. If I wanted you jelly right now, you would be."

His eyes roam my face. "I don't doubt you for a second."

"So. You figured me out. How?"

"I think you wanted me to."

"That so?"

Joey nods. "Hannah saw you. You had to know she'd tell me that you were there right before you Mary Poppins'ed the house, paid everything off, and filled the place with food." His thumb runs over my cheek, and I hate that I can't read on his face how he feels about it all. "Why?"

"Why what?"

"Why did you do it?"

I break our gaze, looking at my hands, not even sure if I can talk about it. I use ridiculous, over-the-top sayings to stop people from guessing I'm serious. The wilder my life mottos are, the funnier people find them. So putting into words that I help because I *want* to help ... is harder than it should be. "Because no one else would. You're a good person who was struggling, and I could fix it. Simple as that."

"So why didn't you tell me?"

"Because I didn't want you to know it was me. I didn't want you to think you owed me—or worse, to feel like a charity case. You're not. The world isn't set up for people like you."

"Like me?"

"The fighters. The ones who are trying to climb their way out of a broken system. You were in a trap. All I did was slip you the key."

"Artur … You have no idea. You have no idea how much of a struggle it was to make ends meet, to get ahead." Joey's eyes get all glassy. "You did *so much more* than that."

His mouth finds mine again, and I melt into the kiss as he rolls on top of me. It's not heated, not hungry, and I'm not sure how I can tell the difference, but it feels worlds apart from any kiss I've ever had before. It's appreciation and respect. Affection and need. Something that hits deep in my chest and makes me desperate to hold on.

When he pulls back, I get the courage to say, "Please don't tell anyone."

"I won't." His fingers dip below my shirt and scratch along my chest hair. "I promise. No matter what goes on with us, I never would."

"Thank you."

A grin hitches one side of his lips. "So, why Nevele Ounces? Is it a family name? Something you got from a cereal box? It doesn't sound Portuguese, so—"

"Promise not to laugh."

"Of course."

I wish he'd asked me anything but that. "It's … from Eleven Ounces."

"Eleven Oun—wait. Like, the band? *Eleven*?"

"You said you wouldn't laugh."

"Okay, but I didn't know you named your entire sneaky operation around a fucking *boy band*." Joey laughs, and the asshole laughs *hard*. "Are you a *fan*, Art? Do you luuuurve them?"

"I was young. It was a long time ago. I'm regretting every decision that has led me to this moment."

"Don't." Joey kisses me again. "Apparently, boy band groupies are my kink."

33

JOEY

HAVING ALL OF THIS WILD, NEW INFORMATION ABOUT ART IS messing with my head. I'd originally been drawn to him for his fun, flirty, confident side, but this quiet vulnerability, this deep *goodness*? I'd never have known this side of him existed if he hadn't given me the clues. And he did. Hand me the clues. Whether he believes it or not, I think deep down, Art wanted me to know. To know who he really is and to show me that he deserves love as much as the next person, even if I'm going to have to force that emotion down his throat.

Art's worth the wait.

He wanted me to see that. And I do.

I deepen our kiss, lazily exploring his mouth with my tongue. His hands are roaming all over me in that way that makes me feel claimed. Wanted. I'm Art's, and even if it's not something he's ready to admit out loud, he shows me every time we're together.

"Is it time for the clothes to go yet?" he growls.

Fuck yes, it is. I push up onto my knees and strip out of my shirt while Art slowly pops the buttons on his. I'll never get over how sexy he is. How ... how ... *regal*-looking. The urge to kneel at his feet is strong, especially when all he's left in is his open shirt and underwear. All that gorgeous brown skin, ready for me to run my tongue over.

"Pants, Joey ..."

The deep, commanding tone snakes through me like an aphrodisiac. "You didn't say please."

"Do I need to?" he asks.

"Couldn't hurt."

"What if I say *now* instead?"

My exhale is shaky, and I scramble for my fly. "Yep. That works just as well."

Even the cocky glint in his eyes doesn't slow me down. If anything, it stirs the need higher. I feel branded everywhere his hands make contact, and when he pulls me down to kiss my throat, I want to beg him to bite me there. To claim me. To make it obvious to anyone who looks that I belong to him.

Maybe one day, the optimistic voice whispers in my ear. *Maybe one day, you'll be good enough to stand beside him. As equals.*

Art called me a fighter. Well, then he should be prepared for me to fight for him.

As soon as I'm naked, I push Art's shirt from his shoulders and down his arms, then wriggle it out from under him. Through his briefs, his hard cock is pressed against mine, and as much as I'd like to take my time and tease him, I also want to worship him. There's nothing more important to me in this moment than showing him how incredible he is.

I trail my lips down his neck, lingering on his candied scent, and remember with a thrill that *he* left his bodywash for me. Art wanted to smell himself on me.

Oh, holy shit, that thought makes my cock throb.

"You sneaky bastard," I say, then lick a stripe down to his nipple. It hardens beneath my lips as he shifts.

"What now?"

"Like the smell of your soap on me, did you?"

Art chuckles, low and husky and deep. "Maybe."

"Did it turn you on? Marking your territory like that?"

"Seeing you covered in marks I'd put there, smelling like I'd been all over you ... yeah. It was hot as fuck."

"In that case, prepare to find my two-dollar skin stripper smuggled into your shower. I know where you live now. I can do these things."

"I sometimes miss the bergamot."

I lift my head, confused. "Is that what I smell like?"

"Yeah, usually."

"Huh. All it smells like to me is cleaning chemicals. And it always made my skin feel tight after."

"Hmm ... remind me to give you another bottle of mine before you leave."

The promise of smelling like him for a little while longer makes me melt into his chest. My lips follow the path down to his soft belly, to the patch of hair running into his briefs. I curl my fingers under the elastic and pull down slowly, slowly, until the mushroom tip pokes out.

It still makes me nervous and excited, wanting to do good, and being faced with the evidence of how much I turn him on sends lust surging through me.

I wrap my lips around the head of his cock, circling it with my tongue.

Art's hand finds my hair. "God, I love being able to hold on like this."

I love the way he does it too. It's steadying. Powerful. Makes my cock absolutely *ache* at the way he takes charge.

I hum around him, lowering his briefs, revealing more of his steely hard shaft. His precum leaks onto my tongue, and I sink into the taste.

No one has ever made me feel the way he does. Sexually, yes, it's a huge side of our relationship, but the feeling goes deeper than that. Consumes more. Of being wanted, craved, physically and emotionally. No matter how many people I've been with before him and how many people come after, I can't imagine anything coming close to this. This rightness.

Soul mates are bullshit, but here I am, tonsils-deep on his cock and more sure than ever that he's it.

Me and Art?

We're meant to be.

I sink down onto him deeper, suck harder, loving the way he reacts to everything I do. His breathing, his movements, his hold on my hair. When Art likes something, he lets me know, and I've never realized what an amazing thing that is during sex. It gives me room to play and try out new things, and if he doesn't like something I do, he's happy to speak up. Instead of being offended by it, all it does is make me work harder next time.

I trust him to be selfish in what he wants, like I trust him to give me everything I need.

Sex has never been so freeing and *fun.*

I pull off him with a pop and lean in to circle his balls with my tongue. Art spreads his legs, kicking his briefs off the side of his bed and reaching down to stroke himself.

Seeing his big, powerful hand making himself feel good is a complete turn-on.

I push up onto my knees and move between his thighs, then spit into my hand and stroke myself slowly.

"I want you to come on me," Art says. "Then, you're going to finish the blow job you started and swallow every drop I have for you."

I'm only one horny step away from giving him a "yes, sir," but I keep myself under control. Well, as under control as I can be while strangling my cock, desperate for release. The whole time I jerk off, Art's hands explore. My sides and my chest, my thighs, my arms. He pinches my nipples, reaches down to tug on my balls, and even pulls me up to straddle his hips so he can rub his cock over my ass cheeks.

Having his blunt head skimming my taint and passing so close to my hole is making me crave him. I want to reposition his dick, press it to my entrance, slowly press myself down onto him until I'm fully stretched and impaled.

With no prep, I'm not going to risk hurting myself, but it's good to know Art brings that need out in me.

His thumb sneaks into the furrow between my thigh and my balls, and it sends a spark of lust through me.

"Hot damn, that feels good."

His wicked smirk. Another brush over the sensitive skin. My balls draw up tighter.

"Seriously, Art, that's gonna set me off."

"You think I care? I want you to come. As fast as possible. I'll take any trick that will get you there as soon as I can."

I'm close to sobbing over how good it feels and hating that he so easily found a weakness of mine. If Art's good at anything though, it's reading people, and being in the bedroom is no exception.

My orgasm is building, and the incessant pressure growing under my skin, making it feel too tight, making me want to fucking explode right out of it, is almost too much. My cock swells in my hand, red and angry and ready to blow.

I'm close. So close there's no stopping it. So close I wouldn't want to.

My gaze rakes over Art's gorgeous face, his thick chest, his mouthwatering arms, and heat builds in my gut. Burns south. Singes and sparks along my spine while I jerk off like I'm racing to the finish line.

"Hurry up," Art says. "I want your mouth on me when I blow, and we're running out of time here."

"You close?"

"*Amor*, seeing you touch yourself like that should be criminal. Let me see you come."

And that word, I can translate easily. *Love.* Whether he meant it or not, the word is linked to something deeper, something that craves his affection, and as soon as I hear it, my balls pull tight.

I gasp and aim my cock at Art's chest before the swelling need in my cock releases. Each throb loosens the stranglehold he has on me until I'm milking out the last drops, breathing through the orgasm, sweat rolling down my neck.

"Your mouth, Joey."

I've barely finished coming when I slide backward on the ridiculous-thread-count sheets and suck him down into my throat. Art's moan is full of relief, both hands in my hair as he fucks my mouth with all the restraint he has left. My name falls from his lips as he comes, each warm spurt hitting my tongue and flooding my mouth with his taste. I drink him down, determined to do as I was told as I take every last drop.

Art sags into the mattress and after a few minutes of catching his breath says, "Damn, I should have been bringing men here all along."

I play-gasp as he laughs at me and pulls me up by his side.

"It was only that good because you were with me," I tell him.

"I'm worried you might be right." He wraps his arms around me as his eyes fall closed. "And that's not as terrifying as I always thought it would be."

34

ART

I WANT TO KEEP JOEY.

Not a complete surprise, considering how deep under my skin he's gotten, but it's a surprise in general for me when I've been so happy flying through life solo. A partner isn't something I've ever wanted or needed, but I'm not a goddamn hypocrite, and when my friends found their person, I encouraged them to go for it.

And now I think I've found mine.

So I do what any sane man does when he's about to embark on a life of love and commitment: freak out and send an SOS to my friends.

Keller and Mack show up first, followed by Orson and Payne. Griff is working but sends his contribution anyway: "Whatever it is, I'm sure the answer is sex," which makes me laugh but highlights just how annoying it is when I do that.

"What's up?" Payne asks. "Or is that the problem? I

mean, you're in your forties now. Trouble in that department is to be expected."

I flip him off. "We're not here to talk about your sex life, thanks."

"That'd be a first," Keller throws back. He's normally the calm, levelheaded one out of all of us, but while he's normally quiet and relaxed, his expression looks harder today.

"You okay?" I ask him.

"Peachy."

"That would be a no," Orson points out.

Mack looks between the two of them. "What's wrong, Kells? You know we're all here for you, right?"

Keller inhales slowly through his nose. Probably so he doesn't swear at me for drawing attention to him. "I'm fine. Everything is fine."

"Okay, well," I say, trying to distract. "Back to me. You know, the guy you all came for."

Orson lifts a hand. "I've never come for you."

"Me neither. And never will." Payne cringes, and fuck him very much.

"You'd all be lucky to have me."

"You're a good friend." Mack pats my knees, and I can't tell if he's being sweet or condescending.

I narrow my eyes at him, but his slightly vague expression doesn't change.

"Right. Well. Here's the thing. I might have kinda, sorta, gotten myself involved with someone."

"Joey?" Orson asks.

I pretend not to hear him. "We've been flirting for a while, I thought he was messing with me, then shit got physical, and I realized I don't ever want it *not* to be physical."

"So *you're* the one who gave him all those hickeys?"

I ignore him *again*. "And of course, now I'm scared. Because I'm catching feelings, and I'm not good with feelings."

Mack snorts. "What are you talking about? You're the best with feelings. Why do you think you're always the one we come to when we need someone?"

Ah … "You do?"

Orson tries and fails to hold back his smile. "Did you somehow miss that?"

"Even when your advice is"—Payne makes quote marks with his fingers—"'get laid,' talking to you helps."

"I did not know any of that."

"It's your presence," Keller says. "Makes people think you can handle anything."

"Except for these feelings, apparently." I rub my chest, right over where that warm gooeyness is growing.

"Never thought I'd see the day." Payne grins.

"No need to laugh about it."

Keller shrugs. "Who's laughing? It's called being happy for you. You know, that thing you always are for us?"

"What would you say?" Orson asks, stroking his scruff. "Embrace life with all of its infinite changes."

"And this is a *change*. Capital *C*. Underline. Shouty mark." Payne draws an exclamation mark in midair as though to prove his point.

"None of this is helping."

"What are you worried about?" Keller asks.

"Falling for the guy and being dropped like a hot potato."

"Potatoes can be rinsed."

"And bruised," I grumble.

"But they're hardly ever broken," Orson says, injecting life into his voice.

"This game is fun."

We all turn to look at Mack. He stares back.

"Is it *not* fun?" he asks.

I drop my face into my hand. "I want to tell him that he means something and that I want boyfriends and partners and all that."

"But …"

"Well, for one thing, he keeps disappearing on me. Swapping his shifts and being all shady about where he's going—"

"Well, that doesn't sound good."

"*Thank you*, Mack." Like I wasn't already stressing. "Says he's meeting his girlfriend. Who *doesn't* exist." I add that last part because the looks on their faces make me think they're about to start yelling at me for being so stupid.

"You sure?" Payne asks like he really, really doesn't want to.

"I'm sure."

"Yeah, last time I spoke to him, Joey wasn't seeing anyone," Orson says.

"When were *you* speaking to him?"

"Ford and I were looking for a third." Orson says it so casually, I believe him, right up until he laughs. "Jesus, I didn't know your face went that red."

"Stop channeling Griff and *help me*."

"Stop channeling Payne and *help yourself*," he throws back. "Fuck me. I was supposed to be the straight one, and out of all of us, I think I was the least pathetic about starting a relationship with a man."

"Wait, wait, wait, wait, wait." Keller holds up his hands,

deep line creased between his eyebrows. "Are we talking about Joey, as in the guy who works the bar here?"

"Yeah, why?"

"I thought he was with Will."

I've never snapped my head toward someone so fast. "*Excuse me?*"

"Will's moving in with me since Molly is leaving, but he said it was only for a few months. He was adamant about that, actually. Said he'll be moving in with his friend Joey. He was *blushing*, for fuck's sake. And they've been hanging out a lot. I thought *friend* was code for—"

"*What?*"

The rest of what he has to say is drowned out by the word. Joey's been sneaking off, seeing some girlfriend, which he thinks is hilarious to tell me, but *is* he actually seeing someone?

There's no way when we said we weren't sleeping around with other people. Even if they were out at the club together. Even if he was buying Will a drink that day.

Joey's not a cheater. He's not someone to string along two guys at once.

We've promised each other exclusivity while we're sleeping together, but who knows how long that will continue? How am I supposed to know Joey isn't lining up his next fling?

We're not committed. I couldn't give him that. All I did was give him a taste of dick and avoid every question about what happens in the future, and what if Joey's future isn't with me?

That question is fucking unacceptable.

"Will and Joey?" I burst out.

Keller's mouth is wide. "Maybe I was just assuming, but he was all rambly and flushed and …"

Rambly and flushed over my Joey? *My* Joey?

No one knows he's your Joey though, do they?

I shove to my feet.

"This is gonna be good," Payne whispers as I cross to the banister overlooking the rest of the bar. It's afternoon, and there are a few people in here grabbing post-work drinks, but my gaze immediately flies to my man. Standing at the bar, pulling a drink, and laughing at something the man in front of him is saying.

And the man in front of him has a blond pastor's-son haircut and polo shirt to boot. Fucking Will.

I glance back at Keller. "You *brought* him here?"

"He said he wanted to come and see Joey."

Blood has never pumped so loudly in my ears. To see this man thirsty for a guy who's standing in front of him, smelling like me and covered in bruises I lovingly covered his skin in. I'm feral with rage. Possessive. And unbelievably stupid for not telling Joey he's mine when I had the chance.

Will leans over the bar and swats at Joey's arm, and that's about all I can stand.

"Welcome to Killer Brew," I shout, lifting my hands and drawing the attention of everyone below. I have no clue what I'm doing, but I'm doing it. "I'm Art de Almeida, which I'm sure you already know, considering you're here enjoying my food and drinking my booze." I spare a second for a chuckle, which is echoed below. Behind me, it's more like snickers, but I ignore them. "What you don't know is those things aren't all that's mine."

"Dude, you need to stop," Keller hisses. But I'm a lost cause.

"That sexy bartender over there? Give a wave, *meu lutador.*"

Thankfully, Joey's face is a mask of amused confusion, and he waves like I knew he would. If he didn't, I would have had to derail this thing fast, but with that one wave, we're on the same page. And so I say, with no fear or regret, "That little fucker stole my heart. And if *anyone*—" I pin Will with a glare. "—touches what's mine, they'll be banned from the bar for life. No warning."

Nothing but silence follows, and when I glance back at Joey, he's struggling to hold back a laugh.

Warmth floods me at the acknowledgment that even if Will has a thing for Joey, it's clearly not returned.

My usual cocky smile jumps to my face. "And with that, enjoy! Drink, laugh, and take life for all it has to offer."

A confused murmur passes beneath me, broken by Orson's "*Whoop!*"

Applause breaks out behind me, and slowly, the rest of the bar follows. Hey, at least I know my friends have my back.

I don't give a single shit that I probably convinced my customers that I'm borderline unhinged. Who would have thought that all it would take to get over my fear of committing to someone was the option of it being taken away?

Joey jogs up the stairs a moment later, and before I can say a thing, he jumps into my arms and seals my mouth with a kiss.

"What was that for?" I ask.

"I like having a possessive boyfriend." He grins. "Popped a boner right there at the bar."

I throw my head back and laugh, but Payne's disapproval is louder.

"That's our cue to leave."

"You can stay and watch if you like." I pump my eyebrows at him.

"Yeah, I'm out."

He stands, followed by Orson and Mack.

"I'll watch," Keller says, calling me on my shit.

"You would?"

I glance over at the new voice and find Will's followed Joey up here. But instead of looking pissed off about Joey still in my arms, he's got big puppy dog eyes turned on—*oh*.

Huh.

Well, look at that. I don't know everything.

Keller scrambles to his feet. "Just kidding. Let's go. I want to pick up some things for dinner."

"It's my turn to cook for you, remember?" Will asks, and I don't think he looks away from my friend the whole way down the stairs.

When we're alone, Joey leans in and presses a soft kiss to my cheek. "Wanna tell me what all that was about?"

"Who says it was about anything?"

"Can't bullshit me, remember?"

I huff. "I'm going to hate having a boyfriend, aren't I?"

35

JOEY

MY HEAD IS STILL SPINNING OVER WHAT ART DID. Announcing to his entire bar that I'm his could be bordering creepy territory if not for one thing: I fucking loved every minute of it. Gossip will pass through town, and I'll forever be known as the man who locked down Art de Almeida.

If that's not something to brag about, nothing is.

I drag Art down the hall into his office, where I push him into his desk chair before climbing into his lap.

"Now that you can't escape, tell me more about stealing your heart."

He scoffs and tries to look away, but I hold his face and lean in.

"Do I have your *whole* heart?"

He grunts.

"Do you *love* me?"

"You have to make it weird, don't you?"

"Nope. I just want to hear the words." I lift his hand and run his fingers along my neck. "Do you love these bruises?"

"I do."

I lean in. "Do you love how I smell?"

Art shifts beneath me. "You know I do."

"And how I tease?"

"Yes."

"And my cock." I press his hand to where I'm still achingly hard.

"I really, really love your cock."

"What else?"

We lock eyes, and it's like I can see the hesitation melting away.

"Fuck, you already own me," he mutters. "I'm so ass over tit in love with you, and I don't know how it happened, but it smacked me upside the head. I'm silly for you. Smitten. Totally gone. You own me, and I'm not even scared. I think I like it, and I know I like falling for you. I've never been someone who felt like they were missing anything, and I've lived a full, happy life. There's no reason for me to settle down, except, well, you make my life *better*. And even I'm not stupid enough to ignore something like that."

"Oh, shit." I wasn't expecting any of that from Art. I told him I can read him, but while I knew I'd get him to cough up the L-word, that was more than I was prepared for.

"You're … You …"

"Are incredible?" He smirks. "I know."

"Absolutely zero arguments from me." My heart swells, overwhelmed by the emotions filling me. "I love you too."

"Yeah, but I already knew that."

"How?"

"Because you're only human."

I laugh, but it dies quickly. "Why now? Why today? I didn't want to push you about committing to anything, but as of this morning, nothing had changed."

"Will."

That's not the answer I'm expecting. "*Will?*"

"Keller said he was moving in with you and had a crush, and all I could picture was the two of you growing closer and closer, and … I didn't like it. So I figured I could either go on pretending this was just a thing we were doing, or I could make it completely clear where I stand."

"And you sure as fuck overshot it."

He squeezes my ass. "Maybe. But now everyone knows you're mine."

"You know Will doesn't have a crush, right?"

"Oh, yeah, now it's wildly obvious. All it took was seeing him and Keller together."

"Picked up on that, huh?"

"Your buddy needs to work on being more subtle. And his best friend's *dad*? That's asking for trouble."

"You're my boss. Most people would say the same."

Art sighs, and I guess we've finally reached the point where we need to address that side of things. "It is an issue," he admits.

"It is."

"What do we do about that?"

I wish I had an answer. Instead, I deflect. "Did you actually think I was going to fall for Will instead of you? After I spent so damn long trying to get you all to myself?"

"Well, no, but …"

"But?"

"You're always disappearing on me. Swapping your

shifts. Seeing your *girlfriend*. What am I supposed to think about all the sneakiness?"

I groan and drop my forehead onto his shoulder. "That … that's something else entirely."

"Like …?"

"I don't want to say."

"Why?"

I still can't bring myself to look at him. "Because I lied."

"About a girlfriend? I certainly fucking hope so."

"No, I …" *C'mon, Joey, get it out there.* I pull back to face him. "I never graduated high school. I lied. To get this job. The last few months, I've been working on my high school diploma."

"You …" He blinks at me. "What?"

"My high school—"

"No, I got that." Art takes a second to process, and his face splits into a dopey smile. "I will never fail to be impressed by you."

"Impressed? By me?"

"Nothing holds you back, does it?"

"Look who's talking."

He reaches up to tuck my hair behind my ear, and I warm at the familiar touch. "It's easy to storm your way through life when you have money to ease the way. You really are a fighter. And I want to be there to fight right along with you."

When I can't find the words to tell him how much that means, I lean in and kiss him instead. I've always seen us as me pursuing him, me trying to get to his level, me not measuring up or being worthy of him. But knowing he wants to stand by me, knowing he wants to be there while I fight my way through whatever goals I have? It's the first time I've ever felt supported. Felt like it's not just me against the world. I have someone in my corner who only wants me to succeed.

I cup his face. "I promise that one day, we'll be equals."

Art's eyebrows pull down into a frown. "That's impossible."

Before I even have a chance to ask why, he continues.

"I will never be half the man you are, *meu lutador*. So stop setting me up to fail."

EPILOGUE
TWO YEARS LATER

ART

I HEFT JOEY OFF HIS FEET AND INTO A BRIDAL HOLD BEFORE stepping up onto the table. Joey laughs, and I sway, and it's a teeny tiny bit maybe possible that I'm drunk.

As a cow.

"Wead 'em and reep, fuckers. I'm officially off the market. A cock-one man. One-man cock. Wait. Something about a dick."

Joey's head tosses back before he kisses me and climbs down out of my hold. Then he turns to my friends of crowd —wait—crowd of friends and shouts, "Does anyone want to trade for the night? Beau? Orson? I'm happy to take home a man with tats."

"Mine," I grumble, wrapping my arms around him again. He's so solid and warm. Smells so familiar. Love the way he tickles my nose.

"I really thought this off-the-market party meant we wouldn't be seeing any of *this* anymore."

I blink open my eyes to find Payne shaking his head. "What?"

Joey rubs his thigh into my crotch. "You're kinda humping my leg, but I'm enjoying it. Carry on."

"Off-the-market party?" Will echoes, turning his big eyes on Keller. "I thought this was Joey's graduation party?"

Keller shrugs. "It's been called at least five different things tonight. Just go with it."

"Mmm, happy graduation, *meu lutador*," I murmur into Joey's ear. After getting his high school diploma, Joey stopped working for me and threw himself into college. Between the mornings with Freddy, both his sisters picking up part-time work, and subleasing his spare room, he flew through his business degree. He's spent the last two months learning everything he can from Houston about the brewery, and now he's ready. To run this place. With me.

As my fiancé.

A shot of pure fucking dopamine hits me as I remember why I'm more tipsy than usual. Before everyone got here, I got down on one knee and asked Joey to be mine always. Then, when he said yes, I got down on *both* knees to show him how serious I was about always making him happy.

I hum happily by his ear, rubbing up against his leg again. "Gonna be my hubby."

"Sure am."

"Gonna move in with me and have my babies."

"You're enough of a handful without kids involved."

And after seeing the hoops Beau and Payne had to jump through with their adoption, Joey and I agreed that wasn't in our cards. Alice and Gus are more than enough energy for the both of us.

"I'm so looking forward to our future …" Joey sighs, and it immediately makes me suspicious.

"Why?"

"Well, I'm marrying an old dude. Accidents happen all the time, and when you're gone, I'll have the Killer Brew, and I'll be able to shack up with Will. I'm playing the long game, don't you know?"

I clutch him to me harder. "You're pay to going for that. I mean … going to pay."

"Oh. No. Damn. Definitely not my plan all along."

And I don't know who I was or what I was thinking all those times I joked with my friends about settling down. About saddling themselves with one man for the rest of their lives. Because *this* man? Fucking perfection.

Now he's finished school, I have all the plans for us. Travel and a wedding and running this business like kings.

Joey finally sees himself as my equal.

It took him long enough, and I hate that he ever doubted it.

I'm not someone to aspire to, but Joey? He's everything.

O meu pequeno lutador.

My little fighter.

THANK YOU FOR READING ART AND JOEY'S BOOK!

If you're interested in Keller's story, you can grab it here: https://geni.us/systemoverload.

To find out about my new releases first, don't forget to jump onto my reader list and enjoy the fun.

OTHER BOOKS BY SAXON JAMES

ACCIDENTAL LOVE SERIES:

The Husband Hoax

Not Dating Material

FRAT WARS SERIES:

Frat Wars: King of Thieves

Frat Wars: Master of Mayhem

Frat Wars: Presidential Chaos

DIVORCED MEN'S CLUB SERIES:

Roommate Arrangement

Platonic Rulebook

Budding Attraction

Employing Patience

System Overload

NEVER JUST FRIENDS SERIES:

Just Friends

Fake Friends

Getting Friendly

Friendly Fire

Bonus Short: Friends with Benefits

RECKLESS LOVE SERIES:

Denial

Risky

Tempting

CU HOCKEY SERIES WITH EDEN FINLEY:

Power Plays & Straight A's

Face Offs & Cheap Shots

Goal Lines & First Times

Line Mates & Study Dates

Puck Drills & Quick Thrills

PUCKBOYS SERIES WITH EDEN FINLEY:

Egotistical Puckboy

Irresponsible Puckboy

Shameless Puckboy

Foolish Puckboy

STANDALONES WITH EDEN FINLEY:

Up in Flames

FRANKLIN U SERIES (VARIOUS AUTHORS):

The Dating Disaster

And if you're after something a little sweeter, don't forget my YA pen name

S. M. James.

These books are chock full of adorable, flawed characters with big hearts.

https://geni.us/smjames

WANT MORE FROM ME?

Follow Saxon James on any of the platforms below.
www.saxonjamesauthor.com
www.facebook.com/thesaxonjames/
www.amazon.com/Saxon-James/e/B082TP7BR7
www.bookbub.com/profile/saxon-james
www.instagram.com/saxonjameswrites/

ACKNOWLEDGMENTS

As with any book, this one took a hell of a lot of people to make happen.

The cover was created by the talented Rebecca at Story Styling Cover Designs with a gorgeous image by @xramragde on IG, and edits were done by Sandra Dee at One Love Editing, with Lori Parks proofreading the bejeebus out of it.

Thanks to Tal Lewin for once again creating amazing artwork and to Charity VanHuss for being the most amazing PA I could have ever dreamed up. Without you I'd be even more of a chaotic disaster and there isn't enough space to cover the many hats you wear for me.

Eden Finley, thank you for being there for all the doubt spirals and hand-holding. Whether you wanted to be or not.

AM Johnson, Becca Jackson, and Riley Hart thank you so much for taking the time to read. Your support is incredible and I really appreciate it!

And a huge, huge thank you to the amazing Ana Ashley who helped me make sure Art was portrayed properly and answered my many (many) questions. Any mistakes made with his character are entirely my own.

And of course, thanks to my fam bam. To my husband who constantly frees up time for me to write, and to my kids whose neediness reminds me the real word exists.

Ingram Content Group UK Ltd.
Milton Keynes UK
UKHW040802300523
422560UK00001B/37